Magic & Mayhem

Book 9 of
The Warden

Felicia Jedlicka

Felicia Jedlicka (FelJed)
Find me on Facebook: www.facebook.com/feljedauthor
Visit my website feljedauthor.wordpress.com

To my loyal and PATIENT fans.

SISTER WITCHES
THE DEVIL'S SHADOW
THE DEVIL'S SOUL

DESTINY REJECTED
DESTINY RECLAIMED
DESTINY RAZED
DESTINY RESTORED

DÉJÀ VU

SAVE THE HUMANS

THE NECROMANCER'S CHILD

<u>**THE NEBRASKA APOCALYPSE NOVELS**</u>
CORN COWS AND THE APOCALYPSE
COW TIPPING AFTER THE APOCALYPSE
CORN HUSKING AFTER THE APOCALYPSE

<u>**THE WARDEN SERIES**</u>
SUCCESSORS
RIVALS
LOVERS AND LIARS
BAD BLOOD
TENANTS AND TYRANTS
THE RING BEARER
GODS AND MONSTERS
BEASTS AND BURDENS
MAGIC AND MAYHEM
FORK IN THE ROAD
DETAILS AND DEADLINES
*CURSES AND SACRIFICES**
*WITCHES AND WOLVES**
*SAINTS AND SERPENTS**
*ENEMIES AND ALLIES**

*MARRIED TO DEATH**

Magic & Mayhem

Felicia Jedlicka

1

G YPSY LEANED ON THE stucco pink wall, watching the cars pass with an attentive eye. She could smell the noxious Mexican food that permeated the street and ostensibly the whole fucking country. She had already smoked an entire pack of cigarettes to alleviate her olfactory sense with a different abuse, but apparently, she hadn't burned enough of her nose hairs to diminish the experience.

She knew it was important for Callin to get the allegiance of Mexico's clans, not just to help overthrow Frederique—which was now a definitive outcome of their efforts, give or take a few loose ends—but also to make Leona's rise to power uncontested. Since she didn't trust anyone else to handle Callin's security, she made the trip with him.

Still, she hated Mexico on principle.

Maybe it was the obnoxious bright colors that pretended to compensate for the rampant poverty. Or perhaps it was the cuisine that only redeemed itself after it escaped the borders. Better still, it was probably the endless potential threats lurking in the shadows. There were always a good number of bottom feeders poised to benefit from the hubbub of a parked limousine and private security.

Even now, she could sense movement in the alley across the way. So far, she couldn't get a bead on the voyeur. She couldn't tell if it was a man or woman, human or werewolf, but she wouldn't take any chances. She leaned over to the large picture window that was barely a window since the entire menu was painted on it. She knocked a knuckle on the glass and tapped her wrist. Callin barely glanced away from his dinner party. She signaled for him to take the alley exit, and he nodded.

She repositioned and radioed for the driver to get closer to the alley and keep the engine running. He grunted a "yes, sir" and clicked off. She imagined that the men she led had originally intended to piss her off with the masculine designation, but frankly, as long as it started with *yes,* and ended with them doing what she wanted, they could call her *sugar lips* for all she cared.

They were under the mistaken impression that she was sleeping with their boss in order to get the privilege of leading such an esoteric operation. Little did they know she hadn't even met the mysterious benefactor. She had hoped someday to meet him, but had resigned herself to the *Charlie's Angels* feel of her contracted employment. The money was good, and the work was helping to hone her skills, so she couldn't really complain.

After another half hour, the heavy metal door leading from the restaurant kitchen into the alley opened and a small Mexican man stepped out to peek around the alley. He caught sight of her and his mouth dropped open slightly as he took in her hard-edged military style.

The only color on her was a silver crescent moon necklace. A *gift* from Frederique that she had graciously accepted after their first face off. She had never gambled to wear the necklace in front of her, but now that the fem-wolf was blind, the risk was minimal.

The little Mexican man tucked back behind the door and said, "Si, si, una chica."

Gypsy gripped her gun and stepped to one side to see around the door. Callin tipped the man generously, and he thanked him before scurrying back to his kitchen duties. She narrowed her eyes on the werewolf and waited for an explanation.

He stepped into the alley, making sure the door was properly latched before turning back to her. He was only wearing blue jeans, and a white-collared shirt, with a V-neck gray cardigan, but it could have easily been an Armani suit, since he was never without his suave demeanor. "Well... " He paused to place his money clip in his front pocket. "You can't be too careful."

She waggled her head. "I suppose, but it does present the appearance of mistrust."

"Not at all. I trust you implicitly," he said, bowing his head slightly.

"But not with your life?"

He shrugged apologetically. "I appreciate that you are here to keep a watchful eye where I can't, but…" He trailed off, seemingly averse to insulting her.

She crossed her arms. "Oh, please, go on. You won't hurt my feelings. What few I actually have aren't usually wasted on other people's opinions."

His lips turned up slightly, and he tipped his nose up almost imperceptibly to get a whiff of what she wasn't revealing in her expression. His faint smile disappeared entirely.

"Must be the Mexican food," she responded with a brow lift when his sense of smell didn't offer him the interpretation he was seeking.

His smile returned even broader, and he pursed his lips and nodded. "All right, have it your way. Grace, was it?"

"Call me Gypsy," she said, offering the borrowed nickname from Cori—or herself, if she bought into the backstory.

"Gypsy," he rolled the name off his tongue as if he was tasting it, or at least making a point to memorize it this time. Since she had intrigued him, she must have risen above the status of *no-name guard*. "I find it amusing that you are still purporting to be my bodyguard, when it is obvious that anyone who could be a threat to me is clearly going to be a bigger threat to you."

She frowned, looking him over. His face softened, and he raised his hands, surrendering for his rudeness.

He opened his mouth, likely to offer an apology for his chauvinistic—albeit accurate—statement. Rather than let him waste time groveling over the misinterpretation, she interrupted. "So, you don't want me to take care of that red dot that's trying to lock aim on your throat?"

"What?"

2

Before Callin could look down, Gypsy shoved him into the wall behind a dumpster. The bullet meant for his neck pinged off a nearby fire escape. She pulled her gun and ducked down on the other side. Her radio erupted with the babble of her men shouting locations, while the sniper continued to shoot.

She caught a glimpse of movement on the building across the street. The gunman was repositioning behind the roof access door. She waited until he was safely shielded, fired three successive shots just shy of his head, and paused. The gunman did exactly as she intended and popped out to offer his return shots during her hiatus. Instead of the traditional duck and hide, she left herself exposed and fired three more shots.

A spark lit where she hit the gun, and the man stumbled back, clutching his chest. "Damn it." She mumbled, holstering her gun.

"What is it?" Callin asked. He stayed behind the dumpster until she stood and came out into the open.

"He was human," she answered and pulled her radio from her thigh. "Bag him up, guys." The previously lonely street before them erupted with a frenzy of men, each equipped with rifle, handgun, and machete. They had no qualms about taking out humans that dared to step into the crossfire of the werewolf war, but she didn't take any pride in killing humans. It just wasn't good sport.

"Ignorant men following their lovers' orders, no doubt." Callin spoke with an air of condescension.

Gypsy turned her attention back to him. He was none the worse for wear and even looked a little perturbed by the interruption to his evening. "Yes, many a man has fallen victim to being dragged around by their cock. Present company included, of course."

Callin's eyes widened at the blatant insult. She had to fight the urge to smirk at his reaction, since she wasn't likely to recover easily from his retort. Anger flared on his face, but it was gone as fast as it had arrived. He looked her over again, adding another layer to his impression of her. "My, but you are brave, aren't you?"

"Brave... honest, whatever." She shrugged and nodded for him to follow her. "I just call 'em how I see 'em. If you're uncomfortable with that, then we should probably proceed without conversation."

"Uncomfortable?" He stopped next to her at the end of the alley. They each observed the surrounding area before turning to face one another again. "No, I imagine it's not discomfort I'm feeling. In fact, I'm considering showing you how much freedom my cock has."

Gypsy couldn't help but look down to the topic of discussion. She didn't want to make any assumptions about his virility based on the cut of his jeans, but he was ranking high in the preliminaries either way. When she looked back up, his eyes were glinting, and the smirk on his face was full of ardor.

"You're sure Leona won't mind?"

"Do you care?" He took another not-so-cursory view of her body. She wasn't the petite, slender woman that many men preferred, but she was muscular, and that had its own appeal in the bedroom.

"Not really, but I am rather fond of my leg function, and I hate drama."

"You should know that werewolves are not monogamous. Or haven't you been keeping up with the reading?"

Gypsy shrugged. She could sense the heat coming off him, but he wasn't advancing on her. She expected if they went back to his hotel, he would offer her a drink and a long flirtation before instigating any contact. His rating was going up by the second.

"I only got the pamphlet version of werewolves, and it mostly involved how to kill and/or incapacitate them. Sexual habits must have been in a separate leaflet."

"I'd be happy to offer you a lesson myself." He nodded to his ride. "Why don't you accompany me in my limousine? Maybe I can get a better read on you in a closed space." He stepped toward her, keeping his eyes locked on hers as he leaned over to open the door to the waiting vehicle.

She turned to get in, but a flicker of movement caught her attention. The spy she had been monitoring in the alley down the street was still there. *He* was in full view, but the distance and darkness were still covering his identity.

She turned back to Callin's unwavering invitation and presented him with an index finger. "Pop the champagne. I'll be back in a minute."

He glanced at where she had been looking. He sniffed the air, but seemed satisfied that whoever was watching them wasn't a threat. He nodded and slipped into the limo, leaving the door open for her return.

She marched cattycorner across the street toward Callin's would-be stalker. She expected the man to flee, but he was unruffled by her threatening approach. He even went so far as to lean against the wall behind him and cross his arms. She almost had a view of his face. In ten more steps, she would have had a grip on his neck, but the explosion behind her thwarted her efforts.

The impact of the thunderous blast pushed her to the ground. She shielded herself from the barrage of shrapnel and the heat wave that followed. When the spectacle was down to a roaring fire, she looked back to determine what had happened.

Callin's limousine had exploded.

With him inside.

Gypsy leaped to her feet and ran toward the inferno. Her men paced around the blaze in frantic, impotent shock while she headed straight for it. One man grabbed her around the waist in a gallant attempt to stop her rogue firefighter mentality. He obviously expected her to struggle in vain and scream theatrically over her lost comrade, but she didn't.

She went limp, offering him her maximum weight. The unexpected tactic pulled his arms down. While he was bent over, she had enough purchase to flip him over her back. To be sure that everyone learned the lesson; she kicked his crotch on the way by.

She didn't have any protective fire gear, but she took a moment to pour her emergency water canteen on her hair, so she didn't go bald for her efforts. She dove into the back seat of the car, between smoke and flames, and grabbed the first body part she could find.

She yanked on Callin's arm and wrenched him out of the vehicle. He was heavy, much heavier than he looked. To make matters worse, his skin was peeling off as she did it. When she cleared the flames, several men joined her to help drag him away.

One man pawed at her, unbuckling her vest. She grabbed his hands, offended by his proximity. "You're on fire, you crazy bitch!" he practically spat in her face. She released him, and he proceeded to rip at her clothing, patting down any hitchhiking embers.

At some point in the process, he started hissing and seething about a wound on her rib cage—no doubt the reason for the immense pain that was substituting for shock.

"Ambulance is on its way," someone said.

Gypsy looked down at the blackened skin, oozing wounds, and melted clothes on the man that she was meant to protect. "An ambulance won't help him."

"It's for *you*!" her would-be hero yelled. "Fuck him, he's done for! I don't know why you bothered to drag him out in the first place. No one can survive burns like that, werewolf or not."

Gypsy knew he was right, but she wouldn't give up that easily.

3

DANIEL SMILED AS NEVIA trailed gentle kisses down his stomach. Her diamond ring glinted in the moonlight coming through the patio doors. He hadn't bothered closing them since the lapping waves, only footsteps away, provided a nice soundtrack to their lovemaking.

He had never considered himself a romantic, and he probably still wasn't, but there was something special about spending days upon days doting on one's lover in such a beautiful place. Or maybe it was simply because his lover's doting skills had perfected over the last week.

Just as he was beginning to really enjoy himself, a figure stepped into the path of his ocean view. At first, he didn't even bother fully opening his slit eyes to find out who it was, but when Nevia jumped off him and dove for her gun in the nightstand, he decided he should be paying attention.

By the time Nevia's gun was in hand, the visitor was in the room and slapping it away from her. Daniel didn't let the battle escalate further. If this person thought they could rob some unsuspecting honeymooners, they were wrong.

Daniel used his power to shove the thief into the wall. The woman, as it turned out, smashed into a framed flower picture, and buckled to the floor with a groan. "McGrath, stop," she moaned and coughed. "I need your help." She looked up, revealing her face.

"Grace?" Daniel looked over the ponytailed charcoal-brunette that only a few months ago had helped clean up the mess they'd got into with a werewolf horde. He also suspected she was the reason they hadn't had any further attacks.

"Yes." She winced and pulled herself away from the wall. He noticed the blood trail she left on the wall and jumped out of bed, unconcerned for his state of undress. "I need help."

"Clearly." Daniel assisted her rise, while Nevia threw on a robe. When she returned, she had one for him as well. "What the feck are you doing in Mexico?" Daniel asked as he slipped on the proffered robe. He ignored the glares that he was getting from Nevia. He knew she didn't like the woman, but if she was willing to interrupt a man's *happy ending*, then it must have been important.

"I'm here with Callin. He's on a suck-up tour for Leona."

Gypsy eyed Nevia suspiciously as she moved closer to examine her wound. Daniel was glad that she wasn't automatically offering his services anymore, but he could already tell this was an exception to his no boo-boos moratorium.

"Callin?" He tried to place the name with the correct face. "Yeah, yeah. Tall, dark, Gucci model that leaps onto helicopters in single bounds."

"Really?" Gypsy wrinkled her brow, unsure of how sarcastic he was being.

"Oh, yeah, check the resume. How'd you get that little scrape?" he asked. Nevia glanced at him, clearly concerned, and he gave her a slight nod to let her know that he fully intended to help the poor woman.

"I screwed up," Gypsy answered. "Somebody got a bomb on board his limo. He's fried, Daniel, head to toe. He is as good as dead without you. His odds are probably low even with you, but I had to try. Will you help?"

Daniel stepped back and looked to Nevia. He wasn't sure what he expected to see on her face, but he was still surprised to find the eager anticipation for his answer. Apparently, she could tolerate their honeymoon being disrupted if it was to help the werewolf cause.

He wasn't against helping Callin, but extensive burns were a difficult undertaking, even for him. In the end, he would probably have to handle it the same way the doctors would: strip off the old and do his best to heal the new. Gypsy was right, though; it was worth a try.

Rather than scrutinize his obligations to Danato and a slew of nondisclosure agreements—that had gone out the window the minute he'd met Gypsy the first time—he decided to help. He generally avoided any actions that could provoke the warden's wrath, but he preferred being yelled at by Danato than being kicked out of bed by Nevia.

"I'll help him, but let's get you healed up first."

"No, save all your strength for him."

"At least let him stop the bleeding," Nevia petitioned, but Gypsy shook her head. It was obvious the woman was in pain, but she was as stubborn as they come.

"The doctors can handle this. Get dressed and meet me out front."

4

G YPSY LET THE NURSES scrub her wounds without any shots. They explained the reasoning for it, but regardless of the rationale, the end result was still her gritting her teeth and staring at the angry man sitting in front of her. She recognized him as the one that had helped tamp out her fire, but she only recently figured out that he was also the one that she had flipped off her back and racked. Probably the reason he was still bristling, despite the fact that he had come in to check on her.

He was a beautiful man by any standard. His bronze skin and oily black curls looked Spanish, but she was pretty sure he was from Brazil.

"I take it you're still mad," she managed to say in an even tone between the bouts of grating pain.

"Yes, mad; you shouldn't have taken so much of a risk to save him."

"I didn't risk myself to save him. I risked myself to complete the job, which was—by the way—to keep him alive."

"And you think your friend's voodoo will do that?"

Gypsy paused a moment, thinking about the designation *friend*. She wasn't sure she had any, but she was certain Daniel McGrath wouldn't be in that category even if she did. "No, I don't think it. I know it. Did you seriously come in here to lecture me? Because I'm not easily disciplined, especially when I am *your* superior."

"Superior does not guarantee smarter."

"Oh, save me the bullshit. You are just here to regain some of your manhood after I emasculated you in front of everyone. Let me give you a hint: the only place you'll ever be on top of me is in bed, so unless you're flirting, walk away."

Gypsy watched his face contort from anger to shock, then interest, and back to anger again, before he walked out. She could practically see his balls shrivel from the exposure to an outspoken woman. She wasn't sure how fem-wolves managed to find mates. Every man she ever met seemed fascinated by her no-nonsense persona, but they quickly ran off the minute they realized it wasn't a front or an act. She really was a crazy-ass bitch, and there weren't many men that could cope with that. Unfortunately, her best prospect so far was lying in an induced coma with *death*-degree burns.

When the nurse was through with her torture, Gypsy slipped out of the room fashioning her hospital gown in all its non-glory. She found Nevia reading a magazine in the emergency room waiting area. At first she thought she hadn't sensed her, but then she saw her jaw clench. She could smell her; she just didn't want to talk.

"You're going to get TMJ problems if you don't ease up on hating me."

Nevia turned around and looked her over. "I don't hate you," she mumbled. "How are your injuries?" she asked, changing the subject.

"Painful, but supposedly cleaner," she said, sitting down on the arm of a chair near her. "You two got hitched, I see." She nodded to the rock on her finger. She wasn't surprised to see such a large diamond—hunters were paid well. She also assumed that Nevia appreciated the beauty of a large diamond over a small one. She couldn't really blame her. If you're going to commit to one man, he had better be willing to pay up.

"Yes, we got married on the beach. Private ceremony, just the two of us."

"Uh-oh." Gypsy smiled when Nevia's eyes whipped up to look at her. "Private ceremony usually means the in-laws don't get along or that someone disapproved of the match. What's the matter, Mrs. McGrath not onboard with a part fem-wolf daughter-in-law?"

Nevia blinked as if she were lost for a moment. "No, she warmed to me when she realized what I was willing to do to save Daniel's friends. Plus, she could hardly begrudge my heritage when Daniel is so... different."

"So, it was *your* family," Gypsy prodded.

"Do you mind? This is a rather personal conversation to be having with someone I barely know."

"Sorry, just curious. I know a little of your background, but... well, I can only know what I'm told. I can't smell it."

Nevia frowned and turned the unread page in her magazine. Gypsy wasn't oblivious to the subtle hint, but she wasn't quite finished with the chat. "Tell me something, Nevia; you seem flustered around me."

"I'm not afraid of you." Her temper flared, augmenting her displeased gaze to a scowl.

"I know you aren't," she said softly. "I don't imagine much does scare you, but just so you know, you have no reason to be. I don't consider you an enemy. However, since I'm sure we aren't going to be braiding each other's hair anytime soon, I'd like to know what exactly you sense from me that has you on edge."

"What does it matter?"

Gypsy looked around the room, searching for eyes and ears. The only people in the waiting area were an old couple with hearing aids and a mother with two small children. Judging by the incessant whining from both of them, she wasn't likely to have the attention span to eavesdrop on their conversation.

Gypsy leaned in a bit and lowered her voice. "Curiosity again. I know it will get me killed one day. What do you smell from me?"

Nevia slapped her magazine shut and her crossed leg twitched like an unhappy cat's tail. All at once, she stopped moving and looked at her. "Nothing," she admitted begrudgingly. Had they been enemies, she was sure she wouldn't have admitted it, but even had they been friends, she was sure the admission would have been just as difficult.

"Nothing?" Gypsy frowned, a little disappointed.

"Well, not nothing, just nothing more than the basics. I sense your presence, much like anyone. Your pheromones are distinct to females, your age and health, but..."

"You can't read my emotions," Gypsy clarified.

Nevia pondered that a moment. "I sense you're in physical pain, but I don't sense any unease or stress about the evening's happenings. Something I think anyone should feel. Humans, anyway."

Gypsy balked at the suggestion and laughed heartily, while Nevia frowned. "Oh, girl, I think you've been in this job too long. Occam's Razor, remember."

"And what do you suggest the simplest explanation is?"

"I'm not supernatural, I'm—" Gypsy was about to enlighten her, but something, or rather someone, caught her eye just outside the emergency room doors. "Excuse me," she said graciously, before jumping a row of chairs to get to the exit before her potential bomber could flee into the darkness again.

5

C ORI AND ETHAN STALKED through the deteriorated halls of the top level. The bulk of the level had been blocked off for years, because the military only required a small section of it. After the *release* of the elementals, Danato tried, without success, to replace the funds that the military had provided the prison. As a result, the infamous audit was still looming over Cori's head like a guillotine.

She was certain that the threat of being relocated was the worst-case scenario for her indiscretions. However, she was an indentured servant. She had always assumed that meant she was bound to the prison, but in reality, she was subjugated by the same people that dictated to Danato.

She trusted that Danato and Belus would do everything possible to keep her from being banished, and she was sure that it would take nothing short of the collectors to drag her away from her son, but just to be safe she was taking her job very seriously. That, of course, meant following the rules. Although it made Belus's perpetual tutelage easier, it was making her feel less like herself. The more compliant she was, the more useless she felt. After all, her best accomplishments had been achieved in opposition to the rules.

"Do you smell that?" Ethan asked, just ahead of her. His dart gun was drawn, and he was ready to subdue their offending escapee. They didn't have many successful escapes, but those they had were usually repeat offenders.

"Yeah, she must have found a victim," Cori responded, scrunching up her nose from the repugnant smell of carrion. Her only consolation was that it wasn't human.

"Ambrosia," Ethan called and whistled as if he were calling a dog. Not that she would have come to him, but sneaking up on her was as safe as sneaking up on a bear. Better to give a little advanced warning, so he didn't scare her. Fear was always worse than anger with the zoological detainees.

Cori brought up the rear, trying to keep an eye behind them in case she tried to sneak up on them. She bumped into Ethan when he stopped. "Got her," he whispered.

She turned around and caught sight of the massive webbing hanging between the section break and the inner line of cells. The tunneled web design was typical of a funnelweb spider. The ultimate goal was to offer a place for her to hide while she waited for something or someone to stumble into her sticky trap.

The outer edges of the structure were littered with rats. Cori made a mental note to advise the dock manager to put out rat poison to prevent future stowaways from getting into the prison via the shipments. *That* would be a fun conversation.

Unfortunately, the rats were only morsels to Ambrosia. She was half-human and half-spider, and vampiric down to her very core. Blood was not just her preferred sustenance; it was biologically impossible for her to eat anything else. It also happened to be as alluring to her as cocaine to a junky. Hungry or not, she wanted warm, fresh blood.

"She sees me," Ethan said, eyeing the darkened hole in the web.

Cori could barely see anything in the room since the electrical system for the area was trashed courtesy of Efrat's previous proximity. However, she definitely couldn't make out anything in the hole. She stepped in closer to Ethan, feeling the hair-raising creepiness that came with tracking a gigantic spider that was no doubt stalking her as well. He glanced back at her with a telltale smirk.

"Of all the things you've come in contact with, you still get freaked out by a spider."

"A really big spider," she clarified.

"Back off a bit. I need to be able to maneuver."

Cori frowned and stepped away. She knew he didn't mean it to sound cold, but for some reason lately he had seemed indifferent to her. It was subtle and hardly worth mentioning, but she felt it nonetheless. She assumed the recent stresses of a baby, and the audit, had just put a damper on his usual sensitivity.

She directed her tranquilizer gun at the hole, hoping the blob she was aiming at was the dark human torso, and not the impenetrable Linnaean-defying conjoined thorax.

Ethan stepped forward carefully, avoiding the adjunctive structural threads. He couldn't shoot her inside the tunnel. He had to lure her out, otherwise it would be an ordeal to retrieve her from the sticky alcove.

Ethan picked up a piece of broken cinder block and tossed it into the web. Ambrosia leaped forward the instant it hit and started wrapping her web around the precious gift with her lower spider half. Before she could ascertain that the block wouldn't provide her a drop of blood, Ethan shot her with his dart and *missed*.

Cori noted the sudden change in her attitude. Granted, angry wasn't as bad as frightened, but it still wasn't good. Ambrosia's eyes were already bulbous black orbs, but they took on a new shimmer as she looked at Ethan. Her black lips curled, revealing long translucent fangs. Cori knew from drawings that they were partially hollowed out from the tip up so she could sip her victims' blood out faster, like soda through a straw.

While Ethan calmly reloaded his gun, Cori took her turn and shot a dart at Ambrosia. She was pleasantly surprised that she didn't miss. However, the shot in her arm was not enough to drop her. The creature's predacious gaze turned to Cori instead of Ethan.

"Cori!" Ethan snapped, as if she had just screwed up the whole capture. She wanted to remind him that he missed his shot, but that was the type of quarrelsome attitude she was trying to contain. Not to mention, it wouldn't halt the 180-pound—all booty—spider woman that was barreling toward her to skewer her neck.

"Hey!" a voice shouted from behind Ambrosia before electric blue light rimmed her profile and instantly dropped her to the floor.

Cori opened her mouth to yell at Efrat for his fatal attack, but she could already see that Ambrosia was still breathing. She wasn't sure how Efrat had managed to hone his power enough to knock people out for hours at a time, yet still struggled with the simple task of directionality, but she was never more thankful for it than right then.

Ethan approached the downed creature to examine her condition and verify that she was out. When he was satisfied, he aimed his scowl right at her.

"Well, she's alive." Cori shrugged, misinterpreting his annoyance altogether.

"Why did you shoot at her?" he asked.

"Because you missed," she said quietly, in case Efrat wasn't supposed to know he had made a fatal mistake.

"Of course I missed. I wanted to draw her out of the web completely. You think I want to get stuck on that crap?"

Cori shook her head. "I didn't know what your plan was."

Ethan stared at her a moment. He must have been trying to figure out whether her lack of psychic ability was also her fault. "I'm the bait, Cori. Never you," he said softly, but still scolding her for allowing herself to become a target. She wasn't sure why today should be the exception to her usual procedure of stupidly walking into bad situations. She supposed that it had been a while since they were on a retrieval operation together. They were just out of practice. That was all.

"Okay," she said, giving him a slight nod. She normally might have mock saluted him, but she needed to illustrate proper etiquette in front of Efrat. After all, she was a good, loyal, and respectful employee—and Ethan was her pain-in-the-ass supervisor.

Ethan moved to lift the spider woman from the floor. Though he didn't need the help, Efrat jumped in to grab the lower half. At the last second, Cori thought it might be a bad idea for his electrified hands to touch so close to the spinner.

"Efrat, wait!" She jumped over to push him away, but the bulbous back end undulated under his touch. A white film spat out, splattering both their legs. It looked liquid at first, but as they both squirmed away, the intricate webbing revealed itself. The sticky marshmallow matrix left them a small amount of give, but they were effectively stuck to the floor and each other.

6

E THAN DOLED HER OUT another look of disappointment as he inspected their encasement. Cori couldn't take it. She was playing the good little soldier like she was supposed to, and somehow she was still screwing up in someone's eyes. "How is this my fault?" she yelled at him, though he hadn't actually spoken the accusation.

Ethan glanced at Efrat. He got the hint, but since he couldn't leave them alone, he just looked away, trying to find something of interest in the surroundings. "I'm not blaming you."

"Could have fooled me," she grumbled, reaching to tug at her pant leg.

"Don't touch it!" He leaped forward, grabbing her wrist. "Better to be on your pants than your skin."

"I know!" She ripped her hand away. Had Efrat been shorter, she would have backhanded him. As it was, he leaned away to save his shoulder from further abuse. "I was just..." Cori huffed and looked at Ambrosia's unconscious form. "Just take her back to her cell and bring us some solvent."

Ethan looked at Efrat again. He didn't seem to like the idea of leaving them alone. Once again, she wondered why today was any different. She had been helping Efrat train his powers for months—if you could call a three-month-long argument training. Granted, Belus was usually in and out of the sessions, but Ethan was rarely around for them.

He stepped forward and reached to touch her face. She knew what he wanted to do. He wanted to kiss her, or at least exchange an 'I love you' to remind Efrat that she belonged to him, but after being treated so blatantly like an employee, she wanted no part of it.

"Just go." She pulled back slightly. The look he gave her was virulent, and she couldn't help but tone down the anger in her voice. "The sooner you can get me out of this, the better," she rationalized.

He moved away and loaded the spider creature on his shoulder with one smooth lift. Efrat watched him, admiring the display of strength. "When do I get to start taking those steroids?" he murmured after Ethan was out of earshot.

"Yeah, cause that's what we need. Magneto and the Hulk in one package."

Efrat chuckled at that, even though she was being snide as hell. For a couple of minutes, she just stared off into the corridor, trying not to replay the last few months over in her head. What had she done to make Ethan so offish?

Was her newfound reliability and dutifulness turning him off? She had struggled to get back to her pre-baby weight, but she thought her body had trimmed down nicely, and she was sure Ethan would never be that judgmental of her figure. Was she giving the baby too much attention?

Ethan hadn't said much about his trip to China; she knew he was holding something back about the trip. Although she was positive he would never cheat on her, she was wondering whether he had met someone there. Perhaps coming home to his post-pardoned wife, a screaming baby, and the reality of his duty to both of them had broken his spirit.

"Corinthia!" Efrat yowled beside her.

She looked up at him, trying to see what emergency was demanding him to use her given name. He looked over her face and his irritation turned to sympathy. "I know you're having a moment there, kitten, but you are literally freezing my balls off."

Cori looked down at the affected area and found frost caking Efrat's right hip. She looked at her hands and found them both layered with the same snowy coverage. "Sorry," she hissed and focused on warming her hands before wiping off the ice. She even went so far as to hold her heated hands on his hip just to ensure he didn't get frostbite.

"That's nice. Care to move that around to the front?" Efrat smiled at her. It was an honest flirtation, one that reminded her of the way Dr. Frank had seen him. It was a part of him she wanted to encourage to come out, so he could be more like his old self again. Unfortunately, since she was still the only person he could touch without hurting, she wasn't sure how much of what he said was flirtation and how much was invitation.

"I'm already in enough trouble." She rolled her eyes and moved her hands into her pockets.

"He seems on edge or something. Baby blues?" Efrat asked as he tried to find a casual position for his hands. He settled on doing nothing, and holding them out from his sides.

"I guess," she said. Efrat didn't seem to buy her subscribed rationalization.

"Is it us?" he asked.

"Us?" She glanced at him, but he seemed to be serious. She shrugged. "I really don't know, Efrat, and if you don't mind, I really don't want to talk about it."

"That bad?" He whistled and struggled to get away from the webbing again. "Well, if you aren't going to gossip, and I'm no good at small talk since I've been cooped up in this place for seven years, I vote we jump trousers and get out of here."

"Jump trousers?" Cori looked down at her gooey pants.

"Why not? Unless you're going commando?" He tipped his head as if he might see through her pants.

"No!" she quickly amended, which made him smile. "Why would that be sexy? Underwear is not optional for women!"

Efrat shrugged. "It's a penis thing. You wouldn't understand."

"I understand it just fine. I just don't know why I have to be subjected to it every time we are together."

"Because heterosexuality is the only thing we have in common," Efrat grumbled. Cori wanted to defend that point, but he was probably right. Their history was unpleasant, to say the least. Efrat hated everyone she loved. They couldn't talk about the weather because varying degrees of cold made poor conversation, and pop culture was out since neither of them were up to date on current movies or music. "Come on, what's worse, standing here in awkward silence with me, or running around the prison with bare legs."

"Fine." Cori unbuttoned her cargo pants and unzipped them. "Hold me still so I don't nose dive into this stuff."

"Happily."

He gripped around her waist while she lowered her pants carefully to the floor. Since her boots were also snagged in the webbing, she had to pull her feet out with some effort. Leaning on Efrat more than she preferred, she finally got free of them.

"Now me." Efrat raised his hands to offer her leave to remove his pants.

"Really?"

He tipped his head. "I can do it myself, but my cock prefers I don't."

Cori crossed her arms and narrowed her eyes at him. "I'll help you, but you have to tell me, once and for all, why you wear that stupid belt—and jeans. Hello, metal!"

Efrat's amusement thinned to near nothing, but he did seem to appreciate her blackmail. "General Clark and I had very different opinions about what good behavior was. He made me wear this because he knew it would be difficult not to shock myself when I was attacking everyone else. He also liked to deny me my restroom buddy when I had been naughty. It's a wonder I can even get a hard-on anymore."

Cori nodded, trying to convey sympathy before she persisted to get more information from him. "Okay, I get that, but why are you *still* wearing it? I sort of took care of the Clark situation."

Efrat glared at her. "Because I can."

She waited for him to continue, but he didn't. "Stubborn." Cori coughed the word into her fist.

"Says the pot to the kettle."

"I'm not stubborn; I'm tenacious. There's a difference." She moved in to disrobe him, starting with his belt.

"I'm going to bite back the 'pain in the ass' reference since I don't want your hands superheated right now," he quipped. She paused, looking at the big belt buckle before tossing it aside. "It's a badge of courage to me," he explained further.

"Badge of stupidity," she murmured as she fumbled with his top jean button.

"You wouldn't understand," he said resolutely.

"Oh, is this a penis thing again?" She knew it was pointless to argue with him, but she didn't want to add silence to her task at hand. She unzipped the pants and was relieved to find that he was a boxer man, and not briefs. "There, I think you can get the—" She paused in her withdrawal. "What is that?" She reached to lift his shirt, but he grabbed her hand.

"Yes, I can get it from here."

Cori eyed his stern gaze suspiciously. She already knew what he was trying to hide, but she didn't like that he was fighting the discovery so vehemently. "Show me," she said simply.

"The tissue is scarred from being shocked. It's nothing."

"I believe you. Now show me."

His palms lit with blue threat.

She glanced down and pulled her hands away. She had learned to deal with Efrat much in the same way she expected she might have to deal with her son in the future. She waited him out with a stern, motherly glare. It took a while, but eventually, like all obstinate brats, he gave in just to get her to leave him alone.

Efrat sighed and lifted his shirt slightly. The round, dark brown scar under his belly button was right where the jean button rested against his skin. She stepped forward, giving him a sympathetic but disappointed headshake.

She pushed his hand to move it out of her vision, but he kept it firmly in place, refusing to raise the shirt further. Cori stood up straight and tried on her motherly tone, which also had benefited her troubled days with Efrat. "You lift that shirt right now, or I will have Ethan hold you down while I do it."

He all but growled as he clenched his jaw and lifted the shirt high on his chest, exposing far more than necessary. Cori examined the halo scar that aligned with the top arch of his belt buckle. She'd expected it to be much the same as the other scar, only larger. However, in addition to its expanse, the center had a greenish black scab that was pulling away from the outer boundary of the injury.

Cori grimaced and crouched down to examine it closer. "Damn it, Efrat! This is necrotic. You have to get this removed. Why didn't you show someone this? Why didn't you...?" She looked back up at him and she saw the same expression she saw every time they had an argument like this. His acrimony went down to the bone. She had hoped that she could help him accept his new lot in life, but it was finally clear to her he would not adapt to this life.

"Am I interrupting?" Ethan's voice broke her from her epiphany.

She glanced over at him. He was back with two pairs of pants looped over his arms and no solvent. He was mad again. She wondered when he had traded in his commitment to never look at her with hatred.

"Actually, we were just getting started. Could you give us a few more minutes?" Efrat answered when she didn't say anything.

Cori looked at Efrat, who was smirking down at her. That was when she realized she was without pants, kneeling before him with her face level with his open fly.

"No," she blurted out before whipping her head back to Ethan. "We were getting free."

Ethan moved around her and tossed her a pair of cargo pants that were a size too big. She moved her head to avoid the near miss to her face, letting the pants land on her shoulder. She turned away, hiding her watering eyes until she could get them under control. She refused to let herself cry when her anger should have taken enough precedence to impede it.

"I couldn't find the solvent. I see you two had the same idea." Ethan helped Efrat the rest of the way with his pants and even went so far as to lift him out of his shoes. It was possibly another show of strength, or just the quickest way to get through the situation. "I might have waited for the pants to arrive myself, but whatever."

Cori brusquely slipped on the pants and grabbed her dart gun from her fallen pair. She tossed the gun at Ethan just as he turned to say something to her. He barely caught the weapon and looked at her with the same irritation she felt. "Efrat has dead, possibly cancerous tissue on his stomach that needs to be removed immediately. I'll stay back and burn off these webs. I've got a lot of fire to use up, anyway."

She moved toward the web, but paused to look back at him. "If that's all right with you, sir?" Her eyes blurred slightly, but she maintained her stoic façade.

Ethan's face dimmed from the dejection. She had finally hurt him. Three months of progressively dismissive behavior, and *he* had the gall to be hurt by *her*. "Yes, Cori, that's fine," he said innocently, ignorant of why she had cut him so deep. "I'll take care of Efrat."

Ethan held her gaze for a moment, and swallowed hard. He probably wanted to kiss her goodbye, but since she'd refused him earlier, he didn't have enough courage to knowingly break his heart again.

Efrat yanked his belt free of his jeans and followed Ethan out. He glanced back at her a couple of times, but Ethan did not.

Cori didn't bother hiding her tears after they were gone. She just used them to fuel her rage, which, in turn, infused her rings with the ingredients necessary to create enough fire to burn down the spider's web.

7

ETHAN SAT IN THE operatory beside Efrat. He wasn't sure if it was necessary to stand guard while the physician removed the blackened tissue on his belly, but he didn't really know what else to do.

His interaction with Cori had left him sick to his stomach. He couldn't blame her for the cold exchange. He knew he had been pushing her away ever since the dragon had warned him that she would betray him. Although she hadn't provided any specifics, his automatic assumption was that Cori was going to cheat on him.

Efrat should have been the last person for him to suspect. Their relationship was so turbulent that no real connection had ever been made. However, Efrat was a smooth talker when he wanted to be. He also wasn't above stealing kisses when the opportunity arose.

Ethan had also considered that his behavior might cause the very problem that he was fearful of, but somehow that didn't stop him from doing it. It was as if she had already been disloyal to him. He wanted to start being angry now, so he could focus on forgiving her after.

Yet, he wasn't sure he could forgive her for that. Not after everything he had sacrificed to be with her.

"This wound should heal normally, but you need to keep your hands away from it," the doctor chided Efrat before helping him sit up. "And this is going in the trash." He picked up the offending belt off the counter and started to walk out with it.

Efrat raised his hand, trickled with swirling blue. The buckle whipped into his hand, dragging the belt and consequently the doctor with it. Efrat looked over the man with a smug smile as he righted himself again. "That's not going anywhere."

The doctor looked at Ethan for help, but he just shrugged. He honestly didn't care if Efrat shocked himself into skin cancer or not. He wasn't a fan of any man that Cori considered a friend, but Efrat was ranking even higher than Cleos had. Happily, Cleos was no longer a problem because he had left the prison as soon as he was pardoned. Efrat, however, wasn't going to be released anytime soon. An untimely disease might just be a humane way to eliminate his presence. Murder wasn't off the table yet, but Ethan knew, with or without Cori's reverence for life weighing on his shoulders, he wasn't a killer.

Efrat looked over the belt as if it was a long-lost friend and his greatest enemy all balled into one. Rightfully so, at least for the latter. "What, no lecture?" Efrat asked when he noticed him staring.

"Hang yourself with it for all I care." Ethan got up and headed out of the room.

"The thought had crossed my mind. One of the reasons I never took it off," Efrat said, following him out, down the hallway, and past the nurse's station.

"Is that supposed to draw my sympathy to your situation?" Ethan didn't turn to see his expression.

"No, not at all. Suicide doesn't deserve any sympathy. It's purely to alleviate one person's pain, in exchange for enhancing another's," Efrat said with a partially mocking philosophical tone.

"Then why bring it up?" Ethan held open the door to the infirmary, so Efrat didn't have to touch the metal handle.

Efrat paused in the doorway and furrowed his brow. "I didn't, you did. I was just making small talk."

Ethan narrowed his eyes at the slight upturn in his lip. This was apparently Efrat's idea of a joke. "I'm not always sure how to take you, Efrat," Ethan admitted.

"By the arm. I don't recommend holding hands."

Ethan allowed him a small smile for the joke. It wasn't really funny to him, but Efrat tended to fight hard to lighten the mood when things got serious, and the least he could do was play along.

"There are very few people on your side right now." Ethan continued to walk, heading toward the animal cells that lined the infirmary. "I'm not one of them."

"I never would have guessed," Efrat said, moving up to walk beside him instead of behind him.

"Belus seems to think that your presence will be helpful in the audit if you can conform to our life here. If you appear useful, then perhaps the auditors will see you as an acquired asset rather than an escaped prisoner, which will make Cori's indiscretion less offensive."

"I'm doing my duties. Crops are being delivered in record time with my help. Escaped prisoners are being subdued without the waste of ammunition. I even say my pleases and thank yous."

"What about after the audit? What about when we all trust you? I've seen this act before from Cori." Efrat gave him a sidelong glance, but Ethan didn't offer any more information to that backstory. "You're just waiting until an opportunity arises to escape. I want to know if all of this is a huge waste of time, because I would rather not waste any more of my wife's time and energy if you aren't serious about being here."

"What does that matter?" Efrat paused and faced him. Ethan stopped to join the standoff. "You've made it perfectly clear what all this feigned camaraderie is about. This isn't about me. This is about protecting Corinthia."

"Don't call her that." Ethan tried to keep the ire out of his face, but he could see it mirrored on Efrat's face.

"I knew this was coming. You've been peeking in on our practice sessions. You must be torn between doing as

Belus asks and sabotaging the plan so you can keep her away from me."

Ethan shook his head. "I'm not sabotaging anything. But yes, I see your flirtation, and I know about your stolen kisses."

Efrat chuckled. "I flirt with Cori because she is a beautiful woman, and she deserves to be flirted with. As far as my stolen kisses..." He shrugged unapologetically. "What can I say? It's been a while."

"Then find yourself a happy whore on level six, and leave my wife alone," Ethan snarled.

"I'll be sure and do that, as soon as I find one that's receptive to the zap they'll get when I climax," Efrat seethed. "Forgive me if I prefer my partners un-fricasseed."

"I understand your condition and situation makes dating a challenge, but I shouldn't have to remind you that Cori is mine."

"I don't know, butch. From what I saw upstairs, all I need to do is hang around in the wake of your asinine behavior and offer her a shoulder to cry on. Another few months of these tiffs and I'll be able to offer my cock for a revenge fuck."

Ethan wanted to punch him. He wanted to grind his head into the glossy white floor until it smeared with red, but he didn't have a chance to.

"Hey, boss!" Duke came jogging in from the next section. "Got the message you needed to meet with me." He stopped beside the two men and looked between them.

"Well, now, what have I gone and stepped in here? You boys are looking fifty shades of pissed off just between the two of ya."

"We were just discussing Efrat's future here at the prison," Ethan said civilly, though he hadn't removed his scowl.

"I reckon his future is looking pretty grim if it needs to be discussed," Duke said cheerily.

"What the fuck do you know about it, hick?" Efrat spat and turned his ferocity on him.

Duke gave Efrat a deceptively friendly smile. "I know which bunk you sleep in. That's what *I* know."

"What's that supposed to be? A threat?" Efrat flaunted his blue trickling hands.

"From what I hear, Sparky, you're only immune to electricity on your hands. I imagine the boys and I could have a lot of fun with that after dark. We aren't above interdepartmental discipline at this prison." Duke twitched an eyebrow, and Ethan resisted the urge to laugh. It was not surprising to see Duke bravely defending himself, but Efrat's retreat was unprecedented. The elemental seemed to understand that his superhuman hands meant nothing, so long as they were attached to his normal human body.

"Enough, you three," Cori said, approaching them.

8

C ORI DIDN'T HAVE TO hear the first half of the argument to summarize it. She wasn't the only one that was having trouble getting along with Efrat. His blasé attitude toward the rules of conduct that the guards proudly adhered to was putting him at odds with the entire prison.

She remembered defending his acrimony to Belus—*he didn't just lose his friends, family, and home, he lost himself.* She had hoped to help him find that missing part of himself, but so far, the only parts she had found were aggressive and intemperate—bitterness turned bitchiness.

"Ma'am." Duke nodded to her. She was disappointed that she hadn't reached the "sugar" stage yet in their relationship, but she was certain it was only a matter of time.

"Everything back to normal?" Ethan turned all his attention to her. She was sure that his face was asking about more than the condition of the level, but she couldn't really answer for something she wasn't certain about yet.

"I may have melted a few things I wasn't supposed to, but I figured the floor's a crap shoot right now anyway," she said with a slight smirk. He smiled at the joke. That was a good start, at least. "I, umm, need to talk to Efrat if you're done with him." Ethan's smile, small as it was, faded. He looked back at Efrat, who modeled a hearty cocksure smile for him. Cori would have been as annoyed as Ethan by it, but she knew it would be gone soon enough.

"Sure." Ethan frowned at her, not quite making eye contact. "I need to talk to Duke, anyway. Will you head home after this?" It was a question, but it almost sounded like a plea.

She nodded, and he moved forward to her. He looked again like he wanted to kiss her, but now with two subordinates in the room, she could tell he didn't want to get too personal. She was almost positive that Duke would simply "woo-hoo" at them if they got carried away, but there was no reason to be unprofessional.

"I'll see you later under the mistletoe." He grinned rakishly at her. She tucked back her coy smile to keep it from turning into a bashful grin. As he brushed past her, he nicked her hand with his.

Duke gave Efrat an eye full of something that Cori could hardly identify since she had never seen the Texan angry before. He gave her a respectful nod before jogging to catch up with Ethan.

"Alone at last," Efrat said smoothly. "I'm not really a foursome type of guy, and especially not with two other guys." He widened his eyes and grimaced for effect.

She nodded. "You were always more monogamous than you appeared to be. Paul used to say you put on your biggest show for women you knew you couldn't attain." Efrat lost his simper. "It was how he knew you really liked a girl. You got shy and tongue-tied."

"Don't." He walked away, and Cori followed behind him.

"Don't what? Remind you of who you were? Or remind you that I still *know* who you were?"

Efrat whipped around to face her. "Don't remind me that my best friend is dead!"

Her eyes watered slightly. It was almost an autonomic response to thoughts of Hirem's death. She was no longer emotionally tied to him. He was just a fading story in her mind, but she suspected that some part of her would always cry at the end of that Romeo and Juliet story.

Cori averted her eyes, and she noticed the belt in Efrat's hand. "Why do you still have that?" she asked, more exasperated than annoyed.

"Get over it, Cori." He walked on, and she followed again.

"Fine, I didn't come down here to argue with you. I came here because I think you deserve to hear it from me first."

"Hear what from you first?" Despite his inquiry, he stepped into the airlock and closed the door behind him, right in her face. She waited for him to pass through the next door before opening her side and going through the irksome decontamination zone that separated the animal level sections.

On the other side, the air was a bit warmer, and offered a new rendition of chirps, chatters, and chitters. Fortunately, they weren't in the water section, or she would be forced to yell over the pumps and aeration units.

"I didn't want to blindside you. I know that you and I have had our differences. Mainly my desire to live, versus your desire to kill me." Efrat turned around and scowled at her for the comment. She shrugged. "Not funny yet?" He clenched his jaw and looked away. "Anyway..." She looked to the floor for a reason to stop or continue, but the impossibly clean white floors revealed nothing. "I just want you to know that what I'm about to say is not out of revenge, or anger, or even frustration."

He looked her over, locking eyes with her. He could see this was serious. As much as he probably wanted to inject his own humor into the moment, he didn't. "Go on."

"I'm going to recommend to Danato that you be released and relocated... after the amputation of your hands." She forced herself to look into his eyes, even though the livid unspoken threat he was directing at her was making her want to shrivel away from him. She raised her chin when he shook his head. "I know you've been trying, but Efrat—"

"I've done everything you asked," he spat.

"Yes," she agreed, "but this is about you as a person, not your conduct, or even your power."

"My power is the only reason I'm here!"

"That's not necessarily true. If you were in control—"

"I *am* in control," he yelled as blue threads twined his fingers, negating his statement.

Cori shook her head. It was useless arguing with him. He didn't even know when to admit he was wrong. "My decision is final. I only told you out of respect for the work that you have put into this."

Efrat charged forward and grabbed her throat, not quite choking her. The tentacles of electricity snapping in her face hurt, so she knew he had intentionally amped his power high enough for her to feel it. It was a useless battle, though; she could feel her rings burning against her fingers to overpower and protect her.

"How could you do this?" he hissed.

Not bothering to defend her neck, Cori drew an imaginary frame around the violent opponent before her. "How can you do this? How long before I stop being your enemy? How long before you rein in this endless temper tantrum you call a personality? How many more people have to die, just so *you* can feel atoned?"

"I will not let you take my hands!"

Cori could feel him press against her throat. She knew it was just a threat, a reminder that he had other ways of hurting her; ways the rings couldn't protect her from. Unfortunately for him, she was done playing the pacifist in this conversation. The bolt she put into his belly hurled him back between two small cells. The twittering red-eyed crows they contained squawked at the disruption and scrambled to be away from the excitement. She hadn't intended him to hit the wall, but apparently being directly plugged into Efrat made her power a lot stronger.

When he got back up, he looked more like a chastised child than her villain. That was good; she could work with that. "This afternoon, you tried to hide your wound from me." He scoffed, but didn't interrupt. "That tells me a number of things. One, you don't trust me." Cori paused in case he wanted to deny that statement, but he didn't falter at hearing it. "Two, you still want to wallow in your misery alone. And three, you are far more stubborn than I ever gave you credit for."

"I developed some bad habits during my incarceration."

"Yes, Efrat, you were wrongly imprisoned. Shit happens!" Cori snapped, losing control of her temper. "You know what else happened? Someone put their livelihood on the line for you and freed you!"

"I am not free, you condescending bitch!" Efrat stomped back over to her. His face was red with the anger she was directing right back at him. "I can't walk away from this prison!"

"Which prison are we talking about? The building or your hands? Because I'm losing track of what I'm supposed to feel sorry for. Hey, here's an idea. How about you kill two birds with one stone?" Behind him, one of the crows squawked in objection to the idiom. "Cut those weaponized hands off and get the hell out of here!"

Efrat panted, seemingly searching for a way to overshadow her anger with his objections. "You said you would help me."

Cori outright laughed at him. "I could train a pig to fly with the amount of time I've put into you, Efrat. You are not worth the arguments with Ethan, and you are certainly not worth the time away from my child. So that's it! I'm done." Cori paused, waiting for him to fight again, but he didn't. His lips were pinched tight. If she didn't know him better, she might have suspected he was on the verge of tears. "I'm putting the recommendation in, damned the audit. Damned be whatever grand plan Belus has. And damned be you... you ungrateful jerk." She only whispered the last part, but it stilled him.

She took a few backward steps, in case he might attempt an attack. When it was apparent he was giving up the fight, she turned around. She should have known he wasn't above shooting her in the back.

9

CORI CRINGED AS THE ball of lightning surrounded her. Her hair turned into a *koosh* ball and every movement created static electricity, but she wasn't being electrocuted. It hadn't even registered on her rings.

She turned back to find out what Efrat had done. He was pacing around the spherical force field he had put around her, feeding it a steady stream of power. She was about to yell at him to let her go, but she realized she had never seen him do this before. This was new. At least to her. He seemed rather familiar with it.

With one hand to secure her confinement, he drew his attention to his other hand. He directed his bolt at a blank spot of wall above the airlock doors. His electrical touch left a blackened trail on the wall. She was impressed by his ambidextrousness, but that was also giving way to questions about how long he had been capable of this feat.

To add to his resume display, the scorched pattern on the wall began to form an image. It was a tree, and not just a kindergarten drawing. The staggered lines provided texture to the bark of the leafless winter tree. She was surprised at his artistic skill, but that was quickly drowned out by the enlightenment that he had enough control to draw with his elemental power. Yet she had struggled for months to get him to attune his aim.

Deception wasn't a suitable description for this hidden information. This was nearing the level of collusion. What was his purpose in hiding this ability?

When he finished, Efrat's blue energy field depleted around her and he lowered his hands. He was panting from the exertion. She imagined the concentration on his energy took as much out of him as potency.

He dropped to his knees, and without looking up at her, changed his previous demand to a plea. "Please, don't take my hands," he whispered breathlessly.

Cori was unfamiliar with this emotion from him. He was finally breaking.

The part of her that wanted to be done with this whole hellish experiment just wanted to walk away. The part of her that knew he still couldn't touch anyone wanted to alleviate his misery, regardless of the fact that he didn't agree with her method. Nevertheless, the part of her that had made so many mistakes wanted to show him that forgiveness was always an option, if you were willing to earn it.

Cori kneeled down on one knee in front of him. There was too much distance between them for her to comfort him, but that wasn't why she had done it. She glanced up at the beautiful graffiti tree that Danato would never allow to remain on his prison wall. "How long?" she asked. "How long have you been able to do that?"

"I've been playing with my powers ever since I discovered the time bubble. An errant bolt pulled me in one day during my explorations. It didn't take me long to figure out that another one would draw me out again." He looked at her sheepishly. "Paul and I knew our best chance at escape was to hone our power, but we couldn't reveal any evolution to Clark. He wanted to weaponize us, but as long as our powers were erratic, he couldn't get approval. Our cooperation was only a secondary problem for him. He had threatened on more than one occasion to find a replacement body for my hands."

He paused, enlightening her to how long that threat had been looming over his head. "Hirem did what he could outside of sight to develop his ability, but meditation wasn't a replacement for practice. In the time bubble, I could practice for a full day before I had to return. As you can see, I was getting pretty good."

"I get why you didn't tell Clark, but why hide it from us?"

Efrat narrowed his eyes. "The same reason."

Cori's brow dipped, and she cocked her head to one side. "You think we want to use you as a weapon?"

"Isn't that what all this training is about? Being useful to you?"

"No, Efrat." Cori crossed her hands over her knee. "Truthfully, your power is pretty useless to us. Although I can see some potential for decorating." She glanced at the tree and smiled at him. She expected him to appreciate her lightening the mood, but her levity was just as unwelcome as his usually was.

Efrat looked around for something. When he didn't see what he wanted, he raised his belt. He focused on the buckle, wrapping it with blue. She expected a display of magnetism, but this was different. The belt rose from Efrat's hand, spinning slowly, floating on the polarity of his electromagnetism.

She was about to say something about the skill being potentially useful, but he shifted his hand, and the buckle was propelled away from them, driven by a burst of energy. The buckle hit the wall beside the glass doors in the section break. The leather strap slapped into the wall right behind it. The drywall only had minor damage, but the buckle had imbedded halfway into it.

She looked at Efrat and he clenched his jaw before speaking. "See? I'm a rather valuable prize for your collection," he seethed.

Cori opened her mouth to object to so many points, but she stopped. They were making progress in honest conversation. For once, she needed to not let him bait her into an argument. Instead, she rose and moved to the wall. With some effort, she pulled the belt free of the sheetrock and turned back to Efrat. He was on his feet again, perpetually ready for the next fight.

"Come with me," she said and passed by his outstretched hand that still wanted the damned belt.

10

Ethan laughed at Duke's mimed performance of the final heist that put him into the penal system for twenty years. With one arm pinned behind him, and the other smashed to his head, Ethan could picture him jammed in an air duct waiting for the police to rescue him.

"That's when I realized that summer jobs are better, because air conditioning doesn't make you sweat."

Ethan shook his head and leaned back in Danato's chair. Somehow, the chair didn't seem as uncomfortable as it used to. The spring no longer poked him, and the back even supported him, despite years of Danato's heavy weight pressing into it.

"You going to tell me what this is about, boss, or are you just doing that quiet contemplation thing for practice?" Duke smirked, but he looked a little worried. "Cause I gotta tell ya, I kind of like talking. Any space you leave open for drama, I might just fill with nonsense."

Ethan chuckled again. He liked Duke. He had considered him to be his first friend outside of Cori, but he wasn't sure that really counted since his draw to her had never been only friendly. It was because of that friendship that he loathed to say what he was about to say.

"Danato tells me that you've declined your parole."

Duke's face melted for a moment, but he put on a fresh smile before he spoke. "Well, sure, signed the paperwork and everything. Done deal."

"He said you've declined your last two paroles."

"Yeah, I guess it's been a few." Duke shrugged. He still didn't show any regret for the self-sacrifice. "I guess I kind of like it here."

"What about your mother and your sister? Don't you want to see them?"

Duke frowned, revealing a glimpse of the love that he held for the only two women in his life.

"I know that you like it here, and with enough paperwork, I'm sure I could manipulate your nondisclosure contract to get you put on as a free agent, like the physicians."

Duke shook his head. "I appreciate that, but I haven't got enough college to get free agent status. If I get paroled, they'll give me a deep wipe. I might get to see my mom and sister again, but everything else..." He trailed off, fiddling with his fingers. "Danato takes care of them. They get my letters. No, I just think I'm a better man in here than I ever was out there. To them I might just be the stupid kin that ended up in the slammer, but if I go back, that's all I'll ever be to myself, too."

Ethan nodded. He had intended to encourage his friend to rethink returning to the real world, but apparently, he had already given it a good deal of thought.

11

C ORI DIDN'T HAVE FAR to go to reach her destination. The cell was just as she remembered, plastic bars and riddled with tree branches and colored rubber toys to entertain the simian inside. He chittered happily and swung over to greet her, as he always did when there was potential for a little affection. She smiled at his enthusiasm and reached through the bars to pet his head.

"This is Fred," she said, not looking away from Fred's contorted body that was begging for more, more, more. She laughed when he twisted so far that he lost grip on his branch and fell to the floor of his cage.

"You wanted to introduce me to your monkey?" Efrat drawled as he leaned on the bars. Fred moved to intercept the newcomer's love, but even as Efrat's hand rose to offer the little guy a scratch, he lowered it again. Disappointed, Fred returned to Cori instead. "That wasn't really the animal I had hoped you would introduce me to, kitten." His smirk pushed through his attempt to look lewd.

"Do you have any idea what we do here, Efrat? What our prison motto is?" she asked, ignoring his flirtation.

"It's a prison. It's kind of obvious."

"I would have thought so." Cori widened her eyes in place of an eye roll. "We contain creatures that are hazardous to the human world." She looked at him to make sure he was with her so far. He did not spare her an eye roll. "What do you think of Fred here?"

"He's a monkey," Efrat drawled with the same waning interest as before.

"Yes, a spider monkey, to be exact. Are you afraid of him?"

"No."

"What if I told you he is responsible for more human deaths than any creature in this prison?" Efrat looked back at Fred, searching for the cause of this destruction. "There was a tribe living deep in the Amazon. They were pushed from their home over and over again by the expanding industry in South America. A shaman of the tribe tapped into some dark magic and took revenge on the deforesting crews in the form of a baby spider monkey cursed with the ability to rust metal with his touch."

Fred screeched as if he knew this story was about him—or she had stopped petting him. "Fred here was happy to find humans that would feed him and scratch his neck. It took about a week, but he devastated millions of dollars' worth of logging equipment, which, in turn, caused a few fatal accidents.

"Unfortunately, he didn't stop there. Someone bankrupted from their employment captured Fred to sell in America. The cargo ship that he got loose on had about 25 crewmembers. When the rusted-out ship sank, Fred survived and floated on cargo debris until he was recovered by a fishing vessel. 13 people died when that boat sank. When he made it ashore in Mexico, his carnage continued in the cities. He collapsed bridges, buildings, not to mention the car accidents he caused. By the time Fred was discovered and contained, he was responsible for 108 known deaths."

Efrat raised his brow, reluctantly acknowledging that Fred was indeed dangerous. "What's your point?"

"Fred's a monkey, Efrat. He's just... a monkey. He doesn't know that he's killed people. He's not vicious. He's not vindictive. He just wants to get his neck scratched and to get the hell out of this stupid cage that we keep him in." Cori pulled a treat from the latched box on the side of the cage to distract Fred so she could stop petting him without being screeched at. "You want to talk about the potential for weaponry. Imagine Fred being released in New York City or Tokyo. It would be cataclysmic."

"Why bother holding him? Why not just kill him?" Efrat said coldly.

She forced her reaction to be calm, despite the fact that every part of her that looked at Fred like a beloved family pet wanted to shove PETA fliers down Efrat's throat. "We don't kill our inmates because they are dangerous. We protect them from others and themselves."

"But you do amputate their limbs."

"That would be the exact definition of protecting you and others. Just tell me you lied about that too, and the topic won't come up again. Cross your arms, itch your nose, scratch your ass." She scoffed, but decided not to let her humor be at his expense. "Fred didn't do anything wrong, but he does *have* to be here. We try very hard to keep him contented, but yes, he is a prisoner. I can't make his power disappear, but I can make yours disappear."

Efrat frowned and lowered his eyes. He was running out of arguments to fight her logic.

"Tell me I'm wrong. I don't want to do this against your will, but... you..." She looked away, trying to get the words right without insulting him. "You can't possibly like who you are right now." He turned away slightly. "You are never going to be the man you once were. I see that now. But that doesn't mean you have to be miserable. You could have a semi-normal life. You'd be handicapped, but you'd be free."

He looked back at her and closed some of the distance between them. "Don't go to Danato."

"Efrat..." She balked, but lost momentum when he placed his hand over hers on Fred's cage.

"Please, I'll work harder. I'll show Danato all my abilities. No more lies."

"It's not just that. I have to do what's right for this prison. You are combative and belligerent. Everyone hates you." She bit her lip and searched for an escape route.

"I can change that. Look at me." He touched her chin just to draw it up again. "You know I'm determined. I can do this. Maybe I won't ever be able to touch anyone again, but..." He rubbed his thumb along the back of her hand. "Don't take away my hope of it."

She glanced at her hand, but didn't pull it away. She raised the belt buckle to him. "You have to let go of all of it, Efrat. You can't keep shoving your past in my face like it's a merit badge that should earn you sympathy for the rest of your life."

He gulped and took the belt from her. He looked at it once more and tossed it into Fred's cage. She smiled at that. He smirked back at her. The deal seemed struck, but his eyes were still locked on hers. The deafening silence made her want to start singing a random eighties song, but she let the moment drag on long enough for Efrat's hand to rise to her cheek.

It wasn't the first time, and probably wouldn't be the last. She told herself it was a minor concession to appease his human need to touch. He never let his fingers go beyond her collarbone, and he hadn't tried to kiss her—again—so she allowed it as a peace offering. It was hard not to, since she was the only human being in seven years he could touch, including himself.

Today, however, a lot of emotions had drifted into his touch and the gaze he pinned her with. She was just about to break the moment when Fred started rubbing against her and Efrat's fingers. The yelp she expected to hear from Fred didn't follow, though.

Efrat took great interest in the soft fur running across his fingertips. Her rings were shimmering with the activation that Efrat's touch inspired, but Fred was not feeling the effects. Curious, Cori intertwined her fingers with his and brushed their hands over Fred's back. Efrat didn't fight her, and when the monkey still didn't get shocked, he took in a deep breath he seemed to be holding.

"I think the rings are absorbing the power. I suppose if you keep calm..." Cori trailed off as Efrat pulled her other hand into his and laced her fingers behind his. Slowly, he drew their hands to his face. He paused and looked at her for permission or encouragement. She nodded, not sure what else to do.

He pressed them against his skin, gently at first, but as it became clear his fingers wouldn't hurt him, he pushed into his cheeks, rubbed his face briskly, yanked at his slightly too long hair. When he brought his hands back to his face, Cori could feel his wet cheeks from between his fingers.

Efrat leaned over, not letting their hands leave as he shielded his face to weep. It was a slow breathy cry at first, but when he fell to his knees for the second time that day, dragging her with him, his cries became howls. Angry, hurt wails that had been pent up inside of him for far too many years.

12

W HEN ETHAN HAD FINISHED with Duke, he intended to go home, but he suspected Cori wouldn't be done with Efrat yet. He went back up to the animal level and found them in a strange embrace. Kneeling together with their hands clasped. Efrat's face was buried in them. At first, his jealousy piqued, and he nearly ripped open the airlock doors to separate them, but as he continued to watch, he could see this wasn't a romantic embrace. It was worse. It was the emotional connection that was missing from their relationship.

13

"I CAN'T BELIEVE YOU are letting us put up a Christmas tree," Cori said as Danato lifted her so she could put a star on the nine-foot evergreen that stood behind his armchair. He had made a special trip out west to chop it down so they could have a proper Christmas. She wasn't sure if it was in response to having a baby in the house, or just the rejuvenation of a life without constant leg pain. Either way, she was thrilled.

"*I* can't believe you requisitioned her that sweater, but you wouldn't order me new lights," Ethan grumbled from the far chair as he tried to untangle and repair a decade-old string of lights.

Danato set her down and frowned at her green sweater. "In my defense, she didn't mention that it took batteries."

Hearing her cue, Cori pushed the star on her shirt. She grinned goofily as the Christmas tree on her stomach twinkled with multi-colored LED lights. Danato shook his head in disapproval, but the curve in his lips told her she wasn't really in trouble.

"*I* can't believe you are making me water down perfectly good rum with eggnog," Belus added from the couch. He had been invited to join in the festivities, but he wasn't so much helping with the decorating as observing... and possibly getting tipsy, if she wasn't mistaken.

"Says the man on his third cup," Cori snorted. "Don't think I didn't see you top them off with extra brandy."

"Well, I don't want *someone* to accuse me of being unseasonable."

"Be nice or I'll pull out the mistletoe." Cori brandished her best kissy lips for him.

Belus let out a deep bass chuckle that was barely audible. He opened his mouth to respond to her threat, but shook his head, thinking better of whatever he had in mind for a retort. "Your star's crooked, kid." He nodded to the tree.

Cori looked up and crinkled her nose at the lopsided star. "Damn it."

"I'll get it, sweetheart. You go grab the rest of the decorations out of the storage."

"You know what this night is missing?" Cori said as she headed down the hallway.

"Functional Christmas lights?" Ethan growled comically after her.

"Unadulterated liquor?" Belus hollered right after.

"Belus to stop drinking, and Ethan to start," she heard Danato add as she reached the laundry room door beyond the master bedroom.

She laughed at all of them. "No, Christmas carols," she said before entering the catchall room. It served as a laundry room, but it was also a pantry and broom closet.

"Well, start singing, kid, 'cause we aren't expecting any carolers," Belus yelled down to her.

"I know. I just miss it," she yelled back as she dug through the deep shelves for the box labeled "x-mas decorations." She was impressed that Danato even had decorations, but assumed he was more sentimental about the holidays in his early years as warden. Time away from the commercialized tradition no doubt tamped out his desire to perpetuate it.

She started to sing to herself just to see if she could release the stranglehold of songs that were pushing into her head. "Oh, come all ye faithful, joyful and—"

"—TRIUMPHANT." Cori jumped back from the abrupt vocalization coming from the shelving. The small room was filled with a symphonic performance. "O COME YE, O COME YE, TO BETHLEHEM."

Cori opened her mouth to yell for Danato, but she was already being pushed, pulled, and thrown from the room before she had the fortitude to speak. She landed partially on the floor and partially in Ethan's arms. He pulled her close and covered her ears with his hands, as if he might protect her from the penetrating music.

Danato clawed at the shelves in the small room, pulling out unnecessary and necessary boxes to get to the culprit. He pulled out a large, antiquated turquoise radio and took a momentary pause to scowl at the device before throwing it against the wall. The force of the impact shattered it into impossibly small pieces.

Belus stepped into the doorway and looked over Danato as he panted and stared at the dent now in the drywall. When he had assessed the danger to be gone, he looked back at her. She shook her head even with Ethan's hands still pressed to her ears. "I didn't know that was there, I swear. I didn't mean to touch it."

Belus dismissed her with a wave of his hand. "No one knew it was there. The blasted things keep showing up."

Ethan released her ears and helped her up. "Is the house making them?" he asked, still keeping her protectively close with a hand on her hip.

Belus shook his head. "So far, the complexity of her skills are plumbing and elevators. The appliances you use are brought in. A radio should be out of her scope."

"How are they getting here, then?" Ethan asked, almost irritated. "I certainly hope we aren't bringing them in on shipments."

"No, we aren't, but—" Belus paused as Danato stomped past him. "But that doesn't mean there isn't another magical force at work here. It's possible that one of the prisoners is making them appear, although I honestly have no idea who would have that skill. The device must not only arrive spontaneously, but it must also psychically link to whoever touches it. I can't think of anyone with that level of skill outside of the wizard's den." Danato passed by again with a trash bag he had retrieved from under the sink in the kitchen. "You want me to get it?" Belus mumbled after him.

"No, it's cathartic," Danato grumbled back.

Belus nodded for them to follow him back to the living room. Belus took Danato's usual chair, and Ethan sat on the couch next to Cori. "So, essentially—" Cori glanced down the hall when she heard something hit the floor, followed by a cuss word. Belus shook his head, instructing her not to interfere. "You're suggesting that one of the prisoners is trying to sabotage us with the device?"

Belus waggled his head. "It's only a theory, and frankly, unless the culprit actually stands up and identifies himself, we would have no way of knowing who it is."

"Why not?" she asked.

"Because the forces being dealt with here aren't tangible. The power behind these devices must be based in magic. Therefore, it could technically be anyone."

"Anyone?" Ethan asked.

"Well, not *anyone*. For example, you and I are both capable of playing basketball, but one of us would be better at it than the other—*me* obviously." Belus tipped his brow and smiled smugly.

Ethan smirked and bowed his head slightly. "Obviously."

"Magic is the same way," Belus continued. "Some have a natural aptitude for it, and some just practice until they are capable. If any of the prisoners are dabbling in the art, they might find themselves quite capable of reining in a significant amount of power, since this area is basically a gigantic petri dish of divine forces. However—"

Danato stormed through the living room toward the front door with his bag of debris. "I'm taking this straight to the incinerator." He yanked open the door and looked back at them. "Ethan, you better have those lights ready when I get back, and Cori, keep Belus away from the mistletoe. He is not a gentleman when he's drunk."

"Yes, sir," they said in unison as the door shut behind him.

Belus stared at the door with a slight smile on his face. He seemed to approve of Danato's bullied persistence to keep the festivities going.

"However?" Cori prompted when he was quiet too long. He looked back at her, blinking in confusion. She tried to hold back her amusement at seeing her mentor daftly befuddled. She hadn't thought he was that drunk, but he was hiding it well. "The prisoners could use the strong magical forces, but..."

"Oh, yes, but much like Ethan's obvious inadequacies on the basketball court,"—Ethan chuckled and shook his head—"the prisoners would have to study and practice the art for years before they would be able to do something as complex as hexing and teleportation. Both of which are even beyond Annette's capabilities, and she has been practicing for a lifetime."

"Is there anyone in the prison capable of that?" Cori asked.

"Ogana," Belus replied.

"The sorcerer in the wizard's den?" Ethan asked.

Belus pinched his face. "He's not technically a sorcerer. He has the ability to draw earth power without the presence of a dragon, which makes him far more advanced than Annette, but he can only access dark magic through his coven. None of that matters though, because as long as he's inside the bubble, his magic is contained."

"So, what you are really saying, Air Jordan," Ethan mocked, "is you have no idea why the radios keep popping up."

Belus shrugged. "In a nutshell."

"Is it possible that the house has taken over one of the prisoners, and they are acting on her behalf?" Cori proposed, with some hesitation.

Belus's gaze froze on her and she thought perhaps she had said something supremely stupid, but she soon saw a slight turn to his lips that he was struggling to contain. "One of my many other theories. Unfortunately, I don't have any way to detect magic, at least not here. It would be like searching for smoke in the fog."

"So, what do we do?" Ethan asked.

"Well, if I were you, I would get back to those Christmas lights before Danato gets back. He's liable to shove the holiday spirit down your throat now." Belus stood up and grabbed his glass from the table beside Cori.

"I, for one, am going back for more nog. Cori, weren't you looking for some mistletoe?" He winked at her and continued to the kitchen.

Cori snorted and got up to head back to the storage closet.

"Great, another man to openly flirt with my wife," Ethan said with more than sarcasm in his voice. Cori turned back to offer him a scowl, which he was already turning away from to tend to his lights.

"That's not flirting." Belus scoffed from the kitchen. "If I were really flirting, you'd have given me a black eye by now."

"Don't mind him, Belus. He's just mad because Efrat found one of his nerves and won't let go."

"Mmm, he's found a few of mine as well," Belus said as he poured himself more eggnog. "We should compare notes."

"I wouldn't exactly say that my wife's fidelity is just a nerve," Ethan snapped.

Cori's mouth dropped open as she tried to hold off her reaction until she had properly translated the word "fidelity" in her mind. She glanced at Belus to see if she might be overreacting, but the stark look on his face only proved what her internal dictionary was telling her. "What did you just say?"

Ethan looked up at her aghast expression and shook his head. "Nothing."

"No, that wasn't nothing. That was an accusation, or at the very least, an insinuation."

"I'm sorry, that was uncalled for. It just slipped out."

"It is a baseless accusation." She glanced at Belus. He took his cue and busied himself into invisibility in the kitchen.

"Baseless? Really?" Ethan's brow crumpled tightly. His teeth were bared in a sneer she wasn't sure she deserved. "He takes every opportunity he can to touch you. I hear more innuendos—"

"I meant it was baseless for me!" Cori snapped just as Danato returned. He glanced over the scene, and Belus gave him a slight head shake to keep him quiet. "I would have hoped you knew that," she said, quieter.

"We can talk about this later," Ethan said, glancing at the new addition to their audience.

"Yeah, right," Cori said acerbically. "Just like we talked about your trip to China later." She walked back to the storage closet to get the decorations. She thought that after recovering from a psychic radio attack that nothing could dampen her spirits, but apparently she was wrong.

14

Danato hated to see Ethan and Cori fighting. He should have been used to their quarreling by now, but this was different. They seemed to be at an impasse. Ethan was obviously distressed by her interactions with Efrat, but instead of showing his territorial side as any man would, he seemed to be shying away from the fight and cowering behind passive-aggressive comments.

He wasn't sure what would cause Ethan's character to change so suddenly, but he suspected it had something to do with his China trip, and apparently, so did Cori.

Ethan had been unusually taciturn about his time there. He mentioned only the basic information about the trip. Descriptions of the location, the people he met, and the disappointment at finding out that he could not hear the thoughts of dragons while under the influence of their blood.

Danato might have thought nothing of it, but then Annette's overdue letter arrived. Instead of revealing more about the events of Ethan's trip, it revealed less. Her normally verbose letter was succinct and without the flowery praise he'd expected she would have for his successor. Annette had always been a fan of Ethan, partially because she sympathized with the burden of Danato's duties and was pleased with anyone willing to ease them, but also because the praise he expressed in his own letters to her left no room for dislike.

Her recent letter only provided a rudimentary description of the ceremonies used to elicit the dragon's communications and then went on to elaborate on her sales trips. Nothing more was mentioned about Ethan's presence, not even her gratitude, which he found highly suspect.

He had wanted to offer Ethan the leeway to expand on his details later, when he felt comfortable with it, but since he was apparently not the only one being shut out, he decided that the time had come to push a little harder.

They managed to get the lights on the tree and most of the decorations with the barest of discourse about technique and style. Eventually, the baby started squawking upstairs, and Cori headed up to feed him. Since she was a trooper and still breastfeeding, he knew he would have enough time to broach China with Ethan privately.

"Ethan," Danato started as he sat down in his chair across the coffee table from him.

"Hmm?" Ethan asked as he focused his attention on gluing Rudolph's nose back on his snout. More than a few decorations had been harmed during his rampage, but most were salvageable.

"I think it's time we talked about China." Danato looked to Belus, signaling him to prepare his offensive face. Unfortunately, Belus had decided to make tonight one of his rare moments of insobriety, so he didn't so much put on his offensive face as just open his eyes a little wider to declare that he hadn't passed out yet.

"China?" Ethan faltered on his task and repositioned the ruby bead. "What about it? I think we've determined without a doubt that I was high as a bloody kite on dragon blood and I thought it was talking to me."

"Yes, I think that much has been cleared up, and as relieved as I am about that, I think—"

"Relieved?"

"—there is more to your trip than just that."

"Why are you relieved?" Ethan persisted, ignoring his statement on the whole.

"I think being able to communicate with an ancient species would not only be a burden on you, but I'm afraid such a privilege would take you away from your current position." Ethan's brow crumpled. "Annette is one of my best friends and I owe her a great debt. I would never deny her the ability to expand her understanding of the dragons, but I have no doubt that she would commandeer your time without any regard to how it would affect this prison."

Ethan nodded and looked down at his decoration pensively.

"Ethan, you've hardly spoken about your trip since you came back. I thought it was just me you weren't making privy to it, but apparently Cori has questions as well."

"There is nothing more to tell. Would you like the details of my meals?" Ethan snapped.

Danato refused to give in to his anger. The more irritated Ethan got, the more he knew he was right to ask the question. "Perhaps you might explain what's going on with you and Cori, then."

"That is none of your business," Ethan said, firmly pinning him with his eyes.

"Perhaps I should pretend to go have a cigarette during this topic," Belus interjected into the stalemate.

"Don't bother, Belus." Ethan raised a hand to stop him. "We are done with this conversation."

"No, we really aren't, Ethan," Danato said evenly. "You may not like me interfering with your life, but I still don't have an adequate account for your time in China, and when Annette's letter arrived, I knew it was time to speak with you again." Danato could see Ethan hesitate at that disclosure. He glanced at Belus, hoping that he would help circumvent the truth about the letter's lack of information.

"You might as well tell us your side of things, kid," Belus said on cue.

Ethan huffed and put down his decoration, careful not to lose the nose again. He sat back in his chair and, for a moment, appeared to be refusing to speak, but his face softened and he leaned forward again. "What if I was withholding information about part of my trip, but it was at the orders of someone whom I feel compelled out of respect to obey? Am I supposed to deny their request to honor yours?"

Danato sighed and leaned back to contemplate that question as well. He didn't like the idea that Annette might keep a secret from him, but he also didn't like putting Ethan in a position of breaking his promises to her.

"Clearly, I am no one to pass judgment on keeping secrets, but I do feel that the question marks you are leaving all of us with are disrupting our relationships."

Ethan glanced at the stairs. "I know. I'm trying not to let that happen, but that is a separate issue... to some extent." He pinched his lips, seemingly debating his next sentence carefully. "Adrianna, the woman I told you about."

Danato clenched his teeth, hoping against hope that Ethan was not about to divulge anything that could hurt Cori. He nodded rather than spoke in case his voice held any threat.

"She was apprenticing with Annette. I'm sure she never mentioned her before because she had flubbed up an attempt to make her a magnifier for earth power. The poor girl unfortunately absorbed some pretty intense magic. Instead of becoming a magnifier, she became a vessel."

"How could she survive that?" Belus inquired.

Ethan shrugged. "I'm not sure she technically did survive it. I mean, she was alive, of course, and sane—luckily—but she was using Levi to alleviate the burden of powers just to stay that way."

"She was hurting him?" Danato asked.

Ethan smirked. "No, uh, it was a sexual ritual. Consensual, although she never let him remember it. If I hadn't come along and let the cat out of the bag, it might have stayed a secret."

"I see." Danato nodded and relaxed. There had been some speculation about his relationship with Adrianna. It was too hard to tell if he was happy or sad to speak about her. The conflicting emotion had left Danato wondering if Ethan had succumbed to an indiscretion with the woman. Although he trusted Ethan's values and character, he also knew that it was easy to fall short of one's own expectations. "Why didn't Annette just remove the magic?"

Ethan shook his head. "She couldn't. When I found out that Addy was basically on her deathbed, I wanted to help." He paused as if he was waiting for someone to give him a reason to continue. Danato waited patiently, as did Belus. "The ceremony that Annette originally performed left Addy full of dark magic—human magic. In order to balance the human magic, she had to take in the power of the earth as well."

"That's insane." Belus's brow furrowed. "You're talking about creating a sorcerer. Even if it was possible with only one conduit, the host would—" Belus stopped before he said the word aloud. He glanced at Danato as if he had inadvertently discovered why Ethan had been so reluctant to share his trip details.

"Annette actually performed the second ceremony?" Danato asked gingerly.

"Yes, at my and Levi's and Addy's request. Annette was reluctant, with good reason, but I convinced her it was the right thing to do."

"You convinced her?" Danato asked, struggling to keep the disappointment out of his voice.

Ethan raised his chin. "As an alternative to letting her die, or go completely insane. Levi and I helped with the ceremony, and Addy survived." Belus's eyes widened, much like Danato suspected his own had. He didn't interrupt, though. "She was in a coma when I left. I haven't heard any news to the contrary, so I can only assume that she still is. Unless Annette's letter..."

Danato stared back at Ethan a moment before he realized what he was asking. "No, I'm sorry. Annette didn't mention her status."

Ethan nodded, searching the room for nothing in particular. The silence dragged out as Danato contemplated the questions that needed to be asked and the statements that needed to be made. Belus must have assumed he wouldn't speak, so he jumped in—somewhat indelicately due to his inebriation.

"Sorry to splash vinegar on an open wound, Ethan," Belus said, rubbing his face, "but I'm trying to fathom what the hell you were thinking encouraging this ceremony. With your knowledge of the wizards—why would you think it would be wise to imbue a human with earth power?"

Ethan pinned him with a blank-faced stare. "Adrianna is a very strong woman. I knew she could survive—"

"You weren't just endangering *her* life," Belus snapped, surprising both of them with this modification to their usual good cop/bad cop routine. "Do you even comprehend the magnitude of power Annette put in that girl?"

"Yeah, I got a pretty good idea, since I was right next to her when it happened," Ethan said snidely. "It was a stupid choice based on too many opinions. I'm regretting it daily, but I can't do anything about it now."

"You still aren't getting this." Belus scowled. "There is a reason that Annette didn't tell Danato what went on there." Belus glanced over at him, asking permission to continue. Danato nodded. This normally would have been his speech to give, but he didn't want to tell Ethan the hard truth any more than Belus did. "If that girl wakes up with even half the power you three idiots put into her, she will be the most powerful being on earth. Taking into consideration that she won't be bound by ancient scrolls, she might even be stronger than a genie."

"She's not malevolent, if that's what you're worried about." Ethan wrinkled his nose as if the suggestion was not just impossible, but downright asinine. Danato could tell that Ethan had affection for the girl, and that was what made the next statement so hard for him to say.

"Ethan..." Danato waited for him to look at him. "We have to execute her."

15

"Execute who?" Cori asked, coming in on the tail end of what looked like an incredibly tense discussion.

"What the hell are you talking about?" Ethan stood, ready to fight against the words Danato had just thrown at his feet.

"Even Ogana doesn't possess the power you are talking about!" Belus yelled at him. Cori jumped at the sound of her usually calm mentor raising his voice.

"Ogana is a destructive nutjob!"

"And how do you think he got that way?" Belus continued. "Some idiot wizard coven thought they could magnify the earth's power."

"It wasn't like that! Addy is *good*!"

"Power corrupts!"

"You can't just kill her!" Ethan's teeth clenched.

"Who's Addy?" Cori asked meekly as she crept closer to the living room area. She wasn't sure *now* was the right time to be jealous, but watching her husband vehemently defend a woman she didn't know was making her more than a little uncomfortable.

Ethan glanced at her, but didn't stop his argument to explain. "Annette won't just let you kill her."

"Ethan—" Danato started.

"Oh, don't try to fucking pacify me! Just say it like you're the warden of the prison and not my friend. It won't make me hate you any less, but at least I'll have to respect you for it."

"Ethan!" Cori scolded, but he didn't take his eyes off Danato.

The big man's face melted at the heartless insult, but he soon committed to his role as warden—aka bad guy—and stood up. He stepped forward, allowing his height to be a factor in his dominion over the declaration. "I'm sending the collectors." Ethan cringed, almost near tears from the statement. Cori wanted to go to him and hold him, but the situation seemed to be beyond kisses and hugs.

"Regardless of what you feel about this, Ethan, I..." Danato paused and took a step back, his body visibly more relaxed. "Regardless of how angry you are right now, I know you know that I would never willingly kill an innocent woman. And even though I am acting in accordance with the rules set by my predecessors, it doesn't mean that I'm any happier about it than you are. You might hate me for this, but you're not alone in that sentiment."

Ethan rubbed his face harshly. "If I am given an opportunity to save her, I will take it."

"Don't threaten me," Danato warned.

"It's not a threat, Danato. It's a declaration from the future warden. I won't do anything to endanger my family, but just know that I now consider Adrianna an extension of that family. You might have to follow the regulations, but I'm pretty sure you can change them too. So I will find a reason for you to rescind that decision." Ethan didn't wait for a response from Danato, nor did he acknowledge Cori's concern. He snatched his jacket and stomped out the front door.

"Was I ever that obstinate?" Danato asked after the door had slammed shut. He shrugged, either not remembering, or not willing to be bluntly honest about it.

"It was different for you," Belus rationalized. "Your father had lower expectations."

Danato's brow crumpled, contemplating that observation.

"Does anyone want to explain what that was just about, or should I just smile and nod?"

Danato turned to Cori and gave her a sympathetic look. "It seems during his trip, Ethan and Annette's assistant helped her perform a ceremony that may have produced a full-fledged sorceress."

Cori tried to remember her intensive studies on sorcerers. She knew it took a very complex set of magical circumstances to create one, and the closest any coven had gotten on this side of recorded history was Ogana, but he wasn't even a full sorcerer.

"That's bad," Belus snarled sarcastically. She gave him a stern look that he acknowledged and returned.

"Ease up, Belus. You're not mad at her." Danato gave her a reassuring shoulder squeeze before sitting back in his chair. "Ethan was trying to save this girl by giving her more power."

Cori broke away from Belus's drunken gaze and sat on the arm of Danato's chair. "And now, after rescuing her from death, you are signing her execution order."

"Yes," Danato said simply. Cori thought about that for a moment. "Aren't you going to call me a monster and plead for a stay of execution, too?"

"You're not a monster, Danato. An ogre maybe." She smiled at him and he allowed his mopey lips to turn upward. "I suppose if I knew her, I would have more to say, but..." Cori definitely didn't like the idea of killing anyone, but if she had learned anything from her experience with Gypsy, it was that some people are just better off dead. She looked between the two of them. "Can we put her in the time bubble, like the others?"

"If she has the full power of a sorceress, then the bubble won't be enough to hold her. It barely holds Ogana. The only reason we were able to entrap him was because we confiscated his wand," Danato answered.

"Can her powers be reduced or removed?" Cori asked.

Danato shook his head. "It's kind of a one-way street once you get to that level."

"I don't suppose there is a chance that she will be Glinda the Good Witch?"

"Even if she could," Belus submitted, "do you really want to risk the entire human race on that gamble?"

Cori took in a deep breath and shook her head. "No, I suppose not." She looked at Danato. "Do you want me to talk to Ethan?"

"No, sweetheart." Danato grabbed her hand and kissed it. "It's best that he sees *me* as the bad guy."

"Go figure," Belus said, standing up. "She's the one on our side."

"I'm always on your side." Cori stood and escorted him to the front door. "Sometimes you just need to be reminded which side *is* your side." Belus chuckled and wobbled slightly. "Are you going to make it home, okay?"

"I'm not going home. I have a social call to make at the infirmary." He paused at the front door. "Speaking of social calls, where's that mistletoe?"

"Belus," Danato chastised from his chair.

He smiled at Danato and motioned for Cori to come closer, and pointed at his cheek. She smiled at his friendly affection and wondered if she preferred him a little sauced. She leaned over and gave him a peck. "Merry Christmas, Belus."

"Merry Christmas, kid. Danato." He waved back at him.

"Belus." Danato nodded to him with a slight smirk on his face, and Cori let him out.

16

"WAKE UP!" ETHAN KICKED the dragon Penelope. He wasn't sure what he expected her to do. Even with superhuman strength, it was hardly more than a poke to her. "He's going to kill her!" Ethan kicked her again, but when she only rumbled out a snore, he leaned against her and buried his face in his hands. "Stupid dragon. You're screwing up everything! I saved Addy for you, and now Danato is going to kill her anyway. My marriage is falling apart, and now so is everything else."

Pray tell, how am I responsible for your marital bliss-less-ness?

Ethan looked up and saw the dragon still happily sleeping, snoring, and drooling. "Are you sleeping?"

Penelope is, but the psychic link between us dragons is open, even in our unconsciousness.

"How...? Never mind. Are you the dragon that asked me to convince Annette to do the ritual?"

My designation is irrelevant since the decision was unanimous... but yes, I am. What further woes do you wish to lie at my feet?

"Danato is going to execute Adrianna."

Why do you say this?

Ethan shook his head and rolled his eyes, hoping his thoughts could convey that. "He just told me he is going to send the collectors to get her. He said to my face that he will execute her."

Words spoken are not actions. Saying it does not guarantee it will happen.

"But he means to do it."

Conviction is an indication of path, but not destination.

"What the hell does that mean?" Ethan wasn't sure a sigh could be thought, but he was almost sure the dragon interjected a rather purposeful pause.

It means that the future is not written by one man.

"What about you? All of you have been hinting about my future."

We are not man... and we are significantly better at foretelling the destination of an event path.

"I don't suppose that Penelope was wrong about Cori?" Ethan paused, but the dragon didn't respond. "I can't lose my wife."

Penelope has not foretold the loss of your wife.

"I know, but... I don't know if our marriage could survive infidelity."

A marriage is not a being. It is a bond. A bond is only as strong as each partner's predisposition to accept the attachment.

"Can you tell me something that will help me, and not a riddle?" There was a long pause and Ethan thought the creature might have given up trying to communicate with his human brain.

Don't worry.

Ethan laughed at the ridiculous simplicity of the statement. "Easier said than done. Can I ask you something else while I've got you on the psychic phone?"

Yes.

"Why me? Why did Penelope choose to speak to me? You didn't have to drag me to China to convince Annette. You could have told Levi to convince her."

It is true that another might have convinced Annette to complete the ceremony. However, Levi was not strong enough to keep Adrianna safe through the procedure.

"You needed my strength for the ceremony?"

No, your power.

Ethan opened his mouth to ask what that meant, but the door to the gym opened and Belus strolled in.

17

"Little late for dragon fighting, isn't it?" Belus asked from the red line across the gargantuan room.

"I wanted to work off a little steam, but she's not budging." Ethan patted the dragon's shoulder before moving out of the hangar. Belus met him halfway in the center of the gym. He gave the sleeping beast a few furtive glances, but eventually relaxed. "Don't you have something to say?"

"I have lots of somethings to say. Something you'll listen to..." Belus shook his head somberly.

"This isn't right. You have to know this isn't right." Ethan and Belus rarely saw eye to eye on anything, and he clearly felt strongly about the subject, but he was hoping to find the diplomatic side that Cori always referred to.

"If I handed you a box, and I said that it either contained world peace or human extinction, but I didn't know which one, would you destroy it and lose our chance at peace or would you open it and risk the human race?"

"That's not what this is." Ethan could feel his defenses rising again, but he kept his volume civil.

"Yes, it is," Belus said, even quieter, no doubt also trying to keep his anger out of the conversation. "I know you don't want to believe ill of your friend, but power and magic change people. Humans are not meant to be gods. That's why we live finite lives, mostly sleeping and eating."

"How can you be so blithe about murdering an innocent...?" Ethan trailed off as Belus's eyes hardened with the accusation.

"I know better than anyone what it means to choose the job over a friend. To make a risk assessment twenty different ways and still come out with the same horrific solution." Belus swallowed hard.

"I don't understand how you don't hate him for making you..." Ethan trailed off again, but only because saying the words would make the verbal wound bigger.

"We've never glamorized this job, Ethan. It's hard work, and it's even harder when your heart is involved. For the record, though, Danato didn't make me do anything. I chose to alleviate the warden of his duty, because it would have been too much for him to bear. As far as hate goes, Danato and I used up all our hate on ourselves for that incident."

"I don't think I can forgive Danato for this."

"You think that, but until you have to make the decision yourself, you'll never understand the gumption it takes. I know you weren't kidding about finding a way to save her, and if you find a way that doesn't harm anyone in this prison, you better believe that Danato and I will be on your side a hundred percent."

"But?" Ethan offered.

"But..." Belus looked back at the dragon. "I wouldn't be flaunting your ascension to warden in the same sentence that you defy the current one."

"I have a right to argue my point."

"The only argument you have right now in her favor is that she's an innocent girl and your friend." Belus frowned. "Trust me... that won't be enough to save her."

18

Gypsy stepped into the club and gauged the crowd of drunken dancers. Two meaty men, werewolves of course, eyed her entrance with suspicious interest. They hadn't met her personally, but she was developing a reputation. As unfounded as the rumors were getting, she didn't mind the attention. It didn't make things any easier, but it made them more entertaining.

One of the doorstops placed a hand on her shoulder. She looked over at the knobby fingers, unimpressed. Before she could cater to his invitation to violence, the club door opened behind her and she heard a low guttural growl; an aphrodisiac she had come to appreciate. The grip on her shifted and eventually slid off.

Callin stepped up beside her and smiled slyly as he surveyed the crowd, much like she had just done. He was, as usual, dressed in quality luxury fabrics that made him look delicious. She could hardly claim to be his girlfriend, since neither of them was monogamous, but she had to admit, his was the only bed she had been seeking lately. She kept thinking the sex would taper off into boring repetition, but so far, every animalistic encounter topped the last. The only thing likely to break their run was the transition her boss had planned for her.

It had been a few weeks since he had illuminated her to his presence and ultimate purpose. She had mistakenly identified him as Callin's bomber and nearly taken off his head before he could convince her otherwise. To say he was an interesting character was like calling the universe pretty big. She had never met anyone like him—and according to him, she never would again.

Despite his tendency to be overdramatic, she got along with him rather well. She especially liked to see him in action, and tonight was the pièce de résistance. The coup against the Council of the Moon had been successful and Frederique was off the throne, but she was still hanging on by her fingernails. Apparently, being blinded, excommunicated, and humiliated wasn't enough reason for her to give up. It should have been no surprise, given that she was stubborn, even for a werewolf, but still... *know when to fold 'em*.

When her boss finally made an appearance at the entrance, in the same fine wears as Callin, he nodded to her that he was ready. She led the march into the crowd. Armed from tits to toes, she was prepared for anything. Even if she wasn't, she had an alpha male werewolf as backup, so there was hardly a risk of strutting through the werewolf bar with her usual cocky attitude.

She parted the crowd on the dance floor—probably because of the machete strapped across her chest—and made her way to the private tables tucked in the back corner, away from the melee that was considered socializing. She could feel Callin at her back, only a step behind. When they approached the curtained-off section, two female guards gave her a once-over before they caught sight of Callin. The two fem-wolves would have been enough to subdue both of them, but not without a messy fight. Since her reputation wasn't the only one that was being aggrandized in the retelling, the women only gave minor glares before conceding to the unspoken request for passage.

The fem-wolves slipped inside the tented table section to announce their presence. After a brief muffled discussion, one woman parted the curtain for her entrance. Gypsy stepped through, wary of any invitation from an enemy.

The tiny table beyond the drape was barely enough to hold a few drinks, but the luxurious padded horseshoe sofa left room for Frederique and her current boy toy to sprawl out, plus room for guests. Frederique still managed to look regal with her perpetual sunglasses and the rhinestone-studded cane at her side.

Her boyfriend was of no consequence, but he looked to be a little young, bordering on bad-teacher-of-the-year young. If he had an ounce of chest hair, it was probably more than his balls had.

"Grace," Frederique's voice chimed like they were old friends.

"Fred. How the hell are you?" Gypsy asked chummily.

"Lacking visual stimuli," she said coldly.

"Now, Freddy, you know I can't take responsibility for that. I only took your peripheral vision."

Frederique sighed. "Oh, how I have missed our banter. Is that Callin I smell with you, or just on you?"

"Both, I imagine," Gypsy admitted without shame.

"Does my sister enjoy sharing with you?"

"Your sister has every werewolf in Europe vying for her pussy. I don't imagine she's pining." Gypsy heard a low growl from Callin as he stepped beside her and gave her a scolding glare. As much as she should have feared any rebuke from him, she couldn't help but hope his punishment for the indiscretion would take place on a mattress. "Speaking of your *lovely* sister," Gypsy quickly changed topics, "have you heard that she's ordered a recount of the werewolf population? The count is now to include half and quarter werewolf heritage."

"Yes, I have actually. A bold first move, watering down our species."

"Seriously." Gypsy furrowed her brow. "You guys are like rabid dogs. I mean no offense to the sane werewolves," she quickly interjected before her mouth got her more discipline than her ass could take. "But wow, Freddy, you *need* some watering down."

"That's amusing coming from you, Grace. I'm not really sure *sane* applies to you either."

"True, but I'm at least pretending to be normal. You… you're just bathing in crazy."

"Ladies." A hand clamped onto her shoulder and her boss pushed her to one side to get into the area. "Could we discuss this later, at a more suitable location, like a tractor pull or a late-night talk show?"

"Who the hell is that?" Frederique's nose sniffed the air, searching for an identity.

"Save your nose, we've never met, and after tonight we never will again," he said, carefully insinuating himself around the two women who were reluctant to let him closer to Frederique. "Now, now, girls. I just need a word with your boss." He brushed their arms and their eyes glazed. Neither voiced another objection to him slipping his slender frame onto the horseshoe couch.

Callin glanced over at Gypsy, and she smiled at him. He had yet to see the man in his element, and this was definitely his element.

"What do you think you are doing?" Frederique's hand latched onto the benefactor's throat, but he didn't flinch. Her hand retracted as quickly as his hand touched hers. "What…?" she said just before her head lolled back.

"Now," he smirked, looking over Frederique, not so surreptitiously. "Let's see if we can't alleviate you of some of your more displeasing personality traits."

19

Ethan and Cori ran up the stairs, while Belus and Danato chose to wait for the elevator. Despite his leg being free of pain, Danato still didn't prefer the cardio of stairs over the elevator. Ethan wasn't sure if it was a point of handicap, or if the big man just didn't want to trouble his knees with the exertion.

It had been some time since Ethan had heard the prison alarms going off. He didn't think Efrat's *Winnie the Pooh* situation warranted the call to arms, but he knew Danato was far more concerned about the reason behind it. Anything involving the bubble tended to make him uneasy.

Ethan pushed on to level five and proceeded through the metal double doors, taking care to shove them wide enough for Cori to enter in his wake. The time bubble was intact, but the slight shimmer effect that the aberration naturally displayed looked more like a pulsation. Inside of the sphere, Efrat remained suspended, apparently stuck.

Chuck broke away from the cluster of guards that he had no doubt called in to help prior to alerting Danato of the problem. He rushed over to them. "Cori!" Chuck said, bypassing him entirely to greet her. The relief on his face was so evident, Ethan half expected the man to hug her. He wasn't sure when he had become secondary in authority on emergencies, but he supposed that the gardening project had strictly been her territory since day one. "I'm sorry, but I can't get him out. He was supposed to come out about twenty minutes ago. When I tried to pull him out by hand, I got zapped all to hell. We can't even touch the bubble without getting a static shock down to the bone."

"I'll try. The rings should protect me," she said less than confidently.

"Has anything like this ever happened before?" Ethan asked, coming back a few steps to join the conversation. Chuck shifted his gaze away before shaking his head. It was a small evasion, but he knew the men were reluctant to report when they were to blame for problems. "Anything, Chuck?" he said firmly.

Chuck shifted nervously. "There was one time he had some trouble getting out."

"Just tell us. It might be important," Ethan assured him.

"A few weeks back, we both went in for a little R&R since the sun was warm. It was only a few minutes, and he said the wizards never bother him." Ethan fought back his initial response. Everyone was getting way too comfortable with Efrat and the bubble. He didn't understand when everyone stopped viewing the den as dangerous. "He bolted the sky, so he could get out and then pull me out after, but it didn't take. He tried a few more times, but it didn't go. He had to give it a pretty big zap before the bubble would pop him out."

Ethan looked at Cori for an explanation. Her blank expression didn't offer much hope of an answer. She stepped forward to examine the dome just as the others arrived. Danato stepped up beside him and he gave him the short version, while Belus hung back, quietly observing.

"Sounds like it's getting resistant to Efrat's particular exit strategy. The bubble is electrified, so Chuck couldn't pull him out manually. Cori's going to try pulling him out."

"Hopefully, the bubble doesn't attach to her this time," Danato said, crossing his arms.

Ethan grimaced. He had forgotten about that particular risk.

Cori approached the sphere and brushed her hand along it. The snapping sound that had hurt Chuck didn't affect her, but it made her rings shimmer defensively. Before reaching for Efrat, she braced herself to avoid being pulled in with him.

Ethan observed her progress carefully, ready to yank her back at a moment's notice. She latched onto Efrat's arm and pulled hard, but Efrat didn't budge. Cori stepped away before trying again. She glanced at Chuck beside her and motioned for him to back her up. Chuck cautiously grabbed around her waist and pulled on her while she unsuccessfully yanked on Efrat's blurry form.

Ethan didn't wait for her to reposition for another try. He waved Chuck away, and he shuffled back, happy to be away from the potential electrocution. Ethan wrapped both arms firmly around Cori's waist. Surprised by the intimate proximity, she glanced back and smiled at her new assistant. "Thank you, sir," she whispered seductively.

"Always a pleasure working with you, sweetness." He pressed his face beside hers and they pulled in unison, she pulling Efrat, him pulling her. When they popped free of the resistance, he hoped they were done, but Cori's hand had only slipped free. She sighed and relaxed against him. "Maybe I could grab him," he said, and her eyes flashed with concern. "If you grab my hand like you do for Efrat." She thought about that and nodded.

They stepped forward with him in the lead, and her fingers trailing against his. The snap and pop of the dome made him jump, but he pushed through. He steeled himself against the pain, but as soon as he reached Efrat, a powerful jolt ejected him that their jury-rigged bond couldn't shield him from.

"This is ridiculous," Cori grumbled as they righted themselves again. "He's right there."

"You know he's not," Belus corrected.

It was true; they weren't pulling Efrat from *that* space. That space was only a conduit in and out of the other side of the time/space fracture. It was not a hollow dome, but rather a solid blob of gelatin. Although he was visibly frozen in place to them, that was only his bookmark. He was actually somewhere far, far away.

"Should I just go in there?" Cori asked.

"No," Ethan objected, with Danato and Belus providing his stereo background. "Why is the bubble even electrified?" Ethan asked, flexing the numbness from his fingers. "It's basically an energy field, anyway."

Belus rocked his hand to let him know that his statement was not entirely accurate. Thankfully, he didn't actually explain it in detail.

"Efrat bolts the sphere barrier to get out," Danato said, more to himself than anyone. "Perhaps the bubble is retaining the energy that he's putting into it."

"What's the read on the field, Chuck?" Belus called over to the anxious guard.

Chuck moved closer to be in the conversation. "Same, sir. The frequency adjusts to compensate for Efrat's exits, just as you asked. We get a slight pitch spike, but the dampener keeps us all from feeling like we just left a Motley Crue concert."

"What about the power input?" Ethan continued with that train of thought. "How much juice is she slurping up?"

"We haven't adjusted the feed, but the shock absorbers are still functional. This baby can tolerate a direct lightning bolt to the building and not feel it. The bubble is stable," Chuck stated rather proudly. He had been a computer hacker in his former life, so operating this system was as close to his field of interest as the prison could get.

Cori glanced at the bubble, then back at him. He knew she had thought of something, but was still figuring out how to put it into words. He raised a brow to ask for her statement.

"Efrat's power isn't exactly electricity," she admitted as if it were a big secret that Efrat's blue rivulets didn't always abide by the standard laws of physics. "The shock absorbers might be controlling the bubble's *caloric* intake, but maybe Efrat's power is like Twinkies vs. steak. Maybe she likes it better."

Ethan looked to Danato and Belus, who were already contemplating that theory.

"If that's true, she might be getting gluttonous," Belus said, glancing at Danato. "She might be holding Efrat in stasis."

"Stasis?" Cori asked.

"Efrat might be frozen in time, not quite in the den, but also unable to get out of it. The bubble is holding him in a position of constant output. It's draining him like a battery."

Cori frowned and looked at Ethan. "Efrat still relies on his natural body to wield his energy. That kind of drain could potentially kill him," she murmured, underplaying her concern for the man.

"Then we best come up with a plan," he said austerely, but he could see her biting her lip. He supposed she was worried that he would not try very hard to save Efrat since he didn't like him. She might have been right, but he loved her, and she didn't like seeing anyone die. "Does anyone have a plan?"

"Maybe I could—" Cori began.

"We can't risk you going in," Danato clarified, in case she had forgotten about the three-against-one vote. "Two people stuck won't do any good."

"What if we shut off the main power?" Ethan asked. Danato's eyes widened in response. "Temporarily, of course," he amended before the big man's eyes fell out of their sockets.

"The main power is still her core stability," Belus explained. "It's like Cori said. She's just getting snacks between meals when Efrat comes along. If we shut off the power, then she will drain Efrat dry. Plus, nothing good will come from pissing her off."

"I think I can get him out without going in," Cori announced. Everyone turned to hear her plan. "Efrat has the ability to adjust his polarity. I just need to create a magnetic field that will draw him out."

"What's stopping you from being dragged in?" Ethan asked.

"Hopefully, you two." She motioned to him and Danato.

There was a long pause as everyone balanced the danger of the plan versus the probability of it working. "Sounds reasonable," Belus declared. "Do you think you can create enough charge to counter the bubble's pull?"

Cori's face crumpled with concern. "I think so. At any rate, if I can't draw him out, I might be able to distract her with *my* Twinkies."

Ethan frowned at Danato. Magnetism sounded like a better description than bait.

20

"**Y**OU GOT ME?" CORI asked, checking Ethan's hand position around her legs. Danato stayed on his feet to pull her back, while Ethan crouched in front of her to push her back.

"I got you, sweetness. I kept the power of the earth from ripping apart Adrianna. I think I can stop your magnetism to Efrat."

Cori looked down at him to see if that was yet another passive-aggressive jab, but he didn't look up to confirm or deny it. Danato tightened his grip around her waist. "We'd have to be dead to let you go, sweetheart." She patted his hand in gratitude.

Cori started to form a field using the metal in the room as a crutch, but just as Efrat had taught her, she drew it away and balled it within itself. The force field he had once used to contain her was essentially an ever-changing polarity of energy.

It took several more moments to flatten the ball into an independent spiral, a force field that circulated like a flushing toilet. When she felt the pull, she knew she was on the right track.

The draw against her strengthened, and she keeled forward as far as Danato's arm would allow. Though there was no wind to speak of, she could feel her hair rise. She hadn't expected the stabbing shocks that made her whole body into a lightning rod, but the men hung on.

The crackling energy between her and the bubble was bright white, despite the blue energy feeding it. She felt another tug, but she was grounded. She increased the power, hoping to drag Efrat out, or at the very least make herself look like a tastier dessert than him.

Ethan grunted and dug his feet in, but they were still being dragged forward over the glossy white floor. "Danato!" he yelled over the sizzling static.

"Got it!" Danato shifted, bracing with his own muscular legs.

Cori felt the halt and increased the feed as high as she could. She was already sweating from an internal heat, and she was feeling faint. She was certain passing out while in control of so much energy was a bad idea, but soon it wouldn't be optional.

At last, she felt something hook and her arms snapped forward. The pull lifted her from the ground. Ethan and Danato were no longer pulling or pushing, but anchoring her, so she didn't fly into the sphere—Peter Pan-style.

The electrical field narrowed into two perfect streams. She had caught Efrat like a fish, or the bubble had caught her. Either way, something was about to be resolved.

A burst of light filled the room, blinding her. Her body flew back in fractionated slow motion. When she eventually hit the floor, she could feel the weight of a number of bodies on top of her. She just focused on breathing, since she couldn't move anything else.

When some of the weight lifted, she opened her eyes. Efrat was over top her, hands clasped with hers, pinning them over her head. His face mirrored her exhaustion as he cooled her with his panted breaths.

Completely forgetting what had caused the compromising position, she yanked her hands to get free of the claustrophobic situation. Losing his precarious balance, Efrat flopped face first against her chest. She grunted, trying to get out from under him, but his hands wouldn't release.

Ethan arrived over them, looking perturbed. "Get off her," he yelled over several layers of cotton in her ears. He pulled Efrat up with one arm, but his hands didn't release. She unwillingly followed in tow behind him. "Let go!" Ethan said directly into his ears. Efrat didn't comply; instead, he leaned against Ethan for support. Ethan manually raised one of his clasped hands and shook it in front of his face.

Efrat looked at their joined hands. He opened his grip and released her fingers. Cori tugged away, but she couldn't gain any distance from his hand. She twisted her hand, feeling the obvious space between them, but the palms would not separate more than a few centimeters.

"I'm stuck," Cori said, just as a tuning fork freed her left eardrum. She flinched at the sudden volume in her voice. Belus moved to her right side and did the same for that ear, while Danato restored Efrat's hearing.

"What do you mean?" Ethan said, shifting Efrat to rest against his arm so he could see their hands closer.

"I can move, but I can't separate any further," she explained.

"Hold him." Ethan shoved Efrat into Danato's chest and came around to view this imaginary connection. He gripped their wrists and pulled. Their hands parted incrementally at first, but once they were about an inch apart, the bond broke with a bright flash. The powerful burst pushed Ethan away and forced Cori to flounder on her remaining leash.

Ethan returned, determined to break the second bond as well. He gripped them both firmly and pulled with strength that always surprised her. When the bond didn't give even a little, Ethan repositioned and tried again. Cori winced at the pressure he put on her wrist.

"Ethan, stop!" Danato scolded. "You're going to rip her hand off."

Ethan stopped and looked at their connected hands. It was, at least for today, the bane of his existence. He was uncomfortable with the time she and Efrat spent together already. She imagined he would go crazy if that time now included handholding.

Ethan pinched his lips and checked her wrist. She was sure that it would bruise, and she wanted to rub it, but she shrugged it off so she didn't make him feel bad for trying. In response to the ordeal, or just his territorial side, he hugged her, pulling her body tightly to his.

She relaxed against him and ignored that Efrat had wrapped his fingers back around her hand.

21

"THAT IS WICKED COOL," Efrat commented in the infirmary waiting room after he found out he could put a piece of paper between his and Cori's hands and not disrupt the connection.

Danato did not agree with the statement. Judging by the increased speed in Ethan's pacing, he didn't find any enjoyment in the revelation either. "I don't suppose you have any theories for this, Belus?" he asked his second, who was trying to get a read on the bond that was preventing their hands from separating.

Belus ripped the paper from Efrat's hand and crumpled it up. "I'm still theorizing," he said, placing his device next to their perpetually high-fived hands. "I thought that Efrat had magnetized to her rings, but there is no magnetic field being produced. And..." Belus waved his probe between their hands. "No electrical current is being exchanged."

"Wait." Efrat lowered their hands. "None? You mean no more than usual, right?"

Belus shook his head. "No, I mean none."

Efrat looked at Cori and grabbed Belus's probe with his free left hand. He peeked at the device, but it showed nothing. He changed course and grabbed Belus's hand. Belus shook his head.

Efrat touched his own face and neck. His smile broadened as he realized the freedom he was being given. The fact that it was at the expense of Cori's freedom meant nothing to him.

Efrat laughed and pulled Cori into an abrupt, forced kiss.

"Hey!" Ethan darted to him, but Efrat shot up, wrapping him in a hug rather than fighting him.

"That was just a thank you. As is this!" Efrat kissed him on the cheek, and Ethan ripped himself out of the hug.

"Efrat, you can't just stay stuck to Cori," Danato grumbled to distract Ethan.

"Your reduced conductivity might not have anything to do with Cori," Belus surmised. "The bubble just drained you of a good deal of your power."

"Yeah, I was there," he muttered.

"I have a few ideas about what's causing this." Belus turned to him. "The most obvious one being that another fragment of the bubble has gotten stuck between them. There must be an intangible element that links the time bubble, Efrat's energy, and those rings."

"Why was Ethan able to break one connection, but not both?" Cori asked, standing up. She looked tired and the frown on her face was one of abject humiliation. He knew she was probably blaming herself for this mishap, but he didn't. This was just another day.

Belus ruminated a moment before speaking. "Which hand did you use to bolt the time barrier, Efrat?" Efrat lifted their conjoined hands. "I imagine that is the answer. Both hands were pulled into the connection, because he's basically two bare wires. But only the active one cemented beyond physical disruption."

"How do we separate them?" Ethan asked, trying to hide his impatience.

Belus looked at Danato. It was time for more brainstorming. "When the time bubble attached to Cori the first time, it took a second bolt from Efrat to stop her jumps," Danato started. "Maybe we can disrupt the connection like last time."

"It's possible, but like Cori said, Efrat's energy isn't just raw electricity, so until he's back to full power, we have no way of duplicating it," Belus volleyed back to him.

"Is it possible to introduce a third magnetism to draw the bubble fragment away?" Danato asked.

"I imagine if we knew what was drawing it to them in the first place we could, but the connection isn't magnetic or electrical. The time bubble itself isn't even electrical energy, it's a matrix of sound waves." Belus paused on that thought.

Danato smiled and nodded in agreement. He was about to announce the solution when Efrat interrupted.

"As much as I'm enjoying this science lesson, I'd like to go flirt with some nurses." He twisted his connected hand around and pushed Cori's hand and his into her back, shoving her toward the nurse's hub.

"The hell we are." She planted her feet. "I'm not hanging out while you pick up girls."

"You should be happy that I can touch someone other than you. Or is that jealousy in your voice?"

"What?" Cori looked at Ethan in her panic. "No! You touch whoever the hell you want."

"*Anyone* I want?" Efrat teased.

Ethan latched onto his shoulder and squeezed tightly. Efrat yielded to the pain. "I would recommend that you not touch my wife, but clearly we are beyond that edict for now. So instead, I will just remind you once again, that she... is... mine."

"Can we get a solution before he starts turning green?" Cori bemoaned.

"Ethan, that's enough," Danato scolded, and he released his grip. "If you three would stop bickering, you would realize that we already have one. We can break the connection with the tuning forks."

Cori and Ethan instantly perked up, but Efrat's excitement dimmed.

22

"WHAT DO YOU MEAN, they aren't working?" Ethan scrambled over to watch as Belus used the final tuning fork in his collection. Efrat and Cori were sitting at the small table on the far wall, their hands perched up for audio separation. When the final tone that was off-the-charts high didn't sever the link, he reached for their hands to pull at them, in the hopes that the connection had weakened.

"Easy, man!" Efrat jerked his and her hand away. "I already have a bruise from you."

Ethan frowned, seeing the bruises on both their wrists.

"He might as well try," Cori suggested. "It's the only thing so far that has worked."

"No, that's enough." Belus put his hand in the way as Ethan reached out for them again. "I think we are on the right track. I just need to do some calculations." Belus looked at the time bubble that was glimmering normally again. "I'll look over the readings and figure out what frequency created this superglue, so we can break the connection with it."

"How long will that take?" Cori asked.

Belus sighed. "I don't know. Depends if we can duplicate the frequency with what we have here. We'll head up to the infirmary and try the ultrasound. Regardless of if that works, the connection will probably dissipate, eventually. For now, though, you are stuck."

Ethan could see Cori wasn't happy about that, but she was trying not to whine about something she couldn't change. Efrat, on the other hand, was grinning ear to ear. "You think this is funny?"

Efrat chuckled when he saw the stern look on his face. "This is the closest I've been to human in years. I'm tickled fucking pink."

Ethan stiffened his frame, preparing to finally punch Efrat like he had wanted to since the day he met him.

"Ethan." Danato's low threat wasn't as ardent as it could have been. It was more of a reminder that violence would not help the situation.

"No, no, Danato, don't stifle the boy." Efrat stood and looked behind him to Danato. "He wants to have a go. We should have a go. After all, it'll finally be a fair fight." Efrat blew on his free palm before clenching it into a tight fist.

"Go ahead." Ethan stepped forward. "Show me your best."

Efrat tensed and lost his smile. Cori stood to break them up, but he pushed her away to open up his stance. She scoffed, but didn't interject.

To Ethan's surprise, Danato's hand didn't land on his shoulder. Belus gave as much attention to the interaction as he deemed worthy before packing up his tuning forks.

"You really want this, sport?" Efrat whispered with a seductive threat.

"Yeah, I do. I want this over with once and for all," Ethan admitted.

"Remember that when you're face down in your own drool," Efrat vaunted right before his eyes lolled back in his head and he dropped to the floor, unconscious.

Ethan furrowed his brow, looking down at the self-fulfilled prophecy before him. He looked at Cori, and she shrugged. "It was easier."

"For who?" he asked sharply. He couldn't help but feel disappointed that he was missing yet another warranted opportunity to pummel Efrat.

Cori frowned at his reaction. "What were you going to do? Beat the crap out of a one-armed man?" She raised her connected hand for reference. "Danato, would you mind carrying him?"

"Of course." Danato brushed past him and flopped Efrat over his shoulder before leaving with Cori in tow.

Ethan cussed under his breath and ran his hands through his hair. It took him a moment to realize that Belus was watching him. He narrowed his eyes at him. "What?"

Belus crossed his arms and leaned against the table. "I was just contemplating giving you some advice, but since you probably don't want it, I think I'll save my breath."

"Save the reverse psychology bullshit, Belus. Been there, done that. You wanna say something, say it."

Belus frowned. "What is with you lately?"

"Aside from my least favorite person being stuck to my wife?"

"Cori," Belus corrected mildly.

"What?" Ethan's face scrunched in muddled disgust.

"You keep referring to her as your wife, like we all need to be reminded of that, but her name is Cori." Ethan didn't bother mentioning that there was no difference to him. "You seem on edge, Ethan. You are usually more controlled than this. Your patience is razor thin. I know the issues in China have you on edge, but I just don't see why that has anything to do with Cori and Efrat. What is going on?"

Ethan frowned and looked away. "You mean besides... all this?" He waved to the time bubble.

"*All   this*..."—Belus mimicked the movement—"happens every day. Cori gets into trouble. Efrat acts like an ass. What's different about today, or yesterday, or the last four months?"

Ethan bit his cheek. He wanted so much to tell someone about the dragon's prophecy, but he could hardly offer that information without revealing the dragons' secret. Defrocking supreme immortal creatures just seemed rude, especially since he was the only one given the privilege of the insight.

"Nothing," he grumbled.

"Which almost certainly means something, but you don't want to share it with me."

Ethan scoffed, trying to force amusement into the intolerable conversation. "What do you want, Belus?"

"Do you want my advice or not?"

"Do I have a choice?"

"Of course. I've spent my life giving advice to Danato. Advice that he rarely takes, mind you, but he is considerate enough to listen to it."

Ethan nodded at the slight dig and took in a calming breath. "Okay, let's hear it."

"I don't know what's going on between you and Cori, but you hating Efrat won't make things any better."

"Please don't ask me to play nice with Efrat, because that's not going to happen."

"Why not?"

"Because... he's an ass."

"Yes, that opinion has been deemed universal enough to be considered a fact, but Efrat isn't exactly getting treated like one of your guards. He's still being treated like an inmate."

"He acts like an inmate."

"The chicken and the egg. Someone has to give a little. Cori is doing her best, but she is not the leader here. You are. These men follow you because they respect you, not because you exert your authority with violent intervention. My advice to you, Ethan, is to start handling Efrat with a little humanity, so Cori doesn't have to feel like she's betraying you when she does."

Ethan wondered if Belus would still offer him that advice if he knew what the dragon had told him. "Noted," he said before heading to the door. He paused and turned back. "Tell Cori I'll wait for her at home."

23

DANIEL WAS HAPPY TO be on a job that didn't require a track medal. So far, all it had required was him and Heaton lounging on a patio, while he watched Nevia crawl around on all fours. Which he was thoroughly enjoying. The only thing missing from the moonlit night was a beer or six.

"Seriously, dude, you can't possibly be getting turned on by this," Heaton drawled from the lawn chair next to him.

Daniel didn't take his eyes off Nevia's backside to respond. "A woman on her knees. What's not to love?"

"And the fact that she is sniffing out a corpse isn't even the slightest turn-off?"

"Hey, so long as *I'm* not a corpse..." He trailed off, leaning his head to one side to look down her shirt.

"I can't believe you got her to marry you," Heaton mumbled.

Daniel finally broke his connection to glare at him. "What's that supposed to mean?"

Heaton smiled and shook his head. "In a million years, I never expected you to sleep with a married woman and not have it be adultery." Daniel wanted to object that he never intentionally went after married women, but he also wasn't above overlooking a ringed finger.

"That's a good thing, though, right? Me and her."

"Yeah, man. It's a good thing. Has she told her parents yet?"

Daniel smiled. "She mailed them her bouquet."

"Ouch." Heaton grimaced. "That pissed, huh?"

"Aye," Daniel said. He wasn't entirely surprised that Nevia's parents didn't approve of him. However, he was surprised she was willing to elope just to piss them off more. "To add fuel to the fire, she sent them a copy of her werewolf registration application, which very clearly claims her grandfather as a full werewolf, and her mother as a half-breed."

Heaton chuckled, finding the same amusement in her audacity. "I take it you're not expecting a Christmas card?"

"No, but I am expecting a big box that ticks any day now."

"Got it!" Nevia declared, concentrating her sniffing to one spot in the yard.

"You're sure that's not just dog crap, Nevia?" Daniel joked, but she ignored him and continued her evaluation.

"Human remains... six, maybe seven months old... male. It has to be her husband," she declared to both of them. Her face was covered in dirt and smeared with grass stains, but Daniel knew better than to question her determination.

He sighed and stood up. "Well, I guess that means it's my turn." He was thankful this transmorph hadn't imbibed his victim, but he still didn't relish the idea of explaining to the wife that her real husband had been murdered six months ago and buried in the backyard.

They waited by the back door for the happy couple to arrive home from their nightly ice cream run. They were both in their early thirties, not yet parents, and boisterously in love, despite being married for nearly a decade already. Daniel could hear the woman laugh and squeal as her *husband* did something playful to her.

He raised his brow to Heaton, who was waiting patiently on the other side of the door. "Let's do this before they start making out." He nodded and pulled out his taser gun. It wasn't enough to stop the transmorph, but the electricity would temporarily stop the creature from transforming—a little tip he had gotten from Efrat the last time he made a drop.

Heaton turned the doorknob, which he had already picked, and crept inside. His movements were fast and concise. The pure stealth of it reminded Daniel that Heaton had trained in the military elite. Sneaking into houses to seize transmorphs or vampires was nothing compared to dodging gunfire and grenades.

Nevia followed with her gun in hand. It wouldn't do any good against the transmorph, but it wasn't unheard of for a spouse to take a few shots at them in defense of their supposed loved one.

When he heard the woman squeal and a zap, he knew it was time for his grand entrance. He moved through the kitchen and into the dining room. He saw Nevia holding her gun on the already cowering wife. Her curly red hair was matted to her face from tears and she was cradling her jaw. He wasn't sure who had hit her, Nevia or Heaton, but either way, it must have hurt, because she wasn't wailing like he expected her to be.

Daniel stepped through the archway between the dining room and the front foyer. Heaton was holding the transmorph, but threw him down the instant he saw Daniel. He stomped past him. "Bitch bit me," he snarled through closed teeth as he clamped his bleeding wrist—apparently the explanation for the overly subdued wife.

Daniel approached the transmorph and looked him over. His balding head was shaved close to magnify the baldness as a choice rather than an affliction. He wasn't sure how the man knew—his cavernous eyes, a preternatural instinct, or just his reputation preceding him—but this one already knew who and what he was. "Don't do this. I'm innocent."

Daniel shook his head. "Are you going to come quietly?" he asked.

"I didn't do anything wrong," the man said vehemently. "You can't take me."

"Do you deny mimicking a dead man?"

"No." He glanced at his wife. "But I didn't kill him."

"That's what they all say. Let's not make a scene."

"I didn't do it!" the man yelled, and Daniel shoved him back with his power. The man hit the stair rail behind him with a concussive force, but he immediately stood and faced Daniel down with vengeful intent.

"No! Don't hurt him!" the wife spouted the anticipated supplication. He heard her run to reach her husband, but he didn't bother trying to stop her. Before the woman could reach him, Heaton's arm latched onto her waist and drew her back again. "Let me go! My husband didn't do anything!" She struggled futilely against his grip.

"That isn't your husband!" Heaton yelled back at her. "Your husband is dead!"

"I know!" she screeched and slumped over Heaton's arm. "I know!"

"What do you mean, you know?" Heaton questioned her.

Daniel turned away from his prey to hear the answer, and the adjustment did not go unnoticed. Before he could exert any force to put him back in his place, the transmorph slipped past him.

Heaton whipped around, throwing the wife aside like a ragdoll to free himself for a fight. Daniel cursed and ran after him, but his opponent had no intention of running away.

Nevia's gun went off just as the transmorph reached her. He lashed himself around her neck and body, teetering on the verge of enveloping her. Her mouth and nose were smothered with the impossible stretch. Daniel watched her struggle and panic, unable to get a breath around his inhuman grasp. The demon parasite behind her raised his lip in a disgusted smile before spitting out the bullet that Nevia had shot him with. "Two can play at this game."

Daniel could feel his temper rise and he knew that there was no amount of breathing or mental preparation that was going to stop it. He wouldn't let this bastard hurt his wife. He turned away from his assignment to the woman lying on the floor in a crumpled heap.

"Daniel," Heaton said, backing up out of his line of sight. "What are you going to do?"

The woman propped herself up, her eyes pinned to his in the ultimate fear. He ignored her increasingly stricken gaze and the screams that followed.

"Daniel!" Heaton yelled hopelessly behind him. He didn't have to learn twice to stay out of his way. "Let her go or he'll kill her!" Heaton yelled at the transmorph. Daniel knew he was probably already trying to claw Nevia from his grasp in a desperate attempt to stop the progressive carnage, but it didn't much matter at that point. He was not playing the game anymore.

"Nooooo!" the husband wailed in anguish as he watched Daniel slowly disintegrate the flesh from his wife's hand, quickly followed by the bone. There was no healing that.

Daniel heard a *thunk* and gasping breaths. He stopped. The transmorph crawled across his path to comfort his wife and stanch her bleeding. He looked back at Daniel with tears beading from his eyes. It was an emulated expression of emotion, but there was no doubt as to the sincerity of it. His eyes pinched and his lips stretched in a tormented grimace. "You monster!" he hissed before looking back at the woman.

It wasn't the first time he had been called a monster, but it was the first time a monster had accused him of it.

Heaton tugged him around to face him. "Wait outside," he said, trying to get through to his numb mind. "Daniel!" He grabbed his face and his gaze flickered over him, searching his face for comprehension. Daniel wasn't sure what he saw that was more alarming than his black orbs, but his eyes misted and he pulled Daniel's head down and kissed his forehead. It wasn't their usual expression of brotherly love, but it didn't feel wrong either. "Wait outside," he whispered this time, and shoved him toward the back door.

Daniel passed by Nevia, who was a little shaken but none the worse for wear. She looked as dazed as he felt. "Nevia, I need you here," Heaton called to her, in case she had thoughts of going outside with him. She squeezed his arm as she passed to assist with the first aid his butchery had necessitated.

He didn't even bother looking behind him before strolling out to enjoy the evening air on the patio.

24

DANIEL HAD FOUND HIS Zen. It was about an hour too late, but he had it once again. Emergency vehicle lights flickered around the house, casting a disco effect on various parts of the yard. He had tucked himself into the shadows, leaning against the building.

Heaton stepped onto the patio soundlessly. Nevia followed behind him, but stopped some distance away. He wasn't sure that was for her safety or just his comfort. Either way, he didn't like it. He liked having her body close.

"She was the murderer," Heaton announced as he stopped in front of him. He searched his pockets for a cigarette, even though he had given it up again. "Husband was abusive as hell, I guess." He continued to glance at Nevia for a confirmation nod. "She *accidentally* pushed him down the stairs. Her neighbor heard the scuffle and came to check it out. She admitted everything, and he revealed his identity as a transmorph to help her cover it up. They fell in love, and were living happily ever after when we showed up."

Daniel nodded. "Sounds about right. Still, she killed her husband."

"Not our department," Heaton scolded, before taking a breath to control himself. "I made a deal with the transmorph. He lets us handle this situation on our own, and we don't reveal the body buried in the backyard."

"And how are we handling this situation?" Daniel asked, meeting his eyes.

Heaton frowned and shook his head. "How do you think?" he grumbled through too many emotions to articulate. "How could you be so stupid?" Heaton got in his face, but his anger wasn't far enough in the lead to make his rebuke sound threatening.

"I'm sorry." Daniel put his hand on his shoulder. "This isn't your fault."

Heaton raised his hand to his shoulder as well and squeezed it hard before backing away from the embrace entirely.

Daniel turned his attention to Nevia, who was crying. He crooked his head to investigate this strange response from his normally reserved partner. He reached out his arm, and she plowed into him, gripping him tighter than he ever could have imagined her tiny muscles could. He wrapped his arms around her and kissed her head while she sobbed quietly into his chest.

When her tears had settled slightly, he dipped down and searched for her lips. Her salty lips clasped onto his firmly, demanding him. He pulled away and trailed kisses along her chin before returning to her lips again. "Daniel," she said, muffled by his lips.

He pulled away. "I love you."

"Can't we just—?"

"No," he said simply, giving her one more kiss that normally would have ushered them into the bedroom. That was going to be a long way off.

"I don't understand why we can't just—" she persisted.

"Because we can't!" Heaton snapped. He didn't meet the glare she gave him. He just stared out into the yard.

"Heaton's just doing his job, Nevia." Daniel tried to mediate the tension between them, but he only ended up getting an allotment of Heaton's ire.

"I am not *just* doing my job!" Heaton seethed, taking a step back to face him. "I—" Heaton's phone chirped, and he broke off his reprimand to answer it. Daniel already knew the ring belonged to Sophie. "Yeah," Heaton answered curtly, turning away from them. "What...? No, I don't think that's a good idea. We just had an incident." Heaton paused and looked back at Daniel. "What makes you think we can if the collectors can't...? We do?" Heaton inhaled and shook his head. "You're shitting me. Why? She—" Heaton groaned and rubbed his face. "Yeah, yeah, I hear you. I understand. Yes, we'll take care of it."

Heaton clicked the phone off and stared at the lawn for a moment before turning back to them. Daniel couldn't imagine Heaton's face could have expressed any more emotions than it had before the phone call, but somewhere in the mix of angry, loyal disappointment was a slew of concern and guilt.

Daniel squeezed Nevia's shoulder before pulling away to meet his friend. "What is it?"

"I can't take you in yet. We have to go fetch someone for Danato, and it takes precedence."

"Aye, but why do you look like your puppy just died?"

"A potential sorceress, she's still in metamorphosis, but she's being protected so the collectors can't get to her."

"Who is protecting her?"

"Annette."

Daniel sputtered. "Is Sophie bloody dense? What does she think we can do that the collectors can't?"

"The collectors won't go past Gog and Magog. Something about brethren code."

"So, on the off chance that we can actually defeat those two big lunkheads, then what? Annette can summon the power of the earth."

"I think Sophie's hoping we can talk some sense into her."

Daniel chuckled again. "Right, because eighty-year-old high-level earth witches usually take advice from dragon-blood junkies." Heaton frowned and shook his head. He knew just as well that this was the type of mission that was liable to get them killed.

Daniel looked back at Nevia. Her curiosity was piqued, but she wasn't battering them with questions as any sane person would. He knew she would step into the path of danger right along beside him, no matter how he pleaded with her. He had already risked his freedom to protect her. He knew, without a doubt, he would risk his life for her. The only problem was that he kind of wanted to avoid the dying part of the hero role.

"We need help." Daniel turned back to Heaton. His partner was already narrowing his eyes suspiciously, which made him smile.

25

C ORI STEPPED THROUGH THE front door with Efrat tucked back behind her. She wanted Ethan to see her face before Efrat's. She had been in the med lab for hours, but so far nothing was breaking the bond between them, least of all her desire to get away from him.

She had expected to see Ethan making supper or reading on the couch, but he was at the dining room table with three other men. The smell of nachos hit her and she realized she was intruding on poker night.

"Hey, Cori!" Chuck raised his beer to her.

Duke nodded to her, as did another man she was chagrined not to know the name of. Ethan turned from Danato's usual head spot at the table and she felt panic wash over her. He was going to be mad, but what else could she do? She wasn't going to just wait out her sentence with Efrat in the prison. She wanted to see her baby and her bitter, angry husband.

To her surprise, he gave her a lopsided smile. "No luck, huh?"

She shook her head.

"Well, bring 'em in. You two might as well eat something. I made enough to feed an army, although my fifth couldn't make it. And it seems Danato would rather play tinker-toys!" Ethan hollered into the living room where Danato was on his chair, leaning over her son and his array of alphabet blocks. His head snapped up to offer her a solemn smile as well. He had left long before the boring part of the tests had begun, but Belus had warned him that the chances of separation were slim.

"I'm not sure he's playing with them so much as tasting them, but yes, I prefer his company to your rabble," Danato retorted.

"Traitor!" Ethan turned back to her and examined Efrat carefully. "You a poker man, Efrat?"

Efrat tucked in behind her to get the door shut, since she wasn't convinced yet if they should stay or make their way to the nearest dog house. "I don't have any money."

The men laughed.

"No one has any money. We play for gloating rights," Ethan clarified.

"I play for the food," Chuck said, raising his half-empty plate.

"Okay." Efrat sidled up next to Cori and put her and his hand behind her back in a sideways embrace. "Mind if my other half joins me?"

Cori could see Ethan's civil resolve fade and the others' enthusiasm dimmed as they waited for him to blow.

Instead, however, his eyes traced her body slowly, and he smiled. "Yeah, bring her along. She's kind of cute."

She smiled at his joke and nearly blushed at his public playfulness. Efrat leaned in closer to her and whispered in her ear. "He's going to kill me in my sleep, isn't he?"

"Maybe," she said and pushed him into the kitchen. Luckily, the meal was finger food, so she didn't have to maneuver a fork with her left hand, but it still took teamwork to get their plates loaded.

Once they were situated, Cori relaxed. Ethan leaned over and gave her a chaste kiss, while Efrat dove into his nachos. He had been eating like a dog for nearly a decade. It was only recently that the cafeteria had started supplying him with glass utensils—a minor compromise to save his dignity. Eating with his hands was probably a dream come true, let alone a home-cooked meal.

Ethan headed to the fridge and returned with two freshly opened beers. He held out the brown bottle to Efrat. "Beer?" Cori stared at Ethan, shocked that he was being so hospitable. She supposed Danato had lectured him about making this experience easier on her, but still, he was being almost friendly.

Efrat stared at the beer forlornly. It could have been a diamond ring as dazed as he was by the offering. He licked most of the cheese off his lips and reached tentatively for the bottle. "Thanks." When Ethan didn't rip it away again, he snatched it and took a long, refreshing drink from it. After which he burped ceremoniously. "Damn, I miss beer."

Ethan hunkered back down behind his hand of cards. "You in?"

"Hmm," Efrat said over another sip. He tipped up his cards on the table and grimaced. "Mmm." Despite his expression, he put in the ante. After all, he had nothing to lose but bragging rights.

After his third beer, Ethan cut him off. He probably hadn't been such a lightweight upon leaving the U.S., but now three beers were enough to leave him with half-slit eyes and grappling for thoughts.

Efrat hissed at his cards and tossed them away. "I'm out." He leaned in close to her and Ethan eyed him carefully, but didn't object to his drunken proximity. "I have a condition that needs attention. Do you want to go back to the infirmary?"

"What's that?" Ethan asked, trying to sound nonchalant.

Efrat cleared his throat. "I usually don't drink this much."

"Yeah, yeah, we know," Duke said, annoyed by his revelry.

"Noooooo," Efrat enunciated with puckered lips. "I usually don't drink much of anything." When no one grasped his point, he groaned. "I have to pee. What is the protocol?" He looked at Cori, and she looked at Ethan.

"I actually kind of have to go too," she said sheepishly.

Ethan looked between them and then to his men, who smartly looked away. "I presume everyone can attend to their own... needs." Cori nodded and looked at Efrat. Since he wasn't electrified, he would not need assistance with his pants or aim. He rolled his eyes and nodded. "Well, I suppose the guest bathroom would offer the best privacy for each of you."

Cori nodded and stood up. Efrat looked at her, confused. "What, he isn't coming?"

"My wife is a grown woman. She can attend to her bathroom needs on her own." He looked at her. "And she knows I'll be there in a flash if she needs anything."

She smiled and leaned in to kiss him. It was a little more kiss than the others needed to be exposed to, but she didn't care. She loved him so much for not making this situation even more humiliating.

As she dragged Efrat to the guest room upstairs, Danato glared at Efrat. Turns out Ethan might not have been the right person to ask permission from.

26

C ORI WAITED ON THE other side of the shower curtain for Efrat to finish the moaning and groaning over a happy urinary release. She wasn't sure if it was his drunkenness making him so theatric or just another way to lighten the uncomfortable situation. He chuckled as the stream ended in drops.

"What?" she couldn't help but ask.

"This is the first time I've held my cock without pain since..." He chuckled again.

"Please don't, Efrat."

"Oh, come on, Cori. You don't have to do anything. In fact, shutting up would be the most helpful."

"Nice. In that case, I'll sing obnoxiously." He didn't respond. "Efrat?" She listened for unsavory noises. "Are you... Efrat?"

"I'm not."

"Are you covered?" She gently pulled back the curtain when he didn't answer. He was still facing the toilet, but he was zipped up. His eyes were wet with fresh tears. "What is it?" she whispered, and he turned to her and looked her over.

"Why did it have to be you?" He looked pained, but it was transforming into bitter anger. As usual.

"Efrat..."

"You still need to pee, you better do it," he grumbled.

"Whatever?" She stepped out of the tub. When he was situated, she undid her pants and sat down to pee. Her desire to do so, however, didn't guarantee the result. "Shit." She leaned over and turned the sink faucet on.

"Shy bladder?" Efrat asked.

"Shut up."

"Silence isn't going to help that. Shall *I* sing?" he asked. Before she could answer, he started to sing a song she had never heard. It was probably an old song. She wasn't into the older music unless it came on a soundtrack. She was surprised that he had a beautiful singing voice and even more surprised that her bladder functioned better with music.

She was done long before he finished, but she didn't interrupt him. When he was done, she left a moment of silence before she spoke. "That was beautiful." She fiddled with her pants, finding that buttoning and zipping up jeans was not as easy as unbuttoning and unzipping. "Where did you learn to sing?"

"Karaoke and too much time in the shower."

"I, um, ouch—I like the song."

"What are you doing?"

"Hang on, I have to zip, but my underwear is caught." She heard him sigh.

"Just let me help."

"No, I can do it."

"Don't be ridiculous." He pulled the curtain aside, and she shielded her blue underwear, peeking through her open zipper. "Hold the buttonhole," he said and grabbed the button from behind. She did, and he threaded the metal button into it. "I'll hold it taut. You fix the zipper." She did so, and he released her.

She thanked him and walked away, but he yanked her back. She panicked, thinking about what his plots might be—alone in the bathroom. "I'm not leaving here without washed hands."

"Oh." She looked at the sink, remembering that clean hands were also her preference. They moved over and turned on the water. With a dab of soap, their hands intermingled, getting each other clean. It felt strange, but perfunctory enough to be innocent.

She glanced up at the mirror as they dried their hands. He had a small smile on his face. "What?"

"And you thought our relationship couldn't get any more awkward?"

She chuckled at the joke, and they headed back downstairs for more gambling.

27

THE GAME HAD BEEN going on longer than usual. Ethan knew he was just stalling the inevitable. As it was, Cori was asleep on the table. He just needed to bite the bullet and let everyone go to bed. He had already suggested that Efrat would fit nicely on the floor next to their bed, but he didn't even like the idea of him in his bedroom, with or without a chaperone.

Ethan shoved his chips into the pile. "All in."

His guards seemed to catch his purpose and went all in with him. Once a winner was established, they could all go home and sleep. Efrat looked over his cards carefully.

"What do you say we sweeten the pot?" he asked, lowering his cards.

"How's that?" Ethan asked.

Efrat's eyes sparkled with the usual condescension, but his expression remained ambiguous. "If I win... I get to sleep on the bed with Cori."

Ethan clenched his jaw and put on a tight, controlled smile. "I don't think so."

"Come on, Ethan. Isn't there anything you'd be willing to put on the table against that?"

"Against my wife's comfort in her own bed? No, I think I'll stay out of that doghouse."

"She's dead to the world already. She won't notice who she's next to." Ethan shook his head. "How about a free punch? Or maybe—"

"You stop working with Cori."

"It's not really my choice," he said, furrowing his brow.

"Belus is the one that wants you trained. Hell, you're training Cori more than she's training you now. If I win this hand, you agree to work solely with Belus and be his good little protégé."

"Okay, deal." Efrat smiled and Ethan laid down his straight. His guards revealed only pairs. When it was Efrat's turn, he smiled proudly. Ethan glared and waited for him to lay down the flush he suspected he had.

Efrat's enthusiasm faded quickly into a harsh grimace as he stared at his cards. The paper blackened and burst into flames. He watched the ashes disintegrate and fall to the table. He looked at Cori before pulling his hand away from the frozen connection. Ethan wanted to jump for joy at the disruption in contact, but the severity in Efrat's expression didn't leave room for anything but stillness.

"Let's call it a night, boys." Ethan gave his men the freedom to escape while Efrat was still quietly raging. They scrambled to the door, not bothering with goodbyes.

Ethan waited for Efrat to explode, but he simply got up and moved to leave. Ethan opened the door for him. "Do you need any help getting into the barracks?"

"They'll let me in... eventually," Efrat grumbled and started out the door.

Ethan put up his arm, blocking his exit. "What did you have?"

"Doesn't matter."

"Of course it does. It's bragging rights."

"I don't care about that." Efrat shook his head.

"Are you really that mad about losing a chance to sleep next to Cori?"

Efrat's brow furrowed, and he pinned Ethan with a hard stare. "It wasn't the girl that I wanted. It was the bed." His eyes flickered, and he raised his hands. A shimmer of blue flowed over them. "It doesn't matter what I had in my hand, because I can't have it now anyway."

Ethan nodded and lowered his arm. Efrat stormed off to mope about life's injustices. Ethan wasn't sure he had sympathized with him much before, but he was realizing why Cori was willing to put up with so much from him. The man really had gotten screwed over and consequently screwed up.

28

"**A**RE YOU SERIOUSLY POUTING?" Gypsy looked over to the stern-faced werewolf walking next to her. Callin was the least emotionally complex person she had ever known, which was probably why their pseudo-relationship had been working so well... up until two hours ago.

"I am not going to have this conversation in the hallway," he said without looking at her.

"Why not? You think the neighbors can't hear us through the walls of my apartment? Trust me, they hear it all." When he didn't say anything, she dug the keys out of her coat pocket along with a pack of cigarettes. She stared at the flattened paper pack and wondered why they were in there. "I still don't know why you are so upset," she mumbled as she put the pack back in her pocket.

"Really?" he said in a low tone that promised that he was not the least bit convinced by her ignorance. They stopped at her door and he leaned against the frame. "It didn't occur to you that your..." He paused to check the hallway for renters and sniff for nearby listeners.

"...*animalistic* boyfriend might be upset if you flirted with another man?"

Gypsy paused with her key in the lock and looked at him. "You're fucking the queen of the werewolves," she spat at him.

"Lower your voice," he hissed and stood up straighter. His movement put her on the defensive, which made his angry gaze turn predatory. The look made her mouth water, amongst other parts of her body. He may have been a dangerous partner, but he was so worth it. "First of all, my feelings for Leona are based on respect as much as attraction. You know very well that I am not currently mating with her."

"Not until she snaps her fingers." Gypsy twisted the key in the lock and pushed through the door.

"That is her right," he said, following in behind her. "I thought you were fine with that?"

"I... am," she enunciated. "What I am not fine with is you scaring off your competition."

To her surprise, Callin laughed as he shut the door of the apartment. "He was *not* competition."

"He is, if I say he is." She clicked on the standing lamp next to her sofa to reveal her messy apartment. She wasn't one for disorganization, but the past few months had left little to no time for anything other than work.

"Is that what you were trying to achieve?" Callin stalked up behind her, pausing momentarily to whisper in her ear. "To make me jealous." He moved past her and sat down in her only clean chair. He rested one foot on the coffee table and pulled his bow tie loose. It should have made him look relaxed, but she could tell he was still hiding his temper under his playful façade. "You do know that it is unwise to make a werewolf jealous?"

"It's unwise to do anything with a werewolf, but I think we are past the tip-toe point of this relationship." She slipped off her corseted black coat and sat on the arm of her sofa, unwilling to get too comfortable. She was dressed in a long shimmering black gown, but she still had her trusty lifesaving knife strapped to her hip. Had the gun not been completely obvious, she would have had that on as well.

"Yes, I suppose we are," he said, studying her body down to the high slit in her dress that exposed part of her thigh. "Then I suppose we shall have to speak bluntly, rather than spare each other's feelings."

"You know I wouldn't spare yours." She shrugged and shifted to prop her leg on the sofa cushion. It was far from a lady-like position, but the only thing she was exposing was more of her leg and the hilt of her knife holstered on the inner curve of her thigh. He glanced down at the knife before settling his determined eyes on hers.

"I don't want you to see other men while I am still available to you."

"I don't want to *see* other men," she said, smiling slightly at the snarl forming on his face. "I want to *fuck* other men."

He clenched his jaw, and she almost pulled her knife, but he was containing his fury well enough. "I don't want another man touching you, let alone that."

She leaned forward carefully, so it didn't seem like an attack. "And who's going to stop me from touching them?"

A low growl sounded from his chest, and she knew he was close to the tipping point. Callin was well controlled, but it seemed she was his Achilles heel. She shouldn't have taken so much pride in summoning his ire, but it was usually worth the bruises she got for her efforts.

She ripped out her knife and jumped over the back of the couch, just before his outrage sparked him to act. She could feel the waft of air behind her as he grabbed for her. She was glad that her hair was in a bun instead of a ponytail, or he might have scalped her.

Her apartment wasn't big enough for a proper game of tag, and hide and seek was always a disappointingly short game with werewolves. Her only option was to stand her ground, but since she didn't have her arm and leg braces on, she was risking broken bones.

She whipped around and stabbed Callin's forearm before he could grab her. The blade was lethally sharp, but it only gave him a flesh wound, since his tightly bound muscle tissue wouldn't allow it to penetrate very deep. He drew back, and she kicked him in the face.

He growled and stumbled back. She tried to kick him again, but he deflected her leg with his palm. She went for a punch, but he ducked and dove to tackle her. She lifted her knee and his nose cracked loudly.

He growled loudly and withdrew to check his nose. When he found blood on his fingertips, he huffed and glared at her. "Again?"

She shrugged, and he attacked again with a vicious, guttural yell. She didn't have time to defend herself, and he bulldozed her into the short wall separating the living room from the kitchenette.

The drywall fractured, and she groaned at the hard impact. He pulled her off it and turned her around. He bent her over the peninsula island counter top and grabbed a fistful of her up-do. He leaned in and hissed, "You'll pay for that." He pushed into her ass and she could feel his length hardened by his arousal.

She groaned again, but this time it wasn't from pain. She was about to get her punishment for being a very bad girl. In another few seconds, she would be half-naked, spreadeagled and begging for his retribution. Or at least she would have been, if the door hadn't splintered open, followed by two men charging in to unwittingly save her from her extensive foreplay. She was still getting a grasp on the interruption when Callin was propelled off her and out the window.

29

DANIEL COULD HEAR THE skirmish inside the apartment. He looked at Heaton, who had the same concern on his face.

"There's a werewolf inside," Nevia said as she joined them at the door.

Daniel didn't have to look at Heaton to know the answer to his next question. They both kicked in the door, splintering the frame. He probably could have used his power, but teamwork was more fun.

"Oh crap, wait," Nevia babbled behind them, but he was already charging in beside Heaton.

Gypsy was pinned between her breakfast nook and a man fisting a bloody knife. He used his double-sided whammy power to push him off her. He wasn't sure that it was necessary to use as much strength as he did, but since the attacker was a werewolf, he didn't want to take any chances of a quick defense. The window he hit shattered against his weight. He fell through and dropped out of sight. Three stories weren't likely to kill him, but then, not much was.

"Daniel?" Gypsy said, still bent over her counter.

Heaton approached her with his gun drawn and peeked behind the counter. "Any more?"

"Any more what?" she asked, smoothing down her upward bunching gown as she stood. He was surprised to find her dressed up. He was also surprised how good she looked. She was too militaristic in fashion and personality for him to consider her a sexual prospect, but he could see how some men might be attracted to her.

Men with high tolerances for strong women.

Or a werewolf.

A werewolf in a designer suit.

"Oh, shite," Daniel cussed.

"What?" Heaton asked.

"It's Callin," Nevia clarified from the door a little too late.

As if on cue, Callin leaped right back through the window he had only recently plummeted from. His suit jacket was off and he was streaked with red from benign little scratches. Scratches he was intent upon reciprocating.

"Callin! Hey bucko! Didn't recognize you at first."

Callin didn't seem to hear his words, since he was still stomping toward him. Daniel backpedaled. He didn't want to use his power again since it would likely only aggravate his werewolf tizzy into a werewolf massacre. If he needed him to stop, he would have to hurt him badly, and that just seemed rude to do before he had gotten in a few punches.

Nevia and Heaton both threatened him and waved their guns. Callin paid them no heed. He grabbed Daniel's neck and lifted him up. The pressure against his chin left him unable to look directly at him. His hand clamped around his throat, reducing his air supply to what was left in his lungs, unable to be exhaled. If he didn't die from suffocation, the stranglehold that was also preventing his blood flow would surely do the trick.

Before Heaton or Nevia felt compelled to act on their threats, a muffled ping sounded and Callin yelled. Daniel was dropped back to his feet, and he stumbled a short distance before he decided that the floor was as good a place as any to recover.

Callin grabbed his side and looked to see where the assault had come from. Heaton and Nevia looked at each other also, but neither could claim the shot since they weren't equipped with silencers. Callin looked behind him and found Gypsy standing by her bedroom door, holding a muzzled gun. He growled and moved toward her.

Daniel, having just received the brunt of his attack, wasn't enthusiastic about drawing his attention back to him, but he was certain Gypsy wouldn't do any better against him than he would. He started to get up again, but two more pings sounded and Callin fell to his knees. Despite the threat of the feral werewolf roaring before her, Gypsy looked nonplussed. "Callin, you remember Daniel, don't you? He saved your life in Mexico."

Callin grunted in pain as he shifted his body to look back at Daniel. The werewolf seemed to lose his edge of anger as the thought processes that made him pass for a human took over. He nodded and huffed out the last of his exasperation with a few weary exhalations.

"And this is his partner, Heaton. You met him at the prison, I'm sure."

Callin looked at Heaton and nodded to him. Heaton lowered and holstered his gun. Nevia didn't seem convinced and kept hers on target.

"And that is Nevia, his other partner and wife."

Callin looked her over and bowed his head slightly. "Yes, of course. I remember all of you." Callin stood with some help from Gypsy. "Must you use the gun?" he murmured.

"Yes," she answered resolutely before disappearing into her bedroom.

Callin rubbed his side and limped over to Daniel, who still hadn't made it to his feet. Although Nevia was still holding him at gunpoint, he didn't waver to pass her up close. Obviously, the first three bullets didn't kill him. Why should one more? Whether he realized she was aiming at his throat was an admission best left for conversations in the past tense.

"Hello, Daniel." Callin smiled and offered him his hand. "Still pissing off werewolves, I see."

Daniel chuckled and took his hand. The overly strong werewolf pulled him in for a half-hug and patted him on the back. "You had me scared there for a minute."

"Yes, I was already rather intemperate when you arrived. It wouldn't have taken much to get me going, but I do apologize." Callin looked at Nevia, who was still holding her gun. There was no exchange of words, but the coy smile on his face seemed to do more to subdue her than the civility he was offering. Nevia frowned and fumbled to put away her gun. Daniel was surprised to see her flustered by the man.

Callin moved to Heaton and shook his hand. "And how about you? Grace told me you had a bad spell with Frederique a while back. Recovered, I see."

"It helps to have my own personal witchdoctor around." Heaton nodded to Daniel, and he rolled his eyes at the comment. He didn't like his powers being utilized as an alternative to surgery, but in that case, he had made an exception. After the incident at the farm, Daniel had drained himself to near death to get him out of "crippled" territory. Scars were one thing, but when the doctors started discussing amputation, it was time to cheat nature.

"Yes, I should think so." Callin turned back to Daniel. "Speaking of your handy healing skills, it seems I owe you my life. Werewolves are not particularly immune to fire, you know."

Daniel shrugged. "Well, Gypsy's the one who dragged me to your bedside." He nodded to Gypsy, who was returning from her bedroom in jeans and a Pink Floyd t-shirt. With her dark hair draping over her shoulders and the remnants of make-up still on her face, she looked almost normal. The knife sticking out of her boot cuff took away some of the conformity in her style. "If you want to thank anyone, it should be her."

Callin looked back at her as she leaned over to adjust her boot. He caught her eye and her movements slowed. "Oh, I assure you, I have thanked her," he said, distracted. "Many times."

Callin pulled his eyes and thoughts from Gypsy and returned to face Daniel. "I consider myself indebted to you."

"Again?"

"Yes, I don't like sitting on my debts. So, if you should ever need my help, you only need to ask."

Daniel looked to see if Heaton was thinking the same thing he was. Heaton tipped his head as if to say, "Why not?"

30

"YOU WANT HIM TO do *what*?" Gypsy shoved her hand through her hair and mussed it up again. She was having trouble concentrating. She felt anxious and trapped.

Her three guests were lined up on the couch with Nevia nearest her and Daniel nearest to Callin in the opposing chair. She probably should have removed the laundry from it, but this was hardly a social call.

"Well," Daniel said with a grimace, "I originally came for your help, but since Callin is laying his services at my feet, I'm happy to have you both."

Gypsy paused, staring at Daniel, then Callin. Neither seemed to sympathize with the fact that she hadn't listened to his initial explanation. All she had really gotten, so far, was that they needed to go to China and fetch a *Sleeping Beauty* sorceress guarded by two giants and an uber earth witch. Maybe that *was* the whole explanation.

"Do you need to take a smoke break?" Nevia asked. The petite woman seemed annoyed by her fidgeting and floundering attention.

"Smoke break? I don't smoke." Gypsy grimaced at the thought.

Nevia scoffed. "I've never seen you without a cigarette in your hand."

Gypsy paused to think about that. The restless energy in her body seemed to be begging for a release. She looked at Callin, who only smiled and looked away. "Oh, that son of a bitch!" she griped and jumped out of her chair.

She found her jacket and ripped the pack of cigarettes from it. She deftly pulled one loose with her lips and searched for her lighter. She knew she had to have one. She moved into the kitchen in search of matches. Her stove was electric, and in a pinch she would use it, but not if she could find something faster and less likely to singe her hair.

She heard a familiar scraping click and turned to see Heaton was sitting at the island, offering her a light from his own lighter. She rushed back and lit her tip. She sucked in her first whiff of smoke and exhaled a most outrageously joyful noise.

Heaton chuckled and lit his own cigarette. She slipped around the end of the island and sat down next to him while Callin continued to get the details from Daniel. She was quickly becoming the backseat guest to their plots anyway.

She looked over Heaton's handsome bronze face before openly taking in his physique. It was true that after dating a werewolf, it took a particularly virile man to get her attention, but Heaton was certainly attractive. A little too tall, perhaps, but she wasn't usually interested in a man's measurements outside of his pants. "So, Heaton, I never got your backstory. I know your statistics—ex-military, hunter/parole officer—but what else?"

"Nothing much. I'm pretty good at a lot of stuff, but no secret powers."

"Single?"

"Single," he admitted. She tipped her brow at him. "And gay as a rainbow-colored fairy in spandex." He threw the information out like it needed to be on the table before any further conversation took place.

"Mmm." She shook her head and looked him up and down again. "Then I am more disappointed than ever not to have a penis."

Heaton chuckled. "I heard you were unabashed, but it's still interesting to see close up."

"I'm especially interesting close up." She tipped her brow again.

"I'll keep that in mind... *if* you ever grow a penis."

She laughed and stubbed her cigarette out on a crumb-covered plate that hadn't made it to her sink. She didn't bother pretending one cigarette was enough and pulled out another one. Heaton lit it for her. "So, what's the deal with this witch?"

"Why do we need you; you mean?"

"No, I get that part," she said, not so humbly. "But this chick is your friend, right?"

Heaton sighed and looked over at Daniel. "Friends don't always make the right choices in the heat of the moment."

"Give me the short, stupid version. Who did what, and why do you care?"

Heaton crushed out his cigarette, but refrained from lighting another. "Annette is a witch. A witch is basically a normal person with a knack for commanding magic. Magic is power that comes from one of two different places: the earth or from humans. Annette can use the power of the earth to do... well, whatever, really."

"She snaps her fingers and poof, I have a penis."

Heaton smiled and shook his head. "No, I think that would be beyond her skills. Also, it isn't the snap of her fingers, because she must summon the power. She is just a ritual witch, so she has to draw her power from dragons or, in a pinch, their blood. She has to phone in her request to the earth, and then she'll get delivery in 12 minutes or less."

"I take it she did something bad with her magic then."

"She put the power of the earth inside of a girl, which means that this girl potentially has the snap-your-fingers-and-poof type of power."

Gypsy nodded. "And that's bad."

"Very bad."

"And assuming Callin and I can help you reach this sorceress, what then?"

Heaton looked away. "Then... we kill her." He looked back up at her. She was surprised to see the coldness in his eyes. He was genuinely ashamed of his duty, but that didn't mean he was going to face it with a coward's heart. "Can you handle that?"

She resisted the urge to smile at his question, since it wouldn't offer him the right kind of assurance. Instead, she snuffed out the remainder of her cigarette and gave him the same look of cold bravado. "Yes, I can handle that."

31

CORI TUGGED ON THE carrots, gently prying them from the unforgivable mud. She had donned her raingear for the day in the bubble, but it wasn't enough to keep her clothes clean, and aside from her torso, she was sopping wet from the steady mist.

She was familiar with picking in the rain, and given her mood, she didn't mind the gloomy cloud cover. Since Efrat had been banned from the time bubble, she was back in charge of vegetable picking. Since it was a light day, she was on her own. It was giving her time to think, which, depending on where her thoughts strayed, was a bad thing.

She slumped back when the final carrot had been picked and tossed it in her basket. There was still time until she was retrieved, so she headed down to the lake. She could at least partially wash up.

She meandered through the trees that preceded the treasured lake. She heard a twig snap behind her, and she whipped around, drawing her gun. The thin wilderness offered little room for hide and seek, so she holstered her weapon when she didn't see a wizard stalking her.

She and Efrat had never had any trouble with wizards in this area, but Danato had warned her against complacency. He now only allowed her to bring darts into the bubble, just in case they tried to use her gun against her, but *shoot first and run like hell* was still the prescribed response to a wizard attack.

She made it to the water's edge and looked around again before crouching to rinse her muddy hands off. Her nails were in desperate need of a manicure, but she had long since given up the lifestyle that provided that, the job that allowed it, and the personality that cared about it.

She checked her watch and turned to head back to her vegetables, but her path was blocked.

Cori gasped at the seven-foot man before her. She was relieved she could still breathe, but that was as far as her respite from terror went. She should have been grabbing her gun, as she had been instructed by Danato, her natural instincts, and her general determination to preserve her life, but she had only ever prepared herself for a wizard.

This was not just some clumsy, slightly insane, partially brain-dead egomaniac. This was the sorcerer that all those wizards had created—or at least tried.

Ogana hadn't been seen in years, but he was just as his photo depicted: a nearly bald man with effeminately hollowed cheeks. He wore the traditional gauzy robes that provided just the right mixture of coverage and aeration for the vacillating climate. However, the drawings depicting him as a radiant giant with fire for eyes didn't seem nearly as exaggerated as she'd once thought. She wasn't sure that his eyes were fire red so much as just brown, but that detail might change in the retelling of this story. Assuming she actually made it out alive.

"Do you know who I am?" Ogana asked. It wasn't the deep baritone voice that she'd expected from a being with such a violent reputation, but rather a silky tenor that might read her a book by the fire. Whether or not she was *in* that fire while he was reading was still up for debate.

"Yes." Cori genuflected slowly, opting for a safer suck-up defense. "Sorcerer Ogana. Your legend is incontestable. I humbly submit."

"Don't bother placating me, girl. I'm not as damaged as the rest of my clan. Not yet, anyway," Ogana added, tipping his brow.

Cori swallowed hard and stood. She made a point to look at her watch again. Five more minutes. Just long enough to get killed. She debated her gun again, but decided that patience was a better option since she had no chance of getting away before he passed out. The bubble dampened most of his power, but he was still dangerous.

"I have been watching you for some time." Ogana tipped his head, examining her. "Your gardens are a nice addition to *my* territory."

Cori glanced back in the direction of the gardens. The gardens were northwest of them, and Ethan's favorite sunset spot was to the east of that. She had never had an encounter in any of those spots. It must have all been

Ogana's territory, and the wizards were smart enough to stay out of his way. *There goes her 3.0 brain again.*

"I had no idea you had claimed this land. I never would have trespassed..."

"Stop groveling. I know you are only trying to save your own skin. I also know that you have only minutes until you are pulled out again."

Cori licked her lips and forced herself to converse, even though her voice was shaking. "What do you want?"

"I want... what I have always wanted. Freedom."

"You know I can't offer you that," Cori whispered. "Even if I could, I really have to stop letting prisoners out."

His eyes explored her, still trying to figure her out. "You'd be wise to remember that I could have killed you many, many times before this. My clemency, however, is waning." He raised his hand and motioned to flick her away.

Her body mirrored the movement, abruptly vaulting to one side. The tree she landed against was more than big enough to knock her out, but she had landed in such a way that she could still comprehend every inch of her blooming bruises.

Cori groaned and rolled onto her hands and knees. She didn't bother waiting for round two. She drew her gun and fired on Ogana.

It would have been a good shot, if the gun hadn't jammed. The inopportune malfunction was more than a *minor inconvenience*, but, nevertheless, the shadowy image of the genie in her line of sight signaled her second payment to her debt to him.

"Damn it," she whispered hoarsely. There was still over a minute until she was pulled out to safety, but as Ogana stalked toward her, she knew she didn't have that much time. Her body snapped upright independently, and she felt the pressure on her neck threatening but not quite suffocating her. Her rings were burning, trying to counter Ogana's tactics, but for the time being, they weren't helping her.

She couldn't help but think that this moment would go down on the reports as yet another of her screw-ups. She wanted to grow vegetables in a den full of potentially violent wizards. It all sounded so ridiculous now. Why not just put the stockroom in the basement next to the vampires? Or maybe they could move Danato's office into the dragon hangar. That's a logical use of space, isn't it?

"They are trying hard, aren't they?"

Cori opened her eyes. Ogana was examining her casually as she grappled at her throat. Despite making no progress, he was fascinated by her effort.

Then she realized; he was looking at her rings.

"They are no doubt confused." He released his intangible grip on her neck and grabbed one of her hands. "After all, it was my power that enchanted them."

Shit.

Cori stared wide-eyed at him, not sure how to respond to this new information. What did it mean that she was wearing gold that was enchanted by a coven-created sorcerer? How much trouble was she in? And who was going to suffer for it?

"When a wand won't do..." Ogana shrugged and pulled on her wedding ring. She gasped, feeling it slip, but she couldn't rip her hand away from him to stop him.

The ring stopped at her knuckle and his hand slipped off, just as everyone else's did, save Ethan. Ogana looked at her hand, confused by this development. The gold shimmered, revealing a hint of the power housed within them. He tapped the diamond on top of the ring and looked back up at her. "Who has tampered with my spell?"

The pressure returned to her throat. She was out of time. She had to stall him. Just a few more seconds.

Cori focused on her anger and threw her hands up. The crackling blue ripped out of her, shoving Ogana just as far as he had thrown her. The pressure on her neck was instantly released. She planned to run, but she was halted by a new force.

The momentary relief she felt vanished when she couldn't shut off the electricity pulsating from her hands. Her arms pulled away from her body, tethered by the draw on her power. The blue vines streaked up to the sky, magnetized by the invisible barrier that marked the schism between this time and place and the prison.

She tried to stop the energy flow, but the current was stuck on. The bubble was taking the power from her. She was inadvertently feeding the entity *Twinkies*.

A final surge snapped her back, and the connection broke. She landed on glossy white concrete. She stared down at the floor. As happy as she was to see it, she almost kissed it. She saw feet before her and she looked up to see Chuck standing over her.

"Oh thank God, Chuck. We screwed up big time."

"Yeah, no kidding."

"The rings…" Cori sat up and saw that Chuck's face was stricken with rapt fear.

She whipped around, prepared to unleash her power on Ogana if he had followed her through, but she was relieved to see no one standing behind her. There was nothing behind her.

Some two blocks of vacant white floors and two dozen supporting pillars lay before her. A factory that had once upon a time been built around a breach in time and space.

The shimmering, tangible half sphere no longer tenanted the floor.

The bubble was gone.

32

CORI WAS UP AND running even before the little bleeps and pings started to alert Chuck of the obvious change in the time bubble status. She ran out, giving the metal doors enough of a shove to hit the wall on her exit. She sprinted to the elevator, and for once in its diabolical life, it opened promptly.

She stopped just before entering, remembering the vision of Danato being swallowed up by brick. "I don't trust you," she said out loud, even though she wasn't sure the entity would understand.

As soon as she hit the stairs, the deafening prison alarms sounded, announcing that the worst had happened. Cori wasn't sure what that actually entailed, but she knew she needed to run faster.

She heard stomping above her as a set of guards entered the stairwell. She paid no heed to them as they skipped two and three steps at a time to get down to the main floor, where Danato and the others would be converging for a report. She already heard his voice bellowing over their hand radios in echoed unison. *"Somebody give me a goddamn report!"*

"I gotcha, Warden." Duke's voice sounded just behind her as he trailed the first group of guards. "But I'm as dense as a doorknob. The men aren't making any sense."

Cori grabbed the radio from him on the way by. "Danato, the bubble's gone!"

"What? Cori?"

"We are on our way down now. I'll explain." Cori handed the radio back to Duke, who gave her a worried look.

"That big thing just up and left?" he asked.

"Yeah, I was inside and..." Cori nearly tripped on her feet when her thought process claimed all the brainpower away from her motor function. Duke caught her arm and kept her afloat while they finished the last set of stairs.

"What is it?" he asked, looking her over for an injury. "You were inside and...?"

"Then I was outside of it, but... I can hear you just fine," she answered in a daze as they reached the door to the main foyer.

"I can't see how. These alarms are deafening," Duke said, opening the door for her. He didn't understand, and she was only beginning to.

"What the hell is going on?" Danato said, stomping into the foyer from his office just as she came through the door. Belus came in shortly after him.

"I was in the den getting crops and I met up with Ogana," Cori answered through her daze.

"Ogana?" Danato flushed and looked her over for injuries.

"My gun jammed, so I had to bolt him. It worked, but the bubble latched onto the power and wouldn't let go. It was drawing energy from me, just like it did Efrat."

"Damn it! Duke, get me Chuck on the radio; I want to see those readings."

"Danato, the bubble is gone. The floor is empty," Cori stated carefully.

He stared dumbfounded at her and shook his head. "No, Cori, I doubt that."

"It's a gigantic glowing globe. I didn't just miss it."

"It can't be gone; we're still alive," Danato answered caustically.

"If the frequencies shifted, it might just be invisible," Belus stated before Cori could begin to question what Danato meant.

"It's not the frequencies," Cori said.

"If the entity left, the elevators would be gone." Danato jutted a finger at the lift. "Speaking of which, let's get these shut down, in case she has another temper tantrum and tries to drop someone." Danato moved amongst the guards to instigate a series of protocols that Cori knew wouldn't help this situation. She knew he wasn't intending to be dismissive, but of course, the situation at hand was just too pressing for him not to take some immediate action. However, since she already knew what the situation was, she wasn't going to stand in line for his attention.

"It's not the frequencies!" Cori screamed at his back. Danato turned around slowly, staring at her with the severity of a general to an undisciplined new recruit. The guards blanched, looking between the two of them. A few even snickered, anticipating the entertainment of watching Danato reprimand her insolence.

"Why do you think that, Cori?" Belus interjected before Danato could combust her with his gaze.

"Because aside from these blaring alarms, I can hear you." Cori glanced at Belus. "I didn't stop for the tuning forks." The tension in the room shifted as silence became the prevailing reaction, followed quickly by illuminating worry. "I haven't left the time bubble yet," Cori answered when no one else wanted to say it.

"It can't be." Danato looked around, still in denial.

"I've been getting some wicked reports from the roof, Warden," Duke added just as Ethan pushed open the stairwell door to join the paused melee.

"You better look at this," he said, nodding to Danato as he passed him by. He walked over to the exit door.

Danato followed right behind him, and Cori joined the trailing line. Ethan pushed open the metal door, and a cool breeze wafted in along with the smell of rain and grass. Cori waited until she was outside to let her panic set in.

The dimming orange sun bloomed on the horizon to the northwest of the prison. Or at least what should have been northwest. Cori chuckled as she looked out onto the rocky cliffs to the far west. The scattered forests to the south and east were dewy with the rain she had only recently left.

The prison and all of its inhabitants were in the center of the time bubble.

33

D ANIEL WAS NOT LOOKING forward to the bored-as-tears journey to China. He hadn't had the privilege of making the trip before, but he had heard from Ethan that it was less than expedient. Unfortunately, that was all Ethan had told him about his trip. He was disappointed that he had kept the information about this sorceress from him, but if he knew the consequences, that was probably why. Ethan was too good-hearted to knowingly turn someone over for execution.

Daniel wondered if he would ever harden enough to make the really difficult calls. As outlandish as it seemed at the time to have a female in charge of the prison, that was one area where he thought Cori might have been a better choice. Granted, she was probably just as opposed to killing a young woman for Annette's stupidity, but she understood the concept of protecting her family. Any doubts Daniel had about her resolve vanished the minute he saw Frederique drowning in her grasp. The look on her face alone was enough to reassure him that she had the stomach for terminal resolutions. She understood that responsibility outranked morality in life-or-death situations.

Fortunately for his wavering attention span, he didn't have to endure the same travel schedule as Ethan. One call from Gypsy and they were on a private jet to the nearest landing strip to Annette's cave dwelling. When they hopped off the flight in Aksu the next morning, there was just enough time to eat before loading up in the arriving helicopter.

"Seriously, who the feck are you?" Daniel asked once again as they all loaded up in the chopper. Gypsy just smiled at him before climbing into the passenger seat and putting on a pair of headphones.

Heaton and Callin sat opposite him and Nevia. He occasionally caught Callin examining her, but he tried not to let it bug him. As far as he understood, Nevia was not fond of her werewolf brethren. And from what he had seen at Gypsy's apartment, Callin was taken. Not that werewolves were monogamous, but he doubted Callin would outright pursue an attached woman, right in front of the attach-ee.

"So how long have you and Gypsy been an item?" Daniel asked abruptly when Callin hadn't readily released the grip on his wife's eyes after she happened to look his way.

Callin dragged his gaze from Nevia and landed on Daniel. He blinked away his confusion and looked out the window. "Since I was healed enough to handle her." He smiled introspectively. "And what about you and Nevia? How old are your wedding vows?" He glanced back at Nevia, but she didn't lock eyes with him.

"We were on our honeymoon when Gypsy came knocking," Daniel said, trying to get his attention back to where it belonged.

"Too bad. She would make an excellent matriarch."

"Nevia isn't interested in that sort of thing," Daniel answered defensively.

Callin bowed his head slightly. "My apologies, Daniel. I don't mean to insinuate anything. It was meant as a compliment to you. It takes a strong-willed man to find balance in a relationship with a fem-wolf, hybrid or otherwise."

Daniel looked at Nevia to see what she thought of this strange conversation. He almost expected her to be sneering at Callin's condescension, but she wasn't. She was looking right back at him, apparently just as curious about his reaction. A small smile curved his lips when he thought it was really she who had reined him in. He wasn't sure any other woman could walk the tightrope of command and sensitivity without tipping into the category of masculine or weak.

He was really going to miss her when he had to turn himself over to Danato.

Nevia frowned, sensing his shift in temperament. She looked away and out her window. He did the same. He could see Callin volleying looks between them, trying to figure out what had changed, but he wasn't as attuned to smelling emotion as Nevia, so he was only left to wonder why their loving gaze had soured. He might have been inclined to ask what it was if the helicopter hadn't tipped irreversibly sideways.

34

DANATO HAD BEEN RUNNING around the prison for what seemed like hours, but he checked the clock and realized it hadn't even been two. He had determined that they were at two-thirds staff. That meant that outside of the prison was another twenty-plus guards that—aside from being free of the time bubble—did him no good, since he couldn't get orders to them.

He had also determined that somewhere outside of his prison walls were thirteen wizards that would no doubt like to formally object to their lengthy incarceration. The guards that were stuck in the building were put on roof duty to monitor wizard activity. They switched to tranquilizers just in case they were forced to point weapons at each other.

Danato stopped at the cafeteria to get some water so he could take his pain pills. His leg was significantly better than it had been before Daniel's intervention, but this much activity was still hard on his old joints. He saw Belus had stopped in for a coffee, or at least the appearance of a coffee. The cup had no doubt gone cold since he was only staring into the distance ahead of him.

Danato got some water from the kitchen staff, who peppered him with questions. He resisted the urge to console them, since that rarely inspired the reaction it was supposed to. Instead, he put on his best indifferent face and grunted about it being, "just another day."

The truth was, it wasn't just another day. Not since the 1960s catastrophe had anything like this happened. He only hoped that there wouldn't be a repeat of that climactic ending. He wasn't exactly interested in seeing his prison become a crater.

He sat down in front of Belus, effectively blocking his view. The small man didn't blink at his arrival, nor did he change his introspective gaze. He just now appeared to be staring at Danato's chest.

"I can only guess what you are thinking about."

"The same thing you are, I imagine," he said, finally tearing his eyes back into focus. "How do we do this without ejecting her entirely?"

"We can't shut her down completely," Danato answered. "Even with a temporary power outage, we risk her expelling the wizards."

"We could try to wean her," Belus suggested. "We just need to turn down the feed. It may take a while, but we might just have to make the time."

"The instruments are useless now," Danato added. "She's feeding off the main generators. I can't adjust that feed."

"Then let's adjust it manually from the sub-basement." Belus shrugged.

"There is no basement." Ethan's stealthy arrival surprised them both. He pulled up a chair from another table and straddled it to sit between them at the end. "The bubble surrounded most of the prison ground to sky, but the basement is outside and so is the eastern end."

"It stops before the dragon hangar?" Belus clarified.

"Yeah. She is happily suckling our power supply, but we are physically nowhere near it. Our only chance is to get outside, so we can dig into the basement from there."

"We still have men on the outside that could potentially pull us out," Danato said, offering hope, but it faded before he could delude himself. "However, we didn't enter from the outside. The bubble surrounded us. Our entry and exit points might be too deep for the outsiders to access."

Ethan huffed with irritation. "Efrat can get out. It shouldn't matter what his entry point is."

Danato was surprised Ethan was the first to suggest it.

"Do you really want to hang your survival on Efrat?" Belus asked.

"As opposed to doing nothing?" Ethan retorted. "I don't think anyone distrusts him more than me, but I was kind of under the impression we were desperate."

"Belus is right," Danato intervened. "Efrat has come a long way, but we can't depend on him to not take advantage of the situation. He could easily just walk away and leave us here."

"Ethan is right," Belus said before Ethan could respond. Danato looked at him, slightly baffled by his change of side. "I never said Efrat would betray us. I just wanted to know if you two wanted to risk it."

"You think he's trustworthy?" Danato frowned, disappointed that Belus could be duped into believing in the man.

"I've never trusted Efrat." Belus shook his head. "I only trust him with Cori." He glanced at Ethan as if he knew the statement alone might send him into a rage. "I don't know if he has an honest connection with her, or if he just can't resist staying on her good side because he can touch her, but for some reason, Efrat listens to her."

"Barely," Danato grumbled before Ethan could say it.

"Yes, barely," Belus agreed, "but I think that's enough to keep him on track.

"You're suggesting that they try to leave the bubble together?" Ethan asked.

"Yes, they both have the power, and to be perfectly honest, if the bubble's bigger, it might take two whammy bolts to get them out anyway."

Danato glanced at Ethan. He didn't want to make this decision on his own. He didn't like the idea of pairing Cori and Efrat up for a rescue mission any more than Ethan did, but they were low on options.

"What if it grows more?" Ethan wisely asked.

Danato turned to Belus for his thoughts.

Belus tapped his mug as he thought about his response. "This was a pretty major expansion. She had to have been saving up for this. I can't imagine that she will push through again this soon. She's still bound to her world. It's a constant effort to maintain her presence in this world."

Danato nodded. "Ethan?"

"We don't really have a choice, do we?"

"We have a choice right now. We can continue to brainstorm."

"No," Ethan mumbled. "This was bound to happen anyway, wasn't it?"

"What do you mean?" Danato glanced at Belus.

"Never mind. I'll go talk to Cori. Maybe one of you can find Efrat." Ethan stood to leave.

Danato frowned at Belus, and he nodded permissibly. "Ethan, wait. There's something you need to know before you agree to this."

35

THE CHOPPER ARRIVED ON the western edge of the Taklamakan Desert. Gypsy could see the marking point of the small vacant village below her. She was surprised she couldn't see the cavern the map was indicating. She was about to ask the pilot where it was over the radio, but a sudden impact forced the helicopter into a barrel roll.

She braced herself while the pilot cussed and fumbled with the controls. "What the hell was that?" he shrieked.

"Get us straightened out!" Gypsy yelled, as she felt her stomach flop a second time.

"I'm trying!"

"Now! I'm not dying because of inept piloting."

After a few frantic adjustments, the pilot balanced out the helicopter, and Gypsy found her bearings. She could feel her heart beating fast and her adrenaline had kicked in, but aside from that, she had control of her faculties. However, the man next to her was practically hyperventilating from the near-death encounter. "What the hell was that?" he repeated.

"That was some shitty flying, followed by some pretty freaking awesome flying," she suggested. "There's the village." She pointed down ahead of them.

"Didn't you see that?" He looked at her angrily.

"See what?" Gypsy bit back.

"Something sideswiped us in midair."

"Something?" She rolled her eyes and looked down at her map again.

"That." He frowned, turning ashen as he looked past her out the side window.

She looked up and saw the massive form flying parallel to them. The pale lavender scales tipped with brown covered the reptilian creature from head to extensive tail. The flapping translucent wings looked relatively normal to her, albeit fifty feet too wide, and not attached to a bat.

"Huh, dragon," Gypsy observed with a little more interest than her tone indicated, but not by much. She had heard about the dragons. She hadn't really put much thought into the grandeur of the creatures. She just knew that they existed. It was one of many creatures she had come to terms with since meeting her employer.

The creature screeched. It was more birdlike than a land animal roar. Its left wing dipped down, and she predicted the shift in its path. "Dive down, it's coming back."

The pilot didn't hesitate to listen, and they barely missed another side impact from the beast. As it was, the updraft threatened to flip them again. "What is that thing?"

"A dragon," Gypsy answered, gathering her pack of gear with several protuberant sheathed blades.

"What?"

"Ask me another question and I will shoot you. Now land this bird before you crash it."

"You want to stay here with that thing?" Making good on her threat, Gypsy pulled out her handgun, cocked it, and aimed it at the pilot's face. "Okay! Okay! Crazy bitch!" he shouted. He landed the helicopter not so gracefully on the desert floor. "Get out!" he commanded.

She holstered her gun. "Stay here," she said as she ripped off her headphones.

"I'm not staying here! That thing is—"

Gypsy dove on the man and shoved her very recently retrieved knife into his throat. "Listen. You don't know me, so you don't know enough to be more afraid of me than dragons. So I'll let this little insubordination pass, but rest assured..." She pulled his name badge from his pocket and held it up to his face. "If you aren't here when we return, you will regret it."

She withdrew abruptly and hopped out of the helicopter. The others were already outside, looking and pointing at the sky. Gypsy gazed up at the majestic creature, blotting out the sun with its wingspan. It should have inspired fear, but part of her just wanted to hop on its back and go for a ride. That was no doubt a suicidal idea, but it might have been worth the ride.

The downwash from the helicopter increased, whipping sand at them. Everyone shielded themselves as their transportation lifted back into the air. When the wind settled, Gypsy pulled her gun. "Oh, son of a bitch!" She aimed it at the escaping helicopter, but Callin ripped it from her hands before she could fire.

"Easy, he's not your enemy," he yelled over the thrum of the distancing rotors. "He's just scared."

She relinquished her fight as the helicopter reached a height beyond her aim. It was no bother since she still had his name and could freely exact her revenge at a later time. With that in mind, she shoved his ID badge deeper into her back pocket.

At the very least, the pilot's cowardice was drawing the dragon's attention away from them. She turned to Callin to say as much, but remembered that he was still babysitting her gun. "Give me that," she grouched and ripped her weapon away from him. He smiled at her irritation and she stomped off.

"What's her problem?" Daniel asked when she looked to be out of earshot.

"She doesn't like it when things don't go as planned," Callin said as he followed her. Daniel fell into stride beside him while Heaton and Nevia followed behind them.

"Nobody likes that."

"No, she really hates it. She's kind of particular, which is surprising since you can rarely anticipate anything in this job."

"I know the feeling." Daniel glanced back at Heaton. He had a gash on his head courtesy of their abrupt course change, but it wasn't worth getting hot and bothered over. Nevia probably had a bruise or two from the shift, but she wasn't asking for any help either.

A bone-shivering caw signaled the return of the dragon. He heard Gypsy cuss and raise her gun to the sky, but he didn't have time to react before she fired it at the dragon.

Gypsy wasn't about to keep dealing with this dragon. She knew enough about them to know their vulnerabilities. When the shrieking beast came back for more, she drew her gun and aimed for its open mouth. She only managed to get a couple shots off before she was toppled face first into the ground.

She expected to feel the weight of Callin on her, but the lean muscle piled on top of her was of normal male weight. "Don't... shoot... the dragon!" Heaton's voice was so close to her ear she couldn't help but flinch at the baritone vibrating her eardrum.

She wanted to retaliate or offer retribution, but he wasn't attacking her, he was protecting her. Instead, she turned her head slightly, rubbing her cheek across his face until their lips were almost touching. "Comfortable?"

He released the pressure of his weight and helped her back up. She nodded to the dragon circling above them. "What do we do about him?"

"Her," Heaton corrected. "Nothing. Don't threaten her. Dragons are relatively peaceful. She's just playing guard dog for Annette. I doubt she was trying to crash us, just scare us away."

"What happens if I shoot her?" Gypsy asked more playfully than she probably should have.

Heaton narrowed his eyes at her. "I said they are relatively peaceful. They'll snap your neck if you piss them off."

"Mmm." She eyed the dragon's vulturine circles. "I guess we have that in common." She turned a hollow stare at Heaton before walking on.

36

ORI DUCKED BEHIND THE concrete rim that surrounded the roof. "See anyone yet?"

Duke looked over at her with the worry that Danato usually had for her. "No, ma'am. We haven't seen any of the wizards. Are you sure Ogana is going to be looking for you?"

"Yes," she answered simply, and watched her rings shimmer unnecessarily. She peeked up over the rim and scanned the trees and rocky outcrops below. "He's out there. I can feel it."

Duke pulled on her shoulder to encourage her to come back down. "I don't know what's got you in such a tizzy, but I can assure you, those wizards aren't getting into this prison."

Cori nodded, but she wasn't sure it was as simple as locking the doors. Ogana didn't abide by the same rules as wizards. He had errantly been imbued with earth magic. The only person with enough power to stop him if he got out of the den was no longer on good terms with Danato.

"We're up, kitten," Efrat hollered as he sauntered over. "Hero duty calls."

"Where's Ethan?"

"He's coming. You don't think he'd let you leave without a kiss goodbye?" He clicked his tongue. "Good thing your bed is outside of the bubble or we'd never get out of here."

Cori ignored his tease and rushed over to Ethan, who had arrived with her baby boy in his arms. Her eyes instantly watered at the thought of leaving both of them behind. She knew Danato and Belus were only estimating around 48 hours to wean the entity, but that meant a month and a half away from her son. At this early stage in his development, it felt like she was abandoning him.

Cori hugged them both, taking turns kissing cheek to cheek, until Ethan eventually caught her mouth up in a deep, sensuous kiss. The emotion behind it was not so much a goodbye as a foretelling hello. She finally pulled back and looked over his face.

"I'm going to get you out of here," she said sternly.

"I know you will." He sounded just as serious, but he still had fear in his eyes. "You know I love you, right?"

"Of course." She leaned her forehead against his. "I love you too."

He lifted his head and kissed her forehead. "Take your son. I need to speak with Efrat before you go."

Cori frowned and looked up. "Please don't pick a fight now. He's so much easier to deal with when he's in a good mood."

He smiled at her and pinched her chin. "I promise I won't pick a fight, but I can't guarantee he'll keep his good mood." He kissed her and handed off the baby.

Danato and Belus arrived and joined her as Ethan headed off for what appeared to be a rather civil, albeit covert, conversation with Efrat.

"Any last-minute advice." Cori looked between the two men.

Danato chuckled. "Stay safe and hurry. We're likely to go stir crazy in here."

Cori squeezed the baby, who blubbered happily. "Oh, believe me, I'll be eager to get back." Cori glanced back at Ethan and Efrat. They both glanced over at her before returning to their dialogue. "I can about imagine what that's about." She rolled her eyes. "Speaking of stir crazy, two days straight with Efrat. Yikes."

Danato smirked at her. "I'm sure your sleeping powers will come in handy."

Cori looked at Belus, who wasn't even pretending to join in the pretense of amusement. "No advice from you?"

He shrugged. "You have your instructions. I'm sure you'll do fine."

"Belus, why don't you take the baby so I can give my girl a proper hug goodbye," Danato suggested. Cori handed off the baby and Danato squeezed her to a near rib-crushing tightness. "I love you, sweetheart," he whispered in her ear.

"I love you too," she whispered back with the last of her oxygenated breath.

When he finally released her, Ethan was back and gave her another kiss. She moved over to Belus and kneeled down to offer her son a kiss. She took the opportunity to hug Belus under the all-inclusive, dangerous mission clause, which he couldn't deny. When she was next to his ear, she whispered, "What aren't you telling me?"

"You have your orders, kid," he whispered back.

She leaned back and saw his unbreakable determination. If he knew something different from what he was telling her, he wasn't about to share it. She gave him a slightly mocking salute before heading over to Efrat.

"You ready?" He glanced back at the others. "I can wait if you need more time."

"What did he tell you?" she asked.

"He told me your favorite sexual positions—"

"What did he tell you?" she seethed, letting the anger feed the electricity she needed for her escape.

Efrat's eyes danced over hers. She wasn't sure she had ever seen him concerned for her, but this was as close as he had ever come. "He told me to take care of you. He told me that he loves you more than anything in the world. Then there were several death threats and a vivid description of a surgical procedure I would prefer to avoid. He loves you, Cori. What do you *think* he said to the man you're about to spend two days alone with?"

Cori relaxed and realized she was reading too much into everything. There were bound to be concerns about being trapped in the time bubble. Without the constant deliveries, food and supplies were going to become very scarce. Not to mention that with everyone sleeping inside the prison, the dream feeders were going to be working overtime.

Everyone was just dreading the unknown.

Cori bolted the sky. She luckily didn't get stuck, but she didn't pop out on the other side of the bubble either. She glanced at Efrat, who seemed to be enjoying her struggle. "You don't have enough juice," Efrat commented. "You're a spark at best."

"Fine then, give me a boost." She held out her hand. He approached and pushed his fingers through hers, interlacing them in a tight grip.

"Ready?" he asked.

Cori glanced back at Ethan. She gave him a pained smile, and he nodded as if giving her permission to go. "Set your phasers to stun, Mr. Alston."

He smirked and shook his head. "It must kill you to live without cable."

She sighed wantonly. "It does. It really does."

Cori felt his crackling blue tickle her skin, but the sensation was gone as soon as the rings kicked in. She reached to the sky.

"Save it up," Efrat corrected before she wasted another shot. "Release it when you think your hair might start on fire."

Cori did as he suggested. When the energy finally released, she felt a whiplash effect, as she was not so gently purged from the time bubble.

37

T HE DRAGON CONTINUED TO dive bomb them, occasionally knocking them down with an outreached claw. However, as Heaton surmised, the creature was only interested in scaring them. If she really wanted to hurt them, they would be stanching bloody wounds instead of shaking sand out of their shirts. Unfortunately, the dragon wasn't the only security they had to contend with.

Daniel jumped at yet another lightning strike from the blooming gray clouds above. The wind had cooled significantly, leaving them shivering even before the rain started. Combined with the unnatural tingle in the air, he was dreading going any further.

Gypsy, on the other hand, was trotting through the unnatural storm as if it was an April drizzle. He admired her bravado, but he couldn't respect her egotistic ignorance. If she thought bullets would protect her from an angry earthen witch, she was going to be re-educated very soon.

"What is this?" Nevia asked, closing the distance between them. Her small frame was covered in goosebumps. Her beautiful chilled breasts begged to be ogled, but he resisted the distraction.

"Annette," he answered, looking over to Heaton, who was a half-step ahead of him. He looked back at him, wearing the same concern on his face.

"Hopefully," Heaton added.

"You think this magic storm might be the sorceress?" Nevia asked. "What if it is?"

Heaton shrugged. "Then it was nice knowing you."

Nevia looked at Daniel to confirm this. "Incarceration is starting to look better and better, huh?" He smiled, even though it wasn't really funny.

"Can't get conjugal visits in hell," Heaton added with his own untimely smirk.

Nevia frowned at both of them for the ill-timed humor and changed the subject. "You said she was your friend. Why would she do this?" Nevia asked as another boom of thunder threatened to pop their eardrums. "Why would she risk the people she cares about to create something so destructive?"

Daniel shook his head. He wanted to know that himself. "She's pretty into profitable witchery, but I can't believe she would go this far." He paused, thinking that through further. "No, I can't believe it."

"If she's not doing it for money, what else is there?" Nevia asked.

"Not to mention, imbuing a witch with that much power isn't a casual spell," Heaton added. "It took a whole wizard's coven to do it last time, and even then it didn't take right. She would be risking her own sanity and the life of her subject just to initiate that kind of possession."

"Yeah, but remember who put those wizards in the den," Daniel said. "If anyone is strong enough to do this, it's Annette."

"That means whoever she imbued has to be that much stronger," Heaton said soberly.

"But why?" Nevia interrupted again. "What would motivate a witch as powerful as Annette to go against Danato and create a being with *more* power than her? One that she can't control?" When Nevia got blank faces as her answer, she continued. "Annette isn't stupid, right? And she isn't a bad person?"

"No, she's ornery, but not bad," Daniel said.

"And what about Ethan?" Nevia pointed out. "You said he was involved with this."

"I'm hoping Ethan just didn't understand the ramifications," Heaton chided their absent friend.

"Even so," Nevia continued, "he's not likely to just allow such a dangerous procedure without proper motive."

"There is only one reason either of them would be involved in this." Daniel shook his head. "The same reason Ethan didn't report it to Danato when he got back. The same reason we all do stupid things." He shrugged. "Whoever this girl is, Annette cares for her. Loves her. I imagine Ethan didn't want to go against her, or perhaps this girl bewitched them both. Either way, Annette is going to protect her, regardless of the rules."

Daniel frowned and exchanged a glance with Heaton. "That means this is going to be that much harder."

38

C ORI AND EFRAT ARRIVED just outside the prison in view of Danato's house.

The high-pitched shriek in her ears was painful. She groaned and pawed at her ears, trying to plug them, but the sound was internal. She felt Efrat still holding her hand. He was beside her in the same doubled-over position. She could see blood in his ears.

She tried to unfurl her hand as she reached into her pocket for their designated tuning forks, but their hands were stuck together again. She gave up trying to free her hand and focused on alleviating her eardrums.

The tuning forks released the cotton and the pain, but it left behind a dull headache and slight nausea. "Are you okay?" she asked when Efrat didn't seem assuaged by the forks she was practically jamming in his ears. He didn't reply, but he threw up, effectively answering her question.

"What the hell?" Efrat said once he was capable of standing upright. "When did that get so trippy?"

Cori looked over the filmy white globe, covering the entire prison. "It's bigger. That probably means stronger, ergo trippy-er."

"What are we going to do about this?" Efrat lifted his hand, which was quite obviously conjoined to Cori's again.

"I don't know. Hopefully, it will wear off again. Come on, we need to get started." Cori tugged Efrat along behind her.

Efrat mumbled. "Where are we going?"

"To the greenhouse. I have shovels there. We can start digging to get into the basement."

"Whoa, whoa, whoa." Efrat put the brakes on, successfully halting her as well.

"You know the plan, Efrat. Get to the basement, reduce the power every few hours, and... pray."

"You just want to dig in right away?"

"Efrat." Cori drew back to face him head on, or at least head to chest. "That prison can't function without regular supplies. It's the downside of being in the Arctic Circle—no mail service. We need to move fast and get them out. We're already pushing it with a month and a half."

Efrat looked around as if he had misplaced his wallet. "That's my point. You, me, and a couple of shovels will take all day to dig into the basement, especially like this." Efrat raised their conjoined hands.

"We can find the guards and they can help."

"Shovels still aren't going to get us through brick. We need power tools or a really big sledgehammer. We need to take the time now to think, so we don't waste more time in the long run."

Cori frowned, realizing he was right. She was rushing in head first as usual, but in this case, it wouldn't help. She needed to think beyond her adrenaline. She needed to figure this out one step at a time. First step, find something to break down brick walls.

Or someone.

Cori gasped and took a step toward Efrat before she realized a hug may not be appropriate for their currently standing *uncomfortable-as-hell* relationship. "Efrat, you are a genius."

39

GYPSY STARED AT THE open gorge suspiciously. She hadn't seen it from the helicopter, and yet there it was, a giant three-story-deep trench, over a mile long and at least a city block wide. Everyone lined up on it, giving it their own evaluation.

The wind was thrashing so violently now. If she hadn't had her hair pulled back, it would slice her face. The rain was turning to sleet as the temperature dropped again. She was shivering uncontrollably, but part of that was her adrenaline.

"Maybe we trick the dragon into flinging us across it," Daniel suggested behind her.

"That's too far to jump, even for me," Callin announced.

"We'll just have to walk around," Heaton suggested.

Gypsy examined the sand on the edge of the drop. It was dry. The rain had been pelting them hard for several minutes. There was no way it could escape the moisture. "I can't wait that long," she said and jumped forward into the cavern. There were successive gasps from everyone, and Callin's hand latched onto her foot.

When she landed on solid, well-disguised ground, no deeper than she'd started, she turned around to look at the stunned faces behind her. Everyone examined the clarity of the magical veil with astonishment. From their perspective, she was standing in midair over the lethal drop.

Callin released her foot and stood up from the position he had landed in trying to save her life. He dusted—or rather smeared—the sand from his shirt. The glower he gave her was a special combination of anger and hurt.

She probably should have probed the area with her foot just to be sure it was safe. She also could have announced her suspicions before literally jumping in with both feet, but she preferred shock and awe. Unfortunately, her werewolf boyfriend didn't find the same amusement in this game as she did.

Callin broke eye contact with her and stalked across the veil. His shoulder clipped hers as he passed her. Normally she enjoyed frustrating him, but this particular nerve had gotten more and more tender the longer they had been together. The poor bastard actually cared about her.

40

C ORI SIGHED AND BANGED her head against the towering bars that held the rock monster Rodan exterior to the prison. "Rodan, I can't get you a bigger cage. You are an eighteen-ton pain in the ass as it is."

"Then bring me a sacrifice." Rodan smiled, or at least the rocks near his mouth shifted to show the diamonds embedded inside.

"Seriously?" Cori glowered at him. "You're already in prison for eating people."

Rodan shrugged—or rather, the boulders adjacent to his head elevated. "Meat is meat. Don't you eat meat?"

"Yes, chickens, and cows, and the occasional fish. I don't, however, eat anything that can carry on a conversation with me."

Rodan grumbled, offering no compromise.

"How long will you last without food?" Efrat asked.

Rodan turned his glowing gaze to him.

"Three and a half weeks before he goes dormant," Cori answered for him. "He can stay that way for years, before he would actually extinguish. I'm told it's a horribly slow death, like living in a coma."

"It will be a while until your next meal if you don't help us," Efrat said with a stern militaristic voice that Cori was unfamiliar with. "What do you suppose happens to you if this prison isn't saved, Rodan?" Efrat paced in front of the creature's cell and she—voluntarily or otherwise—followed him, to buoy his authority. "This isn't about negotiating for perks. It's about maintaining your food supply. You either help us, or we *all* die." Efrat crossed his arms, taking her along with him.

A low menacing growl vibrated in Rodan's throat, but Cori knew he was about to cave. "Fine, I will help you, but this is the last time."

"Oh, come on, Rodan." Cori retrieved the use of her hand and moved to the antiquated winch that raised and lowered his door. Efrat came along in tow to help move the turnstile wheel. "What else were you going to do today?"

41

THE THUNDER ECHOED DOWN the tunnel as Daniel led the way down to Annette's hideout. The effect of the blinding spell was wearing off the others, but it was still dark in the tunnel and he was the only one not affected by either, so he took over as the frontrunner, much to Gypsy's dismay.

He could feel Nevia latched onto his waistband like a frightened child. It made her seem endearing and fragile until he felt the pressure of cold metal pressing on his back. "Nevia, darling, you won't shoot my ass off, will you?" he whispered.

She smiled. "It's not cocked yet."

He stopped and leaned down, kissing her hard and fast, while they were still blanketed by darkness. "That makes one of us."

"Break it up, you two," Heaton scolded.

"What is that smell?" Gypsy asked.

"Collectors," Nevia and Callin answered simultaneously.

"They stink," she groused, hoisting her pack higher on her shoulder. He wasn't sure how many weapons she had brought with her, but the machete and samurai sword strapped to the top of the duffle were enough to concern him about her ultimate goal. As far as he was concerned, this was still a retrieval operation. Assuming the sorceress wasn't active, they would take her back to Danato to deal with.

"Wait till you see them," Daniel mumbled before continuing down the tunnel into the vast cavern that held vehicles and a few too many ugly faces.

"Those are the collectors?" Gypsy asked, sidling up beside him. She was blinking away the last of the blinding spell, but she was having no trouble identifying the twelve-foot twin giants in the center of the room waiting for them to pick a fight. Despite their size, the twins always reminded Daniel of garden gnomes.

"No, those are Annette's doormen. *Those* are the collectors." Daniel nodded toward her side of the cavern, where three bald, semi-human creatures crouched on various protruding rock formations. The creatures snarled at them, revealing serrated teeth.

"That's it?" she asked with the disappointment that everyone had at witnessing them for the first time.

"No, there's three more above you," Nevia said flatly from behind them.

Gypsy twisted to look above her. "Fuck!" She flung herself to the floor and drew her gun on one of the surprisingly close drooling creatures. They were climbing down the wall like surefooted spiders. Their stealth was by far their greatest asset. In a close second was their underestimated intelligence.

Before Gypsy could fire her weapon, Heaton arrived and straddled her supine body, blocking the path of her bullet and the accuracy of her aim. Daniel pinned his lips, so he didn't smile at his audacious friend. *Only Heaton,* he thought.

"Don't... shoot... the collectors," he said with a waggle of his finger.

"Seriously?" Gypsy splayed her arms in frustration. "Why am I here? Are you going to let me shoot anything?"

Heaton offered her a hand up again, and she took it. Once she was up, Heaton pointed up at the hissing collectors. "Those are the good guys. Those..." He turned his finger to the giants waiting for them.

Gypsy rolled her eyes. "Are the bad guys?"

"No, they are the good guys too," Heaton said with mock annoyance. "Haven't you been paying attention the last 24 hours? We have friends here. Don't shoot anyone."

Daniel was pleased that Heaton was having the same concerns about their hired hand. He was also pleased that he had no qualms about reprimanding her.

"Then how do we get past them without guns?" she seethed.

Heaton chuckled and Daniel joined him until he noticed the murderous look she was giving him. "Unless you have a machine gun on you, I wouldn't waste your time," Heaton continued to enlighten her.

"I repeat. How do we get past them?"

"With a great deal of effort," Heaton said.

42

"Ouch!" Cori ducked another dirt clod as Rodan barreled through the ground toward the basement. She shifted back, angling behind Efrat to get away from his haphazard aim. He didn't seem interested in monitoring Rodan's work so much as his own body. He grazed his hands along the skin on his arms and neck.

"I'd ask if you want to be alone, but, well..." She shrugged and swung their conjoined hands.

"Are you sure you want to start the jokes this early? We've got a long *Odd Couple* episode coming up."

"Good point. I wonder where the other guards are?"

"You want to split up and look for them?" Efrat waited for her to glare at him before smiling. She reluctantly smirked before looking away.

"You do realize you aren't as funny as you think you are."

"I am hilarious. I just don't have that many fans." He raked his fingers through his hair. "You're probably the only one, in fact."

"Me? I'm not sure fan is the right word."

"Friend, maybe then," he suggested and turned to see if she was going to object.

She shrugged at him, not wanting to outright decline the title. "I kind of think of you as my ward."

"What is a ward, really?"

"It means to protect." She glanced at his curious expression. "They use it in all those old English novels when someone takes on someone else's child."

Efrat thought about that. "Mother?"

"No," she wailed. "Just go back to touching yourself—above the waist, I mean," she clarified. He raised his free hand to her face, and she flinched.

"Easy, kitten. Just a little dirt." He brushed his bent finger over her cheek, removing whatever abnormality he saw there. He smiled at her, offering her the coy flirtation that he usually did, but this time there was no walking away when he got too carried away. Without the threat of Ethan nearby, she wondered how far Efrat would trespass beyond the title of *friend*.

43

Gypsy opened her duffle bag and geared up. The troll-like giants standing at the center of the cavern seemed no more interested in them than the stinky collectors surrounding them were. Actually, the collectors seemed to be very interested in Callin. He had shifted more than once to avoid the creatures' perusal sniffs. It was unusual to see her lover afraid of anyone, let alone these short doglike beings.

She smiled at him as she snapped her metal shin guard into place. He caught her amusement and his eyes narrowed. "What?"

She looked to the others, who had approached the giants in a vain attempt to barter passage by the beasts. She supposed they were obligated to follow protocol, but if they actually expected that to work, they wouldn't have brought her and Callin with them.

"Are the puppies making you uneasy?" she asked with a childlike pitch in her voice. One of the *puppies* turned and growled at her. She wasn't sure if he understood her or if he was just responding to her taunting tone.

Callin scoffed. "You know nothing about this world. Don't dismiss your fear because of preconceived ideas."

"There's nothing to dismiss," she said, tipping her head.

He paused to look her over. She wasn't lying. Any increase in heart rate was due to the energy in the moment, not any particular emotion. It was true that she was initially startled by their presence, but she wasn't afraid. Survival instincts and sentiment originated from two very different places.

"They couldn't possibly be stronger than you," she said when his gaze shifted into disgust instead of intrigue.

"No, not just one."

"Come on, Callin." She finished strapping a steel brace to her left forearm. With everything in place, she could kick, punch, and block without the threat of breaking bones. Her hands were left free to wield her weapons. "Even with six of them, they couldn't possibly best you."

He took her in, eyeing her weaponized defenses. "Yes, but you are forgetting one very key factor." She perked her brow, giving him permission to educate her. "When they come knocking at your doorstep, they aren't picking a fight. They are catching you." He glanced behind her, and she turned to see what had caught his eye. One of the stinky beasts was right behind her. The same one that didn't like her *puppies* comment.

Once again, the creature's stealth impressed her, but his clicking growl didn't startle her as it had the first time.

He opened his mouth to show off his teeth. His breath alone was a tactical offense.

She wanted to headbutt it, or offer a scathing rebuke, but she was starting to see how unwise that would be. Callin took her hand and drew her forward, away from the beast. When she finally looked at him, he was no longer annoyed with her. He must have recognized her change of opinion and was satisfied that his machismo was no longer in question.

"It's best to ignore them," he murmured, pulling her closer. "They don't like being looked at."

"Then maybe they should bathe more than once a decade," she mumbled. One of the creatures growled behind them, catching Callin's eye. He didn't offer it much of a glance before he closed his lips on hers.

She was more than happy to receive the kiss, but the fervor behind it was more unsettling to her than engaging. She pulled back enough to speak. "This is no time for PDA."

He kissed her again, pushing against her braced arms. She didn't really have the option of complying or not, so she just let him have his way. When he finally released her and looked at her, a small smile played across his lips. "I love you," he whispered.

Her heart jumped into overdrive and a cold sweat hit her fast. Her fight-or-flight instincts went into overdrive, and since flight wasn't on her list of qualifications, she did the only thing she could think of.

She punched him.

44

CORI DUCKED THROUGH THE makeshift entrance, entering the prison's basement near the east elevators. The quiet floor surprised her; their arrival hadn't prompted an orchestra of vehement screeches. As usual, it smelled like piss though.

Efrat pushed in behind her, forcing her forward faster than she intended. He offered no apologies for almost tripping her, but he increased the tension in his grip to help keep her afloat while she traversed the rubble heap.

"How is this the least dangerous floor, and yet still the creepiest?" he asked as he looked over the long yellow-lit hallway before them.

Cori nodded to the stairwell. "The sub-basement is where the generators are."

"I know." He afforded her a quick glance before leading the way into the stairwell.

One floor down, Cori weaved through piping and ductwork behind Efrat. She supposed it was a feat of magic more than science that the building was still running, even though it was completely disconnected from its power source. The house entity wasn't likely to make such an expansion without compensating for energy flow. The fact that she was trapping the entire prison probably didn't even register as a significant detail to her.

"Why didn't she include the basement?" Efrat yelled over the roar of the incinerators. The excessive warmth was nice for a change, but she didn't dare touch anything with so much metal in the vicinity.

"It's the earth barrier," she yelled back.

"I don't know what that means," he retorted.

She paused, not sure it was worth taking on a conversation of that magnitude while yelling was a requirement. "The ground is like a brick wall to her. She can push through the atmosphere, but strictly to ground level."

Efrat grumbled something and nodded. "Then why not just take the whole prison? Why did she leave the east end exposed?"

"Belus thinks it's because the dragon is there."

"Dragons are immune to time bubbles?" He glanced back, and she shrugged.

"You tell me. That's where I stop sounding like I know what the hell I'm talking about." Cori thought she heard him laugh, but it was hard to tell.

Beyond the intense heat and noise, they found the generators. They made the appropriate adjustments to reduce the feed into the building. Cori checked her watch. It would be another two hours before they could make another change.

They made their way back upstairs to the main basement level. When they pushed open the stairwell door, seven guards greeted them with their weapons leveled at their faces.

"Whoa!" Cori held up her hands and Efrat joined in. "Easy guys, it's me, Cori." The men didn't shift the weapons. "Stand down!" she shouted, lowering her hands. The weapons were lowered one by one. "What is wrong with you?"

"The bubble appeared around the prison," Cori's least favorite guard, Dirk, answered. The over-muscled, over-tattooed and undeservingly cocky meathead stepped to the front of the other men. "We went out to investigate and found Rodan out and a hole in the prison. We suspected sabotage." Dirk locked eyes with Efrat.

"Efrat and I just came out of the time bubble. Everyone else is still trapped inside. We're adjusting the electrical feed in the hopes that the bubble will shrink back to normal."

Dirk looked back at her and then down at her and Efrat's joined hands. "Stuck again?"

"Yes." She moved forward, pushing through the men.

"What are our orders?" Dirk asked when she and Efrat had reached the entrance. She turned back and saw several faces turn to hear her answer. She suddenly realized that for the first time since she arrived at the prison, she was in charge. Ethan had always been in charge of the men, and Danato had always been in charge of the prison, and Belus had been in charge of her, but she had never been in charge of anything but vegetables. She vaguely remembered a time that she had purported to be worthy of the warden position. It seemed laughable now.

She cleared her throat and took on the duty of reporting to the men more than ordering them. "The feed needs to be adjusted every two hours. We are estimating two days for any change in the bubble size. That will put our men inside at a month and a half, so we'll need to prepare emergency supplies to get things back on track once the prison is accessible. I assume the barracks have emergency supplies?"

She got more than a few nods. "All right, we should do a full inspection of the bubble to see if we can pull anyone out, and then meet at Danato's house to put together a more detailed plan."

She wasn't sure if she had inspired respect in the men, but they mobilized. Dirk paused as he passed her. He looked at her and Efrat's conjoined hands again. "Happy climbing." He gave Efrat a lopsided grin that prompted him to squeeze her hand tighter.

45

D ANIEL STARED UP AT the bulbous faces of the twin giants, Gog and Magog. Their features were a mirror image, down to the battle scars that marred their slightly gray skin. They were rumored to be over five hundred years old and had endured battles both magical and manmade since birth. Their particular breed of giants was as much a mystery as dragons, but that wasn't because of elusiveness, so much as detachment.

Neither Gog nor Magog were fond of conversation. Their devotion to humans was out of a deep-rooted inclination to be servile rather than any actual affection for the populace. From what Daniel had been told, giants, like the werewolves, were hunted to near extinction during the Middle Ages. Unfortunately, giants could not conceal themselves as easily as werewolves, since they were huge, ugly beasts all the time, not just during lunar phases.

Heaton stepped up beside him, ready to pander right along with him. Nevia joined him on his left. He could tell she was equally curious and fearful of the giants. Her werewolf blood kept her rock steady, but that little part of her that was human and knew the story of Jack and the

Beanstalk wanted to hide under her covers. The fact that her gun was entirely useless against them probably wasn't helping.

"Gog. Magog." Daniel nodded to them, left to right. He couldn't tell the difference between them, but once upon a time he was told that they always stood in the same position to each other outside of battle. The fact that they hadn't roared in objection told him he got the order of the names right.

"Who trespasses on sacred ground?" they asked together.

Daniel glanced at Heaton, a little unsettled by the synchronicity.

"We are friends of Annette," Daniel responded.

"We have come to speak with her," Heaton added.

"You have come to take her charge," Gog said—the one on the left.

"We have come to secure the human race from a plague of magic," Heaton responded.

"Your ethics have no authority here," Magog spoke.

"And what is your opinion of the creation of this sorceress?" Daniel asked.

Gog tipped his chin, appearing determined in his response. "The sorceress is under the protection of the earthen witch. We serve the witch."

"Don't you understand what she's done?" Heaton appealed to them. "This woman she has imbued will wield the full power of the earth."

"You do not understand the ways of magic," Magog answered.

"I understand that you have seen armies of men laid to waste because of power-crazed witches and wizards," Daniel added to the argument.

Gog started to speak, but Magog interrupted the theme of the exchange. "I have also seen armies of men laid to waste because of power-crazed leaders. Shall I extend my judgment on politicians and help you stop them as well?"

"Actually, that would be great, but we don't have time for that," Daniel said.

"We are not responsible for political wars," Heaton interjected. "We are, however, responsible for breaches of conduct amongst supernatural beings."

"The witch is not by nature supernatural," Gog declared.

"She wields magic; her origin is irrelevant. She has created a sorceress. It is a violation of the prison—"

"We do not recognize your authority on this matter," Magog growled.

"You're damn well gonna start!" Heaton's temper flared, and Daniel held up a hand to stop him from charging. An ironic twist of roles, he thought, but nonetheless necessary. "We are here to detain the sorceress and the earthen witch Mabel Annette for violation of the Ogana Treaty. A treaty, by the way, that *she* created. You will stand aside and let us do our job."

"And if we don't?" Magog asked.

"Then we will make you." Heaton nodded to Daniel for a display.

He did as bid and directed a double spectrum whammy at them. He didn't expect to be able to push them far since they were probably upwards of 10 tons each, but he definitely didn't expect to be flung across the cavern by his own power.

46

Ethan looked at the brick wall that lay between him and what should have been the dragon's hangar. "I suppose I should be thankful that she didn't just leave us with a gaping hole in the side of the prison." He shook his head and leaned back on his cot. The gym was looking like a refugee camp, but Danato preferred to have everyone in one place for the time being.

"I suppose so, but it does make me wonder why she didn't just take the whole prison," Belus said from his cot several feet away. The lights were dimmed, but it was easy enough to make out his features. "Any thoughts?"

"On what, why she didn't take the dragon? How would I know?"

"You're telling me Annette didn't give you gads of useless information about the dragons during your visit? That seems unlike her."

"I'm not sure I got gads." Ethan sighed and thought about the question a little more. "She needs the dragons to perform her magic. Either by proximity or blood. They are connected to the earth somehow. Maybe the entity couldn't envelop Penelope just like it couldn't envelop the basement."

"Good theory; perhaps we should move the dragon's hangar closer to the bubble."

"If earth power can't filter through to the den, it does make sense that the den couldn't invade the earth. Maybe whatever is on the other side knows that, but it can't tell the difference between the dragons and the earth. If they inherently possess earth magic, they might be giving off a vibe that the entity interprets as the earth." He glanced at Belus for agreement. He nodded, but he looked dissatisfied.

"You're a smart kid, Ethan." He turned to look at the ceiling. "It still surprises me that you encouraged Annette to do something so stupid."

"We have a long time in this bubble together, so can you just skip your sanctimonious crap?"

Belus chuckled, once again surprising him with his inconstant reactions to his disrespect. Ethan could only assume that Belus had given up trying to be an authoritative figure to him.

"Sanctimonious?" Belus continued to snicker. "I think you're giving me too much credit." After a long pause, he spoke again. "You've always been very pliant. Strong-minded and brave, certainly, but obedient and forthright. For Danato, anyway."

"I know who I am. Why are you bringing it up?"

"I'm bringing it up, because I want to remind you that *I* know who you are. You and I may not get along as well as the rest of this adoptive family does, but that doesn't mean I can't see you. I can sense when something in your life has changed."

"And what do you sense?" Ethan asked, hiding the depth of his curiosity behind disinterest.

"Anger," Belus answered.

It was Ethan's turn to laugh. "I thought you would be oblivious to that generalized emotion by now."

"Trust me, kid, I've lived and worked with Danato most of my life. I'm familiar with the many facets of anger. Especially sorrowful anger." Belus rolled over to face him. "Why so sad, kid?"

Ethan paused to gather his thoughts and debate his answer. As he had just said, they had a long time in the bubble together, so they might as well drop the crap. He cleared his throat and turned to face the insistent man. "Cori may be about to have an affair," he whispered.

Belus's brow dipped either in disbelief or disappointment. He wasn't sure. "With Efrat?"

"Yes."

Belus thought about that for a long moment. "No," he said with finality.

Ethan shifted onto his elbow. "You can't just... she... I know she wouldn't... I mean, she loves me, but..."

"Ethan, Cori's father essentially abandoned her during the most crucial years of her transition to sexual maturity."

"Wow... that's personal," Ethan stammered, unprepared for a health lesson.

"She holds very tightly to her male relationships. Much to my dismay, some days."

"I get that. And that's why I'm concerned about her relationship with Efrat."

"She won't risk losing you for Efrat. She just can't help sympathizing with him."

"And how far do you think he'll get on that sympathy?"

Belus shook his head. "It's too hard to see your relationship while you're at the center of it. You can't see clearly when it's your heart at stake. I know I don't know the specifics of your connection behind doors, but I do think, as long as you don't abandon her, she won't stray from you."

"Thanks, Belus. I think I needed to hear that." Ethan wasn't sure his statement truly changed his fear, but it reminded him that Cori was not his enemy—a revelation that would have been more useful several weeks ago.

"What made you think she was going to cheat?" Belus asked.

"I just don't like the way they have been interacting."

"Up until recently, they've been at each other's throats and not in a sexual tension way. You've been worried about this almost since you got back from China." Belus furrowed his brow, looking him over for evidence to support his conspiracy theory. "Ethan, this isn't just standard jealousy, is it? You actually believe she is going to cheat on you. Why?"

Ethan took in a breath and plopped down on his cot. There was no winning for losing with Belus. He was just too damn clever. "You know who I am, Belus," Ethan said quietly, so his statement wasn't misconstrued as anger. "So you should know that if I say something, or don't say something, there is a very important reason for it."

Ethan looked over at him, openly revealing the fact that he was still lying about something. Belus examined the determination on his face. He grimaced, but nodded. Ethan went back to staring at the brick wall. Belus's gaze eventually released, and he rolled over to get some sleep. Such as it was with dream feeders shoving in nightmares at Freddy Krueger speed.

47

G YPSY FROWNED AT THE look on Callin's face when he recovered from the shock of her punch. He looked wounded beyond any physical pain she could have inflicted on him. She didn't even know what to tell him. She couldn't have fathomed any man falling in love with her, let alone a werewolf. She had hoped his propensity for polygamy would keep her from having to deal with the messy love stuff, but apparently she had underestimated his romantic side.

She was about to offer an apology, even if she wasn't sure what she was apologizing for. *I'm sorry I hit you. I'm sorry I have no heart. I'm sorry you don't understand the concept of casual sex.* Luckily, she was afforded a reprieve from any groveling when she heard Daniel yowling behind her.

She looked back and saw him finish his descent onto the hood of a rather expensive-looking sports car. She saw Nevia shoving Heaton away from the two giants, but his stubbornness left her scrambling backward toward the beasts instead. One of the beasts kicked them, and they both skidded across the rocky dirt floor.

"Showtime," Gypsy announced, and strapped on her sword and machete before returning her gaze to Callin. He looked less hurt, but only because his hunger for battle was taking the forefront. She didn't want to encourage him, but she could hardly leave things on that much of a cliffhanger. Especially since the possibility of death was looming around every corner—at least the corners she was turning. She shoved herself chest to chest with him and kissed him hard. It wasn't the same endearing kiss he had given her, but that was never what she gave him.

Not now, not ever.

She drew back and she could see the anger had subsided somewhat in exchange for confusion. "If I don't survive, just remember... I want to be buried with my killer." She let her mouth curve only slightly in case he didn't like the not-so-kidding comment.

Callin smirked at her and nodded. "My pleasure," he said. He puffed up his shoulders and put on his game face. He was across the cavern space before she could even take a step.

"Damn werewolves," she grumbled. "Save some for me!"

48

"YOU DO REALIZE AT some point we have to go down there?" Efrat reminded Cori as she peeked over the balcony that overlooked the downstairs. Twenty men dressed in black had politely invaded her home, and were scattered about the open room areas, waiting for her to give them more specific orders. Dirk was the only one that seemed to be indifferent to the antsy panic consuming the men.

"How about I just put up a chore chart and everyone can sign up for a time slot?"

"The point of leadership is not just the distribution of duties. You also have to answer inane questions and prevent dissention."

"I've never been the one to answer questions. I'm always the one with questions."

"Things change," he said with a note of familiar cynicism.

"Maybe I can just put Dirk in charge—"

"Don't put Dirk in charge," Efrat objected fiercely.

"Not a fan either, huh?" she said, perking her brow at him. "The men do respect him."

"Fear him, maybe."

"Same difference."

"No, it's not. Just... don't." His vehemence died away, but she got the impression he had more opinions about Dirk than he was willing to share. She might have asked him what incident had soured his opinion of the man, but the house shuddered, silencing the conversational din. "See? That's fear." Cori jumped at Efrat's mouth near her ear. "They don't need more fear. They need a leader."

"And if their leader is afraid?" she asked dismally.

He looked her over. "Don't worry; I'll be right there beside you." She glared as he winked at her, but he squeezed her hand, reminding her it wasn't just a joke. "Come on, kitten, time to see what Danato has taught you."

She nodded. She didn't like the leader position, but since she had a few more answers than the average employee, she decided she owed it to them to be more translucent than her superiors had ever been with her.

She moved downstairs with Efrat in tow. To his credit, he stayed slightly behind her so they didn't look like a presidential couple. "We are expecting some minor reactions from the time bubble entity, but there is nothing to worry about," she said as they cleared the stairs.

"Of course, there's nothing to worry about," Dirk countered from his lounging position in the living room chair opposite Danato's usual spot. She noted no one had sat in Danato's chair—probably too uncomfortable for the unworthy. "I mean, it's not like the house has ever tried to kill anyone in this room. Oh, wait..." His eyes bugged out at Cori.

"That was a different situation. The house was confused about the emotions she was reading." She could see the men were not convinced. "You have nothing to worry about, unless..." Cori feigned concern and looked to Efrat for backup. "...Dirk, you're not pregnant, are you?" Several men chuckled, excluding Dirk, who was displeased that she had taken back the podium.

"As we continue to lower the power to the building," she continued before Dirk could think of a clever retort, "the entity may cause some disruptions. Danato is expecting most of those disturbances to take place inside the prison, and he is prepared for that.

"Our main focus needs to be on salvaging the prison once it has been released. We will be working over the next couple of days to get the bubble reduced, but inside the bubble, two months will have gone by. That means that food and water need to be rationed for them. We will need to intercept any shipments and hold them until we can get to them."

"Why don't we take it inside to them?" one guard asked.

Before Cori could answer, Efrat jumped in. "We are under strict orders not to enter the bubble."

Cori glanced at him, surprised by his interpretation of Danato's plan. "Since the bubble has grown, we don't know where our entry points will take us. There is a possibility that the land within the bubble has expanded as well. We don't want to drop back in thirty miles from the prison and risk getting our necks broken by a wizard."

"Won't the wizards be busy attacking them?" another guard asked. Cori frowned at the thought of a full-on prison attack.

"No, the wizards are generally suspicious of anything new. They'll stay away unless they are given incentive to attack. Plus, they don't work well together. They generally travel alone. They are just crazy enough to be stupid, but just stupid enough to be dangerous, so we need to avoid them at all costs."

"Not to mention, we would have no idea when to pull you out," Efrat added. "So, once you go in, you might be stuck for a while, and Danato doesn't need another body to worry about."

Cori nodded in agreement. She wondered if he wouldn't have been a better choice for a leader right now.

"Why aren't they dead?" another random question was thrown out.

"Pardon?" She scanned the room for the origin of the question.

"The wizards?" a skinny young man asked.

Cori sighed. "We don't kill inmates." She glanced at Efrat, but he wasn't paying attention to her.

"No, I mean from the bubble," the guard clarified. "If the time goes faster inside the bubble, why don't they just grow old and die?"

"Oh, that's kind of complicated," Cori admitted.

"Which means she doesn't know," Dirk barked.

Cori paused to allow the laughter to die down. "When the wizards were placed in the den, the assumption was that they would live out their lives and eventually die. It was actually intended to be a humane and risk-free death sentence, but they didn't. They have all aged significantly, but not died. The reason is technically unknown to anyone, but Danato and Belus have several theories. Witches and wizards generally draw their power from the earth, but inside the bubble they can't access it. So they are either being sustained by the black magic they took in prior to being incarcerated, or they might be drawing on the abnormal magical energies produced by the entity itself." Cori glanced at Dirk to see if he had another smart remark, but his smartass smirk was aimed at Efrat instead—a smirk that seemed to make him uncomfortable. "It could just be a part of living within the time schism too," she concluded.

"So those wizards have been hanging around in there for like two hundred years or something?" the same skinny man asked.

Cori's mouth gaped as she tried to calculate that particular number. She shook her head. But he probably wasn't far off. "I think we should focus on what we can control from outside of the bubble. If there are complications, then we can evaluate the situation again. Does anyone know how we can get a message to our suppliers to increase the food shipments?"

"We got a backup taps in the guardhouse," the skinny guard said. "Mr. Belus wanted an extra one there just in case the prison went into lockdown."

"That sounds about right for him. I don't suppose anyone knows how to use the thing." Cori paused, hoping for a few hands to pop up.

"I know Morse code," Efrat mumbled. "I can figure it out."

"Okay, Efrat and I will go send a message. The rest of you figure out a rotation to reduce the power. Then, start gathering food and supplies from the storage sheds. The greenhouse should have quite a few fresh veggies as well. But no snacking. From now on, consider yourself to be on a two-day cleanse."

As unimpressive as she considered her speech, the men scattered to do her bidding. She noticed Dirk was still comfortably sitting in his chair still. "Do you need a specific duty, Dirk, or are you just enjoying the furniture?" She smiled, hoping not to appear reproachful, since that wasn't likely to work with him.

"No, ma'am, I have a task I've been meaning to jump on. Just waiting for all the riffraff to get out of the way."

"Well, I know I'm not your favorite person, Dirk, but I do appreciate your cooperation."

Dirk frowned. "Oh, I'm sure you've interpreted me wrong."

Efrat pushed her from behind rather brusquely. "Let's go, time's a wasting." He shoved her again, and she gave him a scolding glare.

"Okay," she seethed and led her pushy partner to the door.

49

DANIEL WAS SURE THE hood of a car was a better landing spot than the floor, but at the moment, he couldn't convince himself of it. He wondered why Annette had a red mustang in amongst her jeeps and dune buggies, but he imagined that her vanity would allow nothing less. How she got it back to civilization was a question left for a non-battle day.

He groaned and rolled off the hood. He could see Callin and Gypsy battling the giants, but gave up any plots of helping them when he saw Heaton crouched over Nevia trying to wake her up.

He ran, or perhaps lobbed, over to them. "What happened?"

"She was trying to get me away before they attacked. I didn't listen. She took the brunt of a Magog kick." Daniel kneeled down beside her unconscious body. "I take it they are immune to your power."

"That part, anyway. I'll try to give them a close shave after the wonder twins wear out. Where did she take the hit?"

"The back," Heaton answered. Daniel turned her over and lifted her shirt. Nevia's back was already turning black and blue from the impact of the creature's foot. She may have been bulletproof, but she wasn't wrecking ball proof. He gave Heaton a shocked and scathing look. "I know!" he grouched at his unspoken rebuke. "Just fix her." He frowned.

Daniel worked while Heaton danced around them, searching for something to do. His gun was useless, and obviously his mouth hadn't helped them. He was surprised that Heaton had been so vociferous in his demand, but he supposed that Annette's betrayal was hitting him pretty hard. Although, it may not have been specific to Annette or even the betrayal. Perhaps it was just the idea that he now had two friends to turn over to Danato.

Heaton ran off, apparently finding something more useful to do than watch him heal Nevia. When he heard her moan, he stopped. He wasn't overheated yet, but he didn't want to waste all his energy in case the others needed some help later.

"Hey gorgeous," Daniel purred to her. "We're kind of in the middle of a fight here. Could you get up off your arse and help?" He helped her flop over and was happy to see a fleeting smile on her face.

"Heaton!" She jumped onto her elbows.

"Heaton is fine," he said, pressing her not to stand.

"No, Heaton!" She pointed behind him.

He looked back and saw his friend peeling out in the cherry red mustang he had previously landed on. "Oh feck," Daniel muttered.

50

ETHAN STRUGGLED AGAINST THE vampiric creature, sucking on his wrist. She was a beautiful blonde with yellow-brown eyes and lips that Botox couldn't come close to. She was a "Day Sith" and by rights shouldn't have been this close to him without being tranquilized, but she was one of the many vampiric prisoners that required fresh blood.

Normally live animals were brought in to satiate them, but since shipments had stopped, they had to resort to more taboo methods of feeding them. The guards weren't happy about the sacrifice, and truthfully, neither was he, but Danato reminded him that the solution to their problem was not to let dozens of inmates die. It certainly wasn't their fault that the prison was in chaos, nor was it fair to ask them to die just because their captors were uncomfortable with bloodletting.

Ethan pulled a little harder, but the woman had latched on so hard, it hurt more to pull than not. "Ethan?" Danato murmured behind him. He wasn't sure if he was concerned for him, or questioning if he should be concerned, but either way, the woman had taken enough and he needed to stop her.

He started to draw his arm away, but a sudden feeling of euphoria came over his mind, relaxing his body into submission. He knew this was part of her attack, but it felt good to not think beyond one-syllable blubbers for the moment.

Danato embraced him and he cuddled into the big man's chest. He loved Danato like a father, but they rarely hugged like this. He breathed in the smell of the century-old cologne brand. He felt a pain in his arm, but it was gone soon enough, and Danato's arm wrapped around him, guiding him to safety.

He babbled on about this and that while Danato dragged him to a chair and started handing him juice and cookies. He loved the cookies, but he would have preferred milk. Milk was hard to come by here. Danato preferred to order necessary beverages like water, coffee, and liquor.

When Ethan's haze wore off, he realized he was in the cafeteria. Danato was sitting across the table, staring at him with undue concern. "What is it? What happened? Did she take too much?"

Danato shifted uncomfortably. "No, she just gave you a buzz. How are you feeling?"

"Tired, but okay."

"It will pass. Your body should replenish blood faster than the average man. Another unwritten side effect of the dragon... serum." Danato stood up and looked around like he had forgotten where he put his wallet and keys. "I need to go assist the others. Will you be okay for a while?"

"Yeah, sure. Are you okay?" Ethan asked, trying to discern the man's fluster. Danato paused and looked him over carefully. Ethan couldn't for the life of him understand why the man was so worried and disturbed. "Look, Danato, if I said something inappropriate, I'm sorry. I don't even remember what I said."

Danato swallowed and looked at the floor. "I know," he said, sullen. "Just don't start moving around until the dizziness wears off."

Ethan nodded, and Danato stalked out the door without another word.

51

GYPSY ARRIVED SHORTLY AFTER Callin, but he was already clinging to the neck of one of the ogres, pummeling his face. The beast roared and grappled to pull him off, but Callin was too quick for that.

Gypsy confronted the other twin, slashing at his extending arm before he could assist his brother. Her samurai sword crashed into the creature's thick flesh, but it barely went deep enough to be considered a paper cut.

The giant drew his attention to her and shifted to bat her away. His hand was easily big enough to crush her head, but she didn't flinch as he swiped it toward her. At the last second, she turned her back and braced her sword under her arm.

The impact was enough to career her across the floor, but it was also enough to jam the sword through his palm. When she looked back, she saw the sword impaled through the bellowing giant's hand. Though his pain was obvious, there was no blood.

Callin's giant finally threw him off. A track of blood followed his descent, but he wasn't hurt. The giant's hand was inexplicably bleeding from a fresh wound that mirrored the one she had caused on her opponent. Gypsy looked over her wailing giant. His face was puce with bruising, even though she had never touched his face.

Callin returned to the battle, unfettered by the possibility of bruised ribs, but incited by his bruised ego. The giants were more than a challenge, but he would kill himself to beat them. Gypsy, on the other hand, was more interested in killing them.

She ran back at her designated beast with her machete drawn. The giant tried to kick her, but she dodged his leg and raked her machete across the underside of his loose-fitted pants—if the baggy diaper could be called pants. She wasn't opposed to castration, but the blade sliced only cloth.

Before she could escape his legs and exit to his back, his undamaged hand lassoed her leg. He pulled her up, dangling her upside down across from his face. "You are not strong enough—"

Gypsy slashed at his open mouth before his monologue could bore her further. He rumbled and threw her to the floor, hard. She could barely inhale from the impact to her back, but she rolled over to see the damage to the other giant. He was bleeding from his lower lip.

Her giant roared and lifted his foot to stomp on her. Sensing her danger, Callin rushed to her aid. She was sure he couldn't withstand the pressure of several tons, but that made no difference to him. He would still try.

Fortunately, neither she nor Callin had to endure their heads being squashed like Gallagher watermelons. Seemingly out of nowhere, a shiny red sports car collided with the supporting leg of her giant.

52

ORI GRIMACED AS SHE entered the guard barracks. She'd expected the door-less segmented brick rooms that left minimal room for privacy, but she hadn't anticipated the smell. She wasn't sure what it was about dozens of men sleeping in close quarters that made it smell like a locker room, but she didn't want to dwell on it. There was a reason God made females, and if it was for no other reason than to make men shower, so be it.

"Which one is yours?" she asked, falling prey to her desire to keep small talk on her resume.

Efrat looked back at her like she was stupid for asking. "The one with the scorch marks," he answered and tugged her along past the cubicles that weren't much different from the jail cells Danato had liberated the men from in return for their service. She noticed the scorched room Efrat referred to, and she slowed to look inside. The space was sparse, with a shelf for his uniforms and a mattress-less bed consisting of just a fiberglass plank with legs. There were a number of scorch graffiti drawings on the walls.

She was about to ask how a singing, drawing man got involved in the military when she saw a sketch that looked remarkably like her face. Efrat tugged her along, refusing to let her linger at his doorway.

"The taps is upstairs," he grumbled and turned them into a narrow stairwell. "I don't want you to talk to Dirk anymore," he blurted out without any explanation.

"Excuse me?" she asked, trying to shift on the stairs to see his face.

"Dirk." He stopped and turned back. "Stay the hell away from him!" he snapped at her with such venom that she actually felt guilty.

"Why are you mad at me?" she asked, truly concerned that she had somehow broken some unwritten guard code.

His face shifted through a few indeterminable emotions before he settled on something akin to the discomfort he had showed at the house. "I need you to stay away from him. He's not a good person."

She shrugged. "I guess."

"No, Cori." He moved closer to her. "I mean it. I know how stupid that sounds coming from me, but... he's the kind of bad that all women should stay away from."

She gulped at the severity of his voice and on his face. She nodded. "Okay."

His eyes danced over hers for a moment, and when he was content that she understood him, he climbed the stairs again.

The upper floor wasn't much better for ambiance, but the smell did seem to be a little less manly. She also noticed the rooms were less sparse—homey even. She presumed that the men on this level were long-time "employees."

Efrat pulled her into a room not unlike the others except for the table full of books in place of a bed. There was a small device that Cori recognized as a Morse code transmitter. Aside from an overabundance of electrical wires coming off it, it didn't look any more advanced than what she saw in old movies.

Efrat sat down at the machine and put on a headset. He tapped out a few letters and seemed satisfied that it was functioning. "What do you want to say?"

"I don't know. Help. Prison taken over by big bubble." He started to tap, and she touched his shoulder. "No, don't tap that. They'll probably just try to blow us up." He quirked an eyebrow at that. "Say this: Prison compromised but contained. Need immediate supplies."

Efrat tapped out the message and paused, pressing on the headphones. He scribbled down a message on a nearby notebook that was already filled with scribbles. He glanced at her and continued to tap.

"What are they—?"

He shushed her and finished tapping his response. He listened to the reply carefully before taking off the headphones. "They'll send out some trucks right away."

"That's it?" she asked, rather impressed that a few pressed buttons on the antiquated technology were going to save the day. "Wow, you're starting to become rather useful, Efrat."

He gave her a slight smile before it instantly soured to a frown. She opened her mouth to object to his persistence to be pessimistic, but the impact to the back of her head was enough to distract her thought processes, let alone her voice.

53

D ANATO TIP-TOED THROUGH THE sparse foliage behind Ethan. It had been a long time since he had been inside the bubble. Even longer still since he had to hunt a worm. With food getting sparse, the only chance of not starving to death was utilizing the abominable meat. He had already lost two prisoners on the animal level because they couldn't spare the massive amount of food they required. It wasn't something he was proud of, but he already knew that tough decisions were going to have to be made and they were barely through the first few weeks.

Ethan raised his hand, and Danato stopped instantly. He couldn't help but be impressed by his stealth. While he struggled to avoid snapping branches and crunchy leaves, Ethan seemed to be walking on pillows. It was one of his many innate skills that neither Danato nor Belus could take credit for.

Ethan pulled his blade from his belt and signaled Danato to follow him. It was a risk bringing a knife out here. The wizards could easily turn it against them, but he hoped that with two of them, they could protect one another.

They entered a clearing with tall corrugated dirt piles that could have easily been mistaken for massive termite mounds. The mud-packed structures towered above them twice over. The bases were as wide as cars, reducing as they rose, until the peaks were only chimneys.

"What is this?" Danato asked.

Ethan's finger shot up, warning him to be absolutely silent. As annoyed as he was at being shushed, he knew it was probably important enough to warrant it.

Ethan stopped next to one of the smaller mounds that, judging by its hard leathered exterior, was older than the others. He kneeled down gingerly and dug into the base of the mound with his knife. His painstakingly slow and silent excavation lasted for twenty minutes. Finally, his blade punctured through a pocket in the base.

Danato watched with interest as he widened the opening. When Ethan reached his bare hand inside the vacancy, he couldn't stop himself from grabbing his shoulder. Ethan looked back at his tether with amusement. *Trust me,* he mouthed.

Danato released him and once again his hand disappeared along with the majority of his arm. When he withdrew, he held a grayish black oblong egg. Ethan smiled at Danato's shocked interest in this discovery and motioned for him to open his backpack.

They loaded the eggs one by one until the bag was at maximum capacity. Danato shook his head at his clever protégé and wondered if he had ever been so cunning. He tossed the pack over his shoulder and chucked Ethan on the shoulder.

Ethan lost his grip on the knife he was attempting to holster. It fell to the ground—the hilt rapping harshly against the dirt mound. Ethan's eyes widened as a low rumble vibrated the ground beneath their feet. He leaped back, pushing into Danato just as mama erupted from the dirt.

Danato landed hard on the ground, but he managed to keep himself from cracking all the eggs in the bag. Ethan rolled back to retrieve his knife, narrowly avoiding a headbutt from the mother snake.

Danato was familiar with the slow, lethargic earthworm-like snakes that tasted like crap, but this egg-layer was even bigger, and considerably more energetic. He knew he shouldn't be surprised. Mothers in any species were liable to kill you for coming near their young, let alone kidnapping them for breakfast.

"Run!" Ethan yelled at him before dodging another strike from the hard-headed beast. It rose easily ten feet over him, balancing on the mammoth strength in its rippling body.

"I can help!" Danato shouted and removed the pack.

"Take the eggs. She can smell them. She won't give up as long as she thinks she can save them."

"What are you going to do?"

"Wait her out," he growled. Danato could see the snake's head bobbing left and right, trying to sense the location of her exposed babies. "Go!" Ethan yelled.

Danato hated to leave him behind, but it was either that or risk losing the food—thereby negating the entire point of leaving the prison in the first place.

54

Daniel watched the Mustang impact the standing leg of Gog. He would have preferred it to be Magog, but beggars don't have time for premeditated attack. The car provided enough impact to topple the giant, as well as set off the airbags in the vehicle.

Magog rumbled and stared down each of them for the offense against his brother. He started to move toward Callin and Gypsy, who were still on the floor. He wanted to try his power again, but he was reluctant to use it against Annette's men if he didn't have to. He also wanted everyone out of his path, since they were definitely not immune.

A gunshot resonated beside him, but the echo bounced around the room. Magog jolted and grabbed his face. Daniel looked beside him and saw his petite little wife brandishing her favorite bedfellow—besides him, of course.

Magog snarled and moved forward. She fired again, hitting him again. As he cradled his eye, she rose to her feet. Callin retrieved Heaton, who was still stunned by the impact. Gypsy withdrew to them and drew her own gun to brandish.

"I thought you said guns were useless," she growled when she was within earshot. She seemed annoyed that this tactic was left out of her ten-second briefing.

"Bulletproof or not, eyes are always vulnerable," Nevia informed her.

Gypsy looked back, eyeing the woman with new fascination. She might have made some assumptions about her character, but more than a few of those earlier opinions were being erased.

"I could do this all day," Nevia hollered, stepping closer to the standing and supine giants. Callin practically dragged Heaton back to their new front line.

"You would eventually run out of bullets," Magog grumbled. Gog sat up, his right eye bloodshot and watering profusely.

"Then I'll aim for your eardrum," Nevia remarked, taking another step forward. Daniel took a few steps to keep her within reach. He wasn't likely to ever stand between her and her target, but he didn't like that everyone was rushing into battle without regard for their limbs. "Partially deaf and partially blind would even the odds, don't you think?"

Magog paused, considering that scenario. Daniel could see the giant wasn't used to giving up and he wouldn't. That was the downside of devotion.

"Or perhaps I could just skin you and let Annette worry about putting you back together," Daniel suggested when the giant's determination was about to stonewall their violent negotiations.

"I wouldn't do that if I were you," a young man said from the back of the cavern.

55

ORI WASN'T SURE HOW much time had gone by between the searing pain of her past tense hit to the head, and the searing pain of her present tense headache. She was on the floor being jerked this way and that by Efrat's flailing arm. She tried to pull away, but not only was her right hand stuck to him, but her left wrist was painfully locked to her right wrist by a single handcuff. The other half of the cuff set dangled freely.

Efrat ducked another punch, but by the looks of his face, he hadn't ducked them all. Dirk growled and aimed for his stomach, but Efrat bent to the side, simultaneously headbutting his arriving forehead. Dirk stumbled back and Efrat gave him a roundhouse kick to the face.

Both men paused, allowing a recovery time for their cardio efforts.

"You won't win, Efrat. Just let me have her." Dirk leered at her, noting that she was awake. "You can have sloppy seconds."

Cori blanched at the threat before her. Efrat had tried to warn her, but she hadn't anticipated Dirk to be *this* brazen. Some part of her was viscerally afraid of the dark leer on Dirk's face. However, the part of her that still believed in the possibility of world peace and sexual equality for all mankind wanted to bash his freaking brains in.

She shouldn't have been surprised this situation was coming up again, since most of the guards were pretty hardened criminals, but she had thought Danato screened his employees better. Then again, just because the docket said armed robbery didn't mean rape wasn't on the resume somewhere. Even criminals have to have hobbies.

The stupid irony was that if Efrat and she weren't stuck to each other, either one of them could fry Dirk to a crisp. But, of course, he knew that. That was why her hands were bound. The power she exerted was just being reabsorbed, and she couldn't get too aggressive without burning Efrat's hand off.

"Do you have any idea what he will do to you?" Efrat snarled at Dirk.

"Do you have any idea how much I don't care?" Dirk licked his lips. "It might be worth it for the privilege of climbing Mount Everest." He winked at Cori.

"You'll have to get through me first," Efrat rasped.

Dirk shrugged. "Not a problem, now that you've been grounded."

"Yet I'm still standing. Maybe you should think twice about going against a Green Beret."

Dirk simpered and dove at Efrat. Cori wanted to help, but all she could do was go limp and let Efrat maneuver around her dead weight. If she threw off his balance, even a little, he was liable to lose the strength behind his punch or kick.

When Dirk came in to bowl him over, Efrat slammed his fist into his kidneys. The big man groaned and kneeled down, huffing his pain away. Cori took an opportunity to kick him in the gut while it wouldn't interfere. Efrat also punched his face while he was down.

Cori was relieved to see him putting every effort into protecting her. She hadn't really thought he would make it his priority. She knew she could trust him enough not to outright abandon her, but Dirk was not exactly easy to stand up to. Furthering her good impression of him, Efrat was holding his own and then some.

It wasn't until she saw the glint of metal that she got worried. "Look out!" Cori tried to pull Efrat back, but he wouldn't give up the last punch, and Dirk took it so he could get his attack by his occupied defenses.

The sharpened dinnerware thrust into Efrat's gut and chest again and again. Cori gasped, shocked by his lethal intent. The tiny stabs made Efrat grunt and retreat, but Dirk held his arm and continued the barrage him with virulent stabs. "Stop!" Cori struggled to stop the angry attack, but Dirk just shoved her away between jabs.

Efrat finally fell to the floor, gushing blood from too many wounds to count. "No!" Cori screamed. She leaped across Efrat, shielding his body from further injury. Dirk panted and gave up the attack. She looked down at Efrat's stunned eyes and his agape mouth. She could already see the blood streaking his tongue. She knew first hand he didn't have much time. "Efrat." She frowned.

"I'm sorry," he whispered over the blood in his throat.

She shook her head, not understanding why he was apologizing to her. She moved their triplicate hands to his face and did her best to caress his cheek. He closed his eyes and nuzzled into her touch. "I'm sorry too."

"Aww, I didn't know you cared," Dirk mocked behind her. "Don't worry, you'll be joining him soon enough, but first." Cori could hear his zipper slide open. "How do you want it? Ass or cunt?"

Efrat's face contorted into disgust, and he squeezed her hand. She probably should have turned around and tried to fight him off, but she was caught up in the feeling of cold metal against her fingers. The free-dangling cuff was pinned between the floor and her hands.

"You probably want it from behind. That's all right. I never really did have much use for your face. Too much sass comes from that fucking mouth, anyway." Dirk undid her pants and tugged them down. She ignored the exposure of her body. "What, no fight? That's the best part." He kneeled down behind her.

Efrat stared up at her solemn face. He seemed saddened that she was giving up, but she gave him a slight smirk. Given the situation, it was probably interpreted as sadism more than amusement. His eyes flickered over hers, and he may have smiled back, but it was hard to tell since he was starting to fade.

"Are you hard yet?" she whispered, not wanting to look at him if she didn't have to.

He chuckled. "Oh, yeah." He leaned against her hip, providing proof of the speculative product. "You like that, don't you? They all like it. Fucking teases just won't give it up."

If he saw her expression, he wouldn't have mistaken her question for interest. She reached back with her newly freed hand and grabbed his member. Between the contact and the sly expression on her face, he must have been intrigued. He looked down at her hand and the rusted cuff continuing to disintegrate around it. The gusto for her connection faded quickly as the coolness of her touch started to register.

Dirk screamed in agony. His expression turned horrified as he stared down at his favorite appendage, turning frosty white.

She couldn't begin to imagine the pain that she was inflicting with the extreme cold. She had never crossed this threshold before, but then again, no one had threatened her in this way post-rings.

Dirk's icy accessory broke off in her hand. She raised it proudly to show him. It was a little more sadistic than she preferred to be, but she was tired of defending her body against uninvited guests. While his stunned eyes were still on it, she smashed it on the floor. He screamed and cradled his vacant crotch. Before he could recover enough to retaliate, she knocked him out with her sleep skill.

56

E THAN FELL BACK FROM the towering snake's jutting head. She wasn't giving up as easily this time. At some point she would surrender the fight, having forgotten why she had even begun it, but the sheer number of missing eggs must have kept reminding her that there was revenge to be taken.

He had no intention of killing the creature, but as it was, he was losing stamina. The damn thing might have been a glorified oversized earthworm, but her head was like a cinderblock and the half-ton body of pure muscle backing it up was becoming less amusing with each dodged concussion.

He rolled left, then right. The divots left in the soil could have devoured bowling balls. He scurried back, trying to get more distance so he could get to his feet. Her quick swiveling tail pushed her forward just as fast.

He flipped himself to his feet and made a break for it, but he was knocked face first into the dirt. He turned over, missing another plunging attack. He was about to be stamped out, not so metaphorically, when the snake froze in place.

Ethan stared up at the faceless head, gasping to replenish his oxygen in the hiatus. The creature's tail twitched slightly, and then she lowered her head to the ground. She slithered back to the hole she had come out of and didn't return.

Ethan was relieved to know that his death certificate wouldn't say, "death by earthworm," but that didn't necessarily mean it wouldn't be typed up either way. His wheezing breaths slowed and a calm sense of doom trickled in to cool his blood and sharpen his senses.

Had it been a wizard, he might have been groveling already, but there was no point to that now. Danato hadn't really given much credence to Cori's previous sighting. That was Danato's mistake. Ethan had all but forgotten about Ogana's presence in the bubble. That was *his* mistake.

57

GYPSY WHIPPED AROUND, POINTING her gun at the short Asian-American man that had popped out of one of the cave tunnels on the back wall. He was unarmed and didn't appear to be angry at their presence. If anything, he looked sad. "Annette has layered them with reversal defenses for supernatural attacks," he said.

"Who the hell are you?" she asked.

The young man turned to look at her, giving her the usual curious inspection that the opposite sex did. It was usually love at first sight or not, but that didn't mean she couldn't change the opinion either way once they got to know her better.

"I'm Levi Sun-Weston. I'm Annette's assistant."

Gypsy glanced to Daniel to verify this, but he reflected the same questioning look back at her.

"Leave us, boy!" Magog roared.

Levi looked at the giant. "Your brother has fallen. Been a few hundred years since that has happened."

"He will rise and fight again." Hearing his brother's words, Gog struggled to stand.

"Save your energy, Gog. There is no battle to fight here," Levi instructed.

"You betray your master!" Magog criticized him.

He stepped closer. "Annette is only doing what she thinks is right. As these people are doing what they think is right." Magog's chin thrust high, but he didn't speak. "Your service is admirable, Magog. I have never seen a more loyal guard, but Addy no longer belongs with us."

"You would let them kill her!" Gog growled in place of his brother.

The boy's head fell and for a long moment he didn't speak. "I would let them save her. If that means she must die, then..." He didn't finish the sentence.

"You love her," Nevia stated more than asked the boy.

"More than I ever knew," he answered, turning his attention to them. "I know why you have come. Annette is still angry... about everything." He looked at Daniel. "We did what we did to save her. It was selfish and stupid, but what would *you* do for love?"

Daniel glanced at Nevia, and she frowned at him.

"Where's the girl, kid?" Gypsy interrupted the monologue before tissues started getting passed around. Nevia glared at her brashness, but she shrugged at her.

"She's on the altar." Levi motioned behind him. Gypsy moved toward the cavern, but Magog leaped to block the path. His stomping footsteps shook several stalactites from the ceiling. "Let them pass," Levi told him.

"I have my orders!" Magog protested.

"Your orders are from a grieving, angry woman who is penancing herself for letting her heart influence her choices." Levi moved forward and touched the beast's leg. His attention on the potential battle wavered. "Adrianna would not want you to kill for her; she also wouldn't want you to die for her. You know that."

"She is not my master."

"She's the embodiment of the earth. That trumps Annette... big time. Let them pass. Let's be done with this."

Magog looked at his downed brother, and the consensus for surrender was reached. He stepped aside and Gypsy didn't hesitate to move forward.

"I should warn you," Levi said as he raised his hand to stop her. "Annette won't release her to you."

"Gypsy," Heaton called from behind her. She looked Levi over while she waited for Heaton to finish his statement. When he finally did, he was right behind her. "Let Daniel and me talk to her first. She won't hurt us. At least not right away."

"Seriously? Why the hell did you guys bring me?" She looked back at him.

Heaton touched her back as he passed her. "It's called teamwork, honey. Get used to it."

Daniel passed her as well, pushing Levi forward. "Show the way, kid."

Levi moved ahead of the dynamic duo, with Nevia fastened to Daniel's belt buckle, lest she get lost. Gypsy was about to follow her, but Callin grabbed her shoulder and forcefully turned her around.

"What the hell was that about?"

"What? He was dragging on."

"No." He huffed out a breath. "I told you I loved you, and you punched me."

"Yeah, well, don't do that. I thought this relationship was based on sex."

"It is based on two people who like to spend time together in and out of the bedroom. Or am I asking for too much to socialize with our clothes on?"

"Look, Callin, I like you. If love is just a stronger word than like, then yeah, let's call this love, but you know better than anyone. I'm just not wired that way. I'm not like other girls."

"That's why I love you. I didn't think I could love anyone more than Leona, but as proud as I am to have created a child with her, she is only a footnote in my life now. You have centralized my attention and my desires."

"I feel the same way," Gypsy admitted and glanced up at Magog, who seemed rather intrigued by the live soap opera.

"Then say it." He grabbed her shoulders. She stared blankly at him. "Say it!" He shook her.

"Why don't you get this, Callin? I'm not capable of that."

"Then why don't you just lie to me? If you have no heart, then why not just lie to me, to keep me happy?"

"I'm honest."

"Bullshit! You're just hard as stone!"

"And you want to crack that stone, right?" She slapped his hands off her shoulders. "Well guess what, Callin. There's nothing inside of a stone. What you see is what you get." She took a step back. "You smell that? It's adrenaline and residual endorphins. That's it. That's all. If you can't handle that, then you shouldn't have started dating a sociopath!"

58

ORI GRUNTED, TRYING TO lift Efrat and drag him. She dropped him again and laid his torso down carefully. She looked him over and stopped at his eyes. Those damn eyes that reminded her of her mother. She couldn't watch them close forever... again. "Efrat, you have to help me. I can't lift you."

"There's no point, kitten. The infirmary is a couple hundred yards away, but it might as well be a million." His eyes softened, as if he had resigned himself to a hero's death. "Thank you for trying, though." Cori knew he was right. First aid kits weren't enough to save him. He needed surgery, or a hell of a lot of magic. "There's something you should know," he rasped with drooping eyelids.

"Wait." She thought about the bubble and its restrictions. There was one place she could take him to help him, and it was on the latter end of the options. "You're not giving up just yet. You have been a pain in my ass since the day I met you. You are going to continue to be long after today."

"Cori..." he objected until she ripped open his shirt. His bloody torso was a massacre of stabs. She knew his punctured lungs were the primary concern, but she didn't want him bleeding to death in the effort to walk.

She shoved her superheated fingers to each of his wounds, searing them shut, albeit probably temporarily. He winced at each one, but the reaction died off, as if he were too worn out to even express the pain. He definitely didn't have long.

"Stay with me, Efrat," she chided and slapped his face when he nearly passed out. "I know you're hurting, but just remember how stubborn you are. You aren't going to let a dick... dick-less jerk like Dirk be your murderer, are you?"

"You're the stubborn one."

"Not stubborn." She pulled him to sit up despite how his face winced. "Tenacious, remember?"

"What's the difference?" he asked, giving her a smile. She was inches from him, trying to figure out how to best wrap her arms around him. She paused, staring into his eyes. He was still trying to lighten the mood even at his death.

Her eyes glossed over with tears, and she shrugged. "One is an act of spite. The other is an act of the heart." He frowned at that, and she didn't bother entertaining his doubt or disbelief. "Now stand!" She pulled up on him, causing him to groan. He moved with her, coughing up blood after a curdled inhalation.

They made it down the stairs before he begged her to stop and rest. She let him lean against the wall while she stared longingly at the door and calculated how many more rest stops it would take to get to the dragon hangar. They wouldn't make it. If she could carry him, it would be fine. If she could separate from him, it would offer more options, but so far the connection was still as strong as superglue.

She caught Efrat's eyes. She could see he had reached the same conclusions. He knew what she knew. Or perhaps she knew what he had known from the beginning. Time and space were a bitch when you were bleeding into your internal organs.

Her tears finally fell, and she shook her head. "I'm sorry, Efrat."

"Shh." He pulled her in by their connected hands. "Tell Ethan that you don't need a protector. You do just fine on your own." He pushed away her tear with his thumb, caressing her cheek as he did. His eyes searched her face for permission before he leaned in to kiss her.

She tipped her chin, allowing the gesture as a goodbye. She could hardly deny a dying man a kiss, especially when there was no chance in hell that it could go any further. She barely felt his lips tentatively touch hers before a meek throat-clearing announced another presence.

They pulled apart and looked at the skinny guard who had eagerly interrogated her earlier. He grimaced, wide-eyed. "Um, sorry, excuse me." He surrendered the scene and slipped out the door.

Efrat and Cori exchanged a glance before screaming after him. "Wait!"

59

Ethan watched Ogana saunter up to him. He didn't have the option of being extracted. His trip back to the prison was a long walk, and Ogana wasn't likely to stay here while he fled for his life.

His starved cheeks and balding head made him look old, but he didn't have the wrinkles of an old man. Whatever kept the wizards alive in the bubble was also renewing him.

"No cowering? No prostrating?" Ogana inquired and stopped at Ethan's feet.

"Would it make a difference?"

"Depends if you think I'll react more favorably to your pomposity."

Ethan nodded to the mound the snake disappeared into. "Why didn't you let her kill me?"

Ogana smelled the air around them. "I can smell earth power on you. I wondered why that might be."

Ethan pushed up slowly, not willing to continue the conversation on his back. The sorcerer didn't flinch or step away from him. He had no reason to be afraid of Ethan. Wand or not, Ogana still had the strength of black magic coursing through his veins, just like the other wizards. It may not have been as much as Addy had taken in, but there was plenty enough to harm people.

"I don't know what you smell. All I smell is dirt and worm poop."

Ogana stepped closer to him and took a deep whiff of his proximity, his eyelids flitting with pleasure before opening to gaze at him. "You smell like power."

Ethan shook his head. "No power, just me."

Ogana reached out and touched his chest. Ethan glared at the contact until his heart started to beat, fast and heavy. He puffed, trying to push more oxygen into his forced cardio. "Where did you encounter this earth power?" the sorcerer asked.

Ethan wanted to hold out, but bravery was useless at gunpoint. "I was part of a magic ceremony, but it was months ago."

Ogana slowed his heart to a jogging pace. "Earth magic stays with you. Who performed this ceremony?" he asked, twisting his fingers to give him heartburn even before he attempted to conjure a lie.

"Annette," he answered in a wail.

The pain stopped, and Ogana lowered his hand. He looked physically impacted by the name. "Mabel?" he whispered. "She is still alive?"

Ethan leaned over his knees, rubbing his chest even though the residual ache wasn't anything that his touch could lessen. "Yes," he admitted, to gain some brownie points.

Ogana's sullen shock turned to repulsion. Whatever memory he was focused on, it was not pleasant. When the emotion passed, he looked up at Ethan with a curious amusement. "You must be rather special to be privy to such a lingering ceremony."

Ethan furrowed his brow, but didn't speak. Whatever danger was lurking behind his eyes would not be deterred.

"Perhaps..." Ogana looked him over. "You are the girl's husband." His head tipped as he inspected him a little differently. "Oooooh," he dragged out the word far longer than necessary. "You *are* special." He chuckled with the high-pitched laugh of a pubescent boy.

"What do you want, Ogana? You've been in hiding for years. What's changed? First Cori, now me?" Ethan queried, too concerned for his life to stay silent.

"Don't you feel it? That fragrant power draping over you like a cloak. It fits you all too well."

"I don't do magic."

"And yet I can no longer wield the power of the gold that rests on your wife's fingers." Ethan's mouth went dry. "You have bound them to her, outside of my grasp." Ogana circled him. "I worked long and hard on that gold. Imbuing it with the last vestiges of my earth power. I admit it was my mistake for letting one of my coven get the drop on me. The poor fool didn't know what he was doing.

'Shiny pretty' was as far as his brain thought. That is also my fault."

Ogana stopped before him again. "I sacrificed their minds for my life." He walked on, pacing slowly in front of Ethan. "The ceremony was going well. Too well. The power was coming in faster than I could receive it. I could feel it dragging me out of my own body. The weight of the earth was crushing me. I was arrogant to think I could take it all, but I thought with the coven backing me that it would be enough to disperse the stress."

Ethan shifted, remembering how extraordinary the earth power weighing on him had been. It took everything he had not to let go of Addy. He couldn't begin to imagine what that burden felt like to her. That was no doubt why she was in a coma. The trauma was too great for conscious healing.

"When I couldn't hold on any longer to myself and the power, I let go of the power." Ogana continued to relay his story. "The boomerang effect was transformative for everyone participating in the ceremony. I was happily left with an increased connection with the earth. My compatriots, however, were further entrenched in mortal magic, which left them with a decreased connection to their mental capacities.

"I expected there to be some fallout with the magical community for our grandiose experiment, but incarceration seemed a bit brash." Ogana laughed again. "Actually, I don't think anyone would have known about the indiscretion if it weren't for my lovely wife. A strange twist of events, especially considering it was Mabel's idea to begin with."

60

DANIEL AND HEATON FOLLOWED Levi to the altar room. The cave chamber was about half the size of the entry area. Aside from the opening they came through, there were large offshoot tunnels that provided dwellings for the resident *pet* dragons, as well as access to the outside. Off to the right was a large circular platform, scribed with symbols.

Annette was on the platform, kneeling over the gauze-bound body of a young woman. Adrianna, the potential sorceress, appeared dead, but Daniel knew better than to assume it would be that easy, especially since two very attentive dragons fringed the platform.

"Annette," Levi announced their presence.

The ragged-looking bleach-blonde looked up at him, simultaneously noticing Daniel and Heaton. "What are you doing? They are the enemy."

"No, they aren't," Levi said softly.

"They'll kill her!" she screamed.

"Then she wasn't meant to live," he continued just as softly.

"Why?" She shook her head. "Why did you make me do this if you were just going to hand her over to them?"

"We shouldn't have done it. We put too much faith in Addy, and not enough fear in the earth. We were all wrong."

Daniel came forward and Heaton followed right behind him. "Annette, you know we have to take her."

Annette looked him over disapprovingly. "You think I'm afraid of you, Daniel McGrath. You can't win."

"I don't have any intention of fighting you, Annette."

She frowned and placed her hand over Adrianna. "I meant her." Her eyes wept as she lowered her hand closer to the mummified sorceress. Before she could touch her, she pulled away, bawling. "Take her if you can," she blubbered and stepped away from the girl and off the platform.

She stopped in front of them, her hard frown further reprimanding their behavior. "Are you proud to be delivering an innocent child to her death?"

"This isn't about pride, Annette, and you know it," Heaton snapped. "Don't pass this blame on to us just because you screwed up."

Annette's mouth gaped, surprised by Heaton's sharp side. "How dare you!"

"How dare *you*!" Heaton crowded her, and Daniel did his best to hold him back without dismissing his right to get his say in. "Why would you risk everything to do this? What would possess you to act so... transcendent? Last time I checked, you are still a human playing with fire. Well, guess what, Annette, someone got burnt; and this time, it was an *innocent child*! Maybe if *you* hadn't been so damn proud, you could have kept this situation under control!"

Annette glared between the two of them, unable to recover from the reverse accusation with any grace. "Just get what you came for, and get out!"

She moved to walk away, but Daniel grabbed her arm. She tried to rip free, but he wouldn't release. He pulled her back and somberly recited his speech. "Mabel Annette, by the order of the warden, Danato Calabria, and the unnamed institution he represents, I am apprehending you for the crime of prohibited witchcraft."

"What? That son of a bitch is arresting *me*? *She's* the sorceress."

"She is the crime, you are the criminal," Daniel clarified.

"I could kill you all with a few choice words," she hissed.

Behind him, a gun cocked, and he couldn't help but smile. "And I could kill you before those words were ever spoken," Nevia stated dryly.

"Either we can take you in, or the collectors," Heaton added.

Annette gave up the fight and sulked. She pulled at her arm and Daniel let her go. He watched her move away, but she didn't go very far. She seemed to understand that she had lost.

61

"**H**OLY SHIT!" TREVOR, THE skinny young guard, stared at the large sleeping dragon before them.

"Never mind that, just help me get him close to her mouth," Cori scolded from the other side of Efrat.

"Mouth?" he yelped.

"She doesn't eat people. She's a vegetarian—well, if you don't count fish."

Trevor helped them move closer to the creature. Efrat was almost gone. The fact that he was still conscious was a credit to his pain tolerance. "I've heard about her, but I just never saw 'er up close."

"She's only scary if you're armed. Put him down and go check on Dirk. If he's alive… lock him up." She debated on saying *kill him*, but that wasn't her call to make. She had already decided on her own to make him a eunuch. That was enough life-altering decisions for one day.

"Yes, ma'am." He lowered Efrat and scurried off to do his duty—far away from the mouth of the dragon.

She adjusted Efrat to sit up against Penelope's massive paw, between the claws. Her head was perched on her leg, snoozing loudly. Efrat looked over his shoulder to the low rumble that was vibrating him and his eyes widened.

"Does she ever stop sleeping?" he asked.

"Not really. They are very old. I assume being that old means you have to hibernate most of the time."

Efrat coughed and choked on the blood filling his lungs. She leaned over to the slumbering beast and pried up her lip to get a good swipe of saliva. "You think that shit will really help? I've got a hole in my lung and in more than a few organs."

"Stop being so negative." She pushed aside his shirt and wiped the sticky substance over his chest and stomach where the worst of the wounds were bleeding again. "I'm being damn clever right now. I want credit for it."

"Yes, I suppose you are." He grabbed her hand. She stared at him, confused. "Maybe this is for the best."

"What are you talking about? We're right here. Ethan says this stuff is a potent healer. You can make it, Efrat." Her eyes flickered over his and he looked down at her hand. "What's wrong with you? Let me help you," she said. "You're like this because of me."

"Dirk is the product of lazy parenting and a corrupt socio-economic system. You are not to blame for his actions. If anything..." He trailed off and looked away from her.

Cori looked him over, trying to find the loose screw in his head. She pulled her hand away from his and tipped his chin up. "You are not going to die, and that is final."

"Is that your tenacity talking?" he asked.

She dithered, not wanting to imply anything with her answer. She reached over and grabbed a scoop full of liquid from the dragon's now slightly agape jaw. She placed it against his lips. "Drink."

He grimaced, but parted his lips to accept the warm liquid. When he was down to slurping it from her palm, she grabbed more.

"Why does everything healthy have to taste like shit?"

She laughed, knowing that the magic was already working if he was making jokes again. She placed another handful to his lips, and he drank it up. She reached for another, but Penelope was freshly awake and moved her head from her probing hands.

"Come on, Pen, don't be shy now. I'll scratch your neck." The dragon rose and stretched. Intentionally or otherwise, she dumped Efrat off her paw. He grunted from the pain of the transition. "Penelope," Cori half scolded, half begged for her attention. The dragon yawned and licked the rim of her jaw before she took notice of either of them. "There, you see?" She exposed Efrat's wounds. "He needs you, girl."

"Does she even understand you?" Efrat mumbled.

Cori shrugged. "She seems to, sometimes, but she's definitely still an animal. The finer points of dialogue escape her, but she does know some words."

"What's the word for *save my dying friend*?" he wheezed. He was turning blue. He wasn't getting better fast enough.

Cori looked at the dragon, which was all but annoyed that her private space was being cramped by the extra bodies. "Penelope," she said firmly. "Help."

The dragon didn't seem any more interested in the words than usual, but she bowed her neck to sniff Efrat. Then she growled, or perhaps it was a purr—either was an apt description. "What is she doing?" Efrat grunted.

"I don't know. Wait, I think she's..."

A long dribble of fresh saliva trickled from her mouth and onto his chest. It didn't look any different from what she had swiped from her lips, but she knew the substance's potency dropped exponentially as it aged.

Cori leaned him forward to drink directly from the pouring ooze. She could tell he was disgusted, but his slow suffocation was making him desperate. He swallowed the liquid, nearly choking on it twice.

"Enough," he rasped and turned his head away. She leaned him back, and he waved her away.

There was nothing more she could do. He would either live or die. She just hoped she hadn't extended his suffering if it was the latter.

62

"ANNETTE WAS YOUR WIFE?" Ethan wasn't sure which statement he was more surprised by, the relationship between them or her encouragement of the magical endeavor.

"Oh, yes. We were quite close. Of course, I didn't realize how self-centered she was when I asked her to marry me. She was all about the magic, and I thought that meant we were destined to be together forever. However, that wasn't her interpretation.

"She was only with me to learn and grow her own skill. She had some natural skill, but not as much as she would have preferred. I think she knew the ceremony would fail. She just wanted to see how it was done."

Ethan tightened his jaw. This was the second time he had to endure a so-called super-being castigating Annette. He didn't like it, especially since he knew she was inherently good. She may not have been motivated by the best incentives, but she wasn't evil.

"When it was clear that the coven was not stable, Annette ran off to tattle on us. She even helped Danato get us into this blasted bubble. I thought that traitorous bitch would be long dead by now." Ogana's eyes glazed in his revelry. "It gives me new hope for the future."

Ogana stepped closer to him, and Ethan tensed, ready to defend himself. The sorcerer clucked his tongue and shook his head. "No need for all that. I'm not going to hurt you. I just need to take something from you." He raised his hand and caressed his cheek in a strangely loving manner. "Not much, just a teaspoon."

Ethan ran through the trees, letting the branches slap him in the face as he went. He couldn't remember the details of the last few seconds, but he did remember punching the snake hard enough to distract it so he could run like hell.

He caught sight of the prison and picked up his pace. The guards on the roof caught sight of him and a few seconds later, the west door slammed open.

"What the hell took you so long?" Danato called out to him.

Ethan slowed down to a stop at the entrance. He pointed back to where he had come from. "Damn snake." He coughed. "She just wouldn't give up. I had to run for it."

"Did you spot any wizards on the way back?"

Ethan shook his head. "No, all clear."

63

GYPSY HAD ALL BUT run from her conversation with Callin. He was a good man, and an even better werewolf, but he still didn't seem to understand that she wasn't. There was a fine line between sociopath and psychopath, and she had skirted it on more than one occasion. The last thing she needed was someone trying to grow her heart. Aside from it being impossible, it was damned annoying.

She found her way to the altar room where Levi and the witch were standing near the door waiting for Daniel and Heaton to figure out how to pick up the sorceress on the altar. They each lowered their hands with the intention of grabbing her, but each of them pulled back like they had been stung.

Gypsy sidled up to Nevia. "Yay, more dragons," she noted, seeing the twitching tails of the guardians. So far, they didn't seem distressed by the men's attempts to take the woman. "What's going on?"

"They can't touch her," Nevia answered.

"Can't?" Gypsy asked, looking for more clarification.

"She's emanating mortal magic," the witch spoke up behind them. "The earth magic was supposed to balance it, but it's just oil and water. Her body is trying to slough it off, but there is nowhere for it to go. My magic isn't strong enough to remove it."

Gypsy glanced back at the woman, unimpressed by the so-called powerful earthen witch. She looked like a new mom: disheveled and desperate for sleep. "And now in English," Gypsy murmured to Nevia.

Nevia looked at her with tear-soaked eyes. Gypsy's brow dipped at this new observation. "It means anyone who tries to get close to her is saturated with intense emotion. So intense it's impossible to touch her." Nevia sniffled. "We've all tried, but she's too potent."

Daniel and Heaton cussed and pulled away from the girl again. They both seemed to be fighting the tearful reaction, but it was only adding to the cussing and yelling and bickering between them.

"Let Grace try," Callin suggested behind them. She glanced back at him, but he didn't appear to be angry. He was hiding his hand. It was probably his way of keeping control of the game, but her cards were all out, so there was no point in playing conservatively.

"I'm game," she said, withholding a smirk for her private joke.

"You might have a better chance than anyone," Nevia said. "You seem to be the only one unaffected by her so far."

"How's that?" she asked.

Nevia nodded back to Callin. "Emotions are running pretty high right now for everyone." Gypsy nodded, seeing the reason for the abrupt confession of sentiment from Callin. "She's exacerbating what everyone is feeling."

"Mmm, so I guess there's only one question." Gypsy looked her over. "What's got *you* so down?"

Nevia looked her over like the question was not only unwelcome, but foreign. She obviously had no intention of telling her, so she moved away to disrupt the ensuing argument on the altar.

When she arrived at the platform, Heaton and Daniel didn't bother stopping their discussion.

"Why are you bringing this up now?" Daniel asked.

"Because we are less than 24 hours from being on Danato's front porch and we need to decide what we are going to say."

"We are going to tell the truth." Daniel threw up his arms. "We are going to do this by the book."

"He'll throw you in a jail cell for the rest of your life, you know that!"

"I *don't* know that. Things between Danato and me—"

"The prison is still his priority," Heaton interrupted. "The deal has been struck; let's just sweep it under the carpet."

"Why would you even consider that?"

"Because I love you, you idiot!"

The men paused, letting the sentiment settle for a moment. "And why do you think I want to turn myself in?" Daniel murmured. "I'm not going to let you throw your career—or Nevia's—down the drain for my mistake."

Gypsy cleared her throat before they started hugging. "Gentlemen, I'm going to take the lady now, if you don't mind." She nodded to the gauze-wrapped body between them.

They backed away and gave her passage to take the woman. They both crossed their arms and watched her come closer. Everyone seemed rather interested to see if she could do it.

Normally, she might have been concerned, but this petite woman looked to be less than a hundred pounds in her malnourished comatose state. She bent down beside her and raised her hands dramatically over the body. She pretended to struggle with an imaginary force for several seconds.

Once everyone's interest was as high as she could get them, she snorted and stuck her hands under the girl's legs and back. She lifted her with ease and situated the bulk of her weight to lean against her shoulder.

"Now what?" She looked at Daniel and Heaton, who were genuinely shocked by her ability to touch her. The dragons lost interest in the event and swaggered their beefy bodies back to their den holes.

"Let's go," Daniel said, stepping off the platform. "I hope you can call another pilot. I didn't opt for the *middle-of-fecking-nowhere* coverage on my cell phone."

"I'll take care of it," Gypsy said, following him to the door. She passed by Nevia and Callin. Neither of them looked happy, but Callin looked completely dejected. Apparently, he wasn't happy that she hadn't exposed her gushy interior. It was official. She was stone cold.

All the way through.

64

Efrat groaned beside Cori on the bed while she read her book. He had been asleep for hours, but his breathing was steadily deepening. She didn't like bringing him into her bed, but the spare bedrooms' mattresses weren't big enough to fit them both comfortably, and since she was still attached to him, options were limited.

The men were generously reporting to her hourly on the electrical progress. She wasn't sure if that courtesy was part of their self-designated protocol or if they had just heard about Dirk and decided it was necessary to suck up.

The lights were gradually dimming, but as Danato had said, the entity would try to preserve her calories. Soon enough, she would have to sacrifice other energy expenditures, namely the bubble.

"Where are we?" Efrat said, looking around the plush but classy bedroom décor.

"My bedroom." She waited for him to make a smart remark, but he just laid his head back down. "How do you feel?"

He took in a deep breath before answering. "Tired and achy. Thirsty."

Cori handed him a bottle of water from her bedside table. He opened it and downed it in a few seconds. The plastic snapped as he sucked the last few swallows out. "Thank you," he said breathlessly.

"You want another one?" she asked, taking the empty one from him.

He shook his head. "No. I just want to lie here. I don't suppose you'll invite me under the covers." He glanced at her. He was downplaying his anticipation of her answer. She remembered the flat bed that he slept in. He must have been overjoyed to lie on a mattress and not inadvertently start it on fire.

"Go ahead," she offered. "You need help?"

He slid out of the bed and she leaned over to give him the slack he needed to situate under the blankets. When he was cozy under the covers, he squeezed her hand. She looked at him, but he said nothing.

After a moment, he looked around. "What time is it?"

"It's after supper. If you want something to eat, I'll make an exception."

"No, I'm not hungry." He tipped his head to read the cover of her book. "Is this okay?" he asked, nodding to the bed. "Ethan won't approve."

She shrugged. "What else is there? I'm not going to ask you to sleep on the floor while you're recovering, and frankly, it's *my* bed."

He smiled and glanced over her body before turning away to cuddle in the blankets. She tried to read her book, but questions kept popping into her head. She finally put down the book. "Efrat?"

There was a long pause, as if he were deciding whether or not to pretend to be asleep. "Yeah."

"Can I ask you a question?"

"What?"

"Why did you try to stop me from saving you?"

"It was dragon saliva, Cori. I was weighing my options."

"I'm serious, Efrat. For once in your life, don't try to play down your real feelings."

"You don't want my real feelings."

"I'm asking now, and I want a real answer. I want to hear something honest come out of your mouth."

He paused for a long time, but she waited him out. "You want an honest feeling?" he ground out. "I'm not happy." She wasn't prepared for that. It was an easy assumption to make given the condition of his life, but to actually hear him admit it seemed to strip away his masks.

"Do you know that at any given time, I could bolt myself with enough electricity to stop my heart?" She didn't bother answering since the question was obviously rhetorical. "Do you know that every night I have to convince myself not to do it?"

Cori wanted to say something. She had started this, and now she was standing by, a mute audience for his displayed pain. She gripped his hand a little tighter. If anything, he would know that she was still listening.

"You were right that I don't like who I've become. The problem is, I don't know who else to be. This is all I am right now." He raised his bare hand and examined it. "I'm a bare wire on the outside and a bare wire on the inside. I keep thinking I should just end it, but I keep hanging on to the hope that it will get better. I guess I'm just as naïve as you and Dr. Frank."

Cori glanced at him, and he looked back at her. She still couldn't think of anything to say to console him.

"This is a miserable life, Cori. The only thing that kept me going before was revenge."

"And now?"

He looked away.

Before Cori could ask him again, Efrat tugged their connected hands and leaned back into bed. "Let's get some sleep."

Cori followed his lead and crawled under the covers. Despite her sympathy for his situation, she still couldn't find anything to say to him. The truth was, there weren't a lot of silver linings in Efrat's life.

65

ETHAN YANKED HIS HAND away from Mezula. The searing pain from her unnatural touch got worse each time he had to see her. She smiled at him seductively and leaned against her bars. "I enjoyed that," she said, her lids drooping slightly from fatigue. He was a little weary from the experience as well, but not enough to pass out.

"The feeling isn't mutual," he snarled. "Why the hell do you have to make it hurt so bad?"

"It feels better that way." She bit her lip hard and made it bleed. "The pain tastes sweeter."

Ethan shook his head and looked at Danato. He was waiting patiently for him to finish unloading his excess of bad dreams into Mezula's mind. "Is she seriously the only psychic who can do this?"

"No, but I can't trust the others not to take advantage," Danato admitted.

"Oh, Danato, let me have some fresh flowers," Mezula said drunkenly.

"No flowers to give you, *Zu*," he retorted and nodded for Ethan to move along with him.

"Oh, Danny-Boy, stay. Stay and let me taste your pain," Mezula whined behind them as they distanced her cell. "You are so sweet. My favorite sugar daddy."

Ethan glanced at Danato to see if he was irritated by her display. He didn't look angry, so much as worried and exhausted. Then again, everyone in the prison looked that way. Between the strict food rations, blood donations, and sleep deprivation, his men were looking like war refugees. Danato was no exception.

The only person who looked worse than him was Belus.

"How much longer can we do this?" Ethan asked.

"As long as we have to," Danato said as they slipped through an airlock.

"And Belus?" Ethan could see Danato tense with the shift in conversation. "I'm not blind. He looks like shit."

"He'll be fine." Danato gave him the knee-jerk response.

"That's a load of bullshit, and you know it," Ethan scolded without constraint. "His eyes are constantly bloodshot and sallow. His concentration is nonexistent. He can barely put two sentences together back-to-back. The other day, he fell asleep in the middle of our conversation. Eyes open and everything."

Danato stopped and threw his head back to take a breath. When he finally looked at Ethan, he still wasn't angry. Just more of the same worried exhaustion. "What do you want me to say, Ethan?"

"I want you to say what Belus would say to me if we were having this conversation about you."

Danato nodded. "Belus is immune to Mezula. She can't help alleviate the burden of the dream feeders. If he doesn't get free of this prison soon, he will have a psychotic break."

Ethan frowned at the reality laid before him. As disappointed as he would be at losing Belus, he knew Cori would be miserable with guilt if anything happened to him before she could rescue the prison. "Cori will rescue us before things get... messy. She's too stubborn not to."

"I know she will." Danato squeezed his shoulder. "And Belus is strong enough to fight off a few bad memories." He moved on, and Ethan followed with him.

Ethan wasn't sure who was trying to convince whom of what, but he didn't find either statement confident enough to withstand doubt.

66

C ORI STOOD OUTSIDE THE shower, watching the steam rise on the mirror. Her scowl was slowly disappearing behind the fog, along with her disapproval of Efrat's mandated shower. She hadn't wanted to further infringe on each other's privacy, but when she saw the amount of blood caked under his bandages, she realized it was probably more of a sterility issue than hygiene.

He groaned obnoxiously loud behind the curtain. "God, this feels so good!"

"You better be talking about the water," she mumbled, yanking at their connected hands.

"I miss free falling water. Sponge baths just don't cut it." He popped his head out, dripping water on the floor. "Last chance, you scrub my back, I'll scrub your front."

"Just hurry up. Trevor will be checking in any minute. The last thing I need is to have him walk in on another easily misinterpreted moment."

"Yeah, remind me to almost die more often. You're nicer to me on my deathbed."

Cori shook her head, resisting the urge to make any jokes about his death, especially considering last night's conversation. Better to avoid honest feelings from now on.

She looked down at the makeshift shirt on her lap. She had cut off his bloody shirt last night to put on the bandages. She hadn't given much thought to how to get one back on him. Ethan had enough t-shirts to sacrifice to the cause, but she was short on safety pins, so he was just going to look a little low rent for the day. Hopefully, just the day. "I can't believe the connection hasn't worn off yet," she pouted.

"Me too. I suppose the bigger the bubble, the stronger the connection."

"Hopefully that's not an exact ratio. That bubble's at least ten times bigger. What was it, about nine hours last time? Great, that's almost four days."

"I'm sure it will wear off soon," Efrat mumbled and shut off the water. "I'm not that lucky," he said and reached out for a towel.

"I know you don't want to lose your tangible freedom." She moved the towel to his probing hand. "But you have to admit, this is no way to live."

"Mmm, not unless Ethan's into polygamy," Efrat said, his voice muffled by his towel. "Speaking of men trying to get into your sex life, how is Dirk?"

"Trevor got him situated and locked up last night. The freezing seems to have cauterized him. He's in a lot of pain, but he isn't bleeding to death."

"Is that a good thing?" he asked, but she didn't answer. "I was surprised you didn't just kill him to begin with."

"I shouldn't have done what I did do. I just..."

"I know."

"No, you don't."

"I know enough." He peeked out of the curtain and gave her a sympathetic look. She wasn't sure how much he knew, but it's not like the origin of her arrival was top secret. Most of the guards had probably heard the rough cut.

"I probably *should* have killed him. Trevor said he's spouting his revenge in Shakespearean proportions."

Efrat drew back the curtain. His towel was precariously hanging from his teeth, blocking her view of the necessities. She did get a view of his sculpted hip bone, and the taut buttock peeking around its perimeter before she could shift her gaze. "Put the pants out and I'll step into them," he mumbled over the towel in his teeth.

She did as he asked and then turned completely to give him privacy to pull them up. When he gave her the all clear, they maneuvered his cut shirt over his torso.

"Remind me to find an insurance carrier with dragon saliva in my PPO network," he said, poking at his healing stabs.

"I think avoiding crazed assholes would be just as helpful to you." Cori looked over the puckered scabs before she pulled the shirt across him and pinned it closed. They were likely to still scar, but the internal bleeding hadn't killed him, and he wasn't in excruciating pain, so that was all that mattered. "Thank you, by the way," she mumbled, trying to downplay the sentiment. She glanced up at him to see if he understood what she was saying. "That's twice now you've saved my life."

"I suppose that balances out the times I tried to kill you," he grumbled.

She shook her head. "I'm not keeping count anymore, Efrat." She glanced up at him. "Really." She continued to focus on the challenge of one-handed safety pinning.

"Truthfully, it's my fault this happened. I knew he'd try something like this eventually. I never thought he'd be *that* bold, though."

Cori remembered his discomfort during her initial interactions with the man. "You seemed to be very sure he was going to harm me?" she probed cautiously.

"Like I said, he's not a good man."

"Sure, I get that, but how did you know that? I mean... did he talk about doing something to me?" She stood up and tugged down his shirt. It was pretty goth-inspired, but it would have to do. She noticed Efrat wasn't answering. He wasn't even looking at her. She didn't want to start a fight so early in the day, but she still wanted an answer. "Efrat? Did he threaten me? Is that how you knew?"

Efrat's breathing increased as he looked at her through the mirror. She looked at his frowning reflection. He licked his lips and swallowed hard. "It was a bet."

67

CORI SLAMMED OPEN THE bathroom door and walked out, although it wasn't getting her any farther away from Efrat. He trailed behind her into the living space, not offering an explanation for his statement. She refused to look at him while she came to grips with his words.

"Why aren't you frantically explaining?" she asked when he stayed quiet behind her.

"Because it won't make it sound any better."

"It may not, but I need context."

"Okay, turn around. I'm not going to talk to your back," he said blandly. She turned around, practically daring him to talk. "I made a bet with that shithead that I could get you into bed before he could." She furrowed her brow despite there being no confusion about the statement. "I'm paraphrasing, of course. The exact nature of the bet was more anatomical."

"Nice." Cori smiled to cover her discomfort and looked away. "Is that why he made the Mount Everest comment? Winning the bet."

"No, the Mount Everest designation came long before me or Dirk."

"What do you mean?"

"I mean, you are known as Mount Everest around the guards' quarters. The unattainable lay." She gaped at Efrat, unable to disguise her reaction to this new level of insult. "It was always just a joke. Something to fantasize about, but nothing anyone would actually try. Too dangerous."

"And you thought you were different?"

Efrat clenched his jaw. "The guys were sitting around discussing previous conquests."

"Rapes?"

"No! Just women," he scolded. "Dirk started bragging about all the women he had *seduced.* Since we were all still talking about consensual sex, someone said he should make a go for you, since he was such a Casanova. He said he was planning on it." Efrat paused, revealing his guilt and embarrassment even before he spoke. "I told him he didn't have a chance. I told him I'd have a better chance than he would. He bet me that he could... before me."

"And you took that bet."

"It was just guys talking, Cori! Guys talk stupid shit all the time!" He looked down and shook his head. "Except Dirk was serious. He got real chummy with me for a while after that. Pretty soon, he was asking how I had gotten so close to you when I attacked you."

Cori frowned, realizing that the betrayal was still not over.

"I told him that your rings would reabsorb the power if your hands were tied together."

She slapped him.

It wasn't the first time; it probably wouldn't be the last.

He waited for her to yell, but she couldn't. Her eyes were watering, but she didn't even have the energy to truly cry. She was emotionally exhausted. Efrat, as usual, had drained her of every ounce of hope and charitable thought.

"Did you really think that I would ever let you climb Mount Everest? Or was that just talk?"

His eyes drifted over her and he shrugged. "Every woman is Mount Everest for me, Cori."

"That doesn't answer my question."

"What do you want to know? You want more of that honesty from last night? You didn't like that, as I recall?"

"I just want to know what the hell you want from me, Efrat. Am I just a game or a bet? Sometimes I think you really do want to kill me and sometimes I think you want there to be something between us. I just don't know how to be with you. You talk about friendship, but then you do such hurtful things."

"It wasn't meant to hurt you!"

"I know, but it did, Efrat!" She squeezed his hand right along with fisting her other hand. "You never *mean* to hurt me, but you do! I get to a point where I think I can trust you with my life, but then it turns out that you were the one endangering it in the first place."

"And I'm on the rollercoaster right with you! You hold my mistakes over my head, and then I have to claw my way back into your good graces. Even when I think I'm doing well, you drag out the amputation card!"

"And even when I think you've been completely honest with me, you pull out a landslide of shit that you've been hiding from me the entire time!"

"And there I am, back to begging for *your* forgiveness. Where's *my* apology, Cori? Oh, that's right! I'm a victim of fucking circumstance!"

"Oh, you're a victim, all right! And that's all you'll ever be! I'm so sick of feeling sorry for you, Efrat! You want your apology? Here it is. I'm sorry I can't make your life better." She turned away, but he pulled her back around.

"You *do* make my life better. That's the problem!"

"What?" Cori frowned at him. They were both panting from their heart-racing argument, but somehow the heightened anger and volume took a nosedive.

"You asked me last night what kept me from killing myself now that revenge is off the table."

She shook her head, but he spoke the words, anyway.

"It's you, Cori."

"No," she denied it.

He moved closer to her, pressing into her personal space. "You wanted to know what I wanted from you. I want the only woman I can touch to want me as much as

I want her." He tipped her chin up and swooped down to her lips.

68

Efrat pinned Cori's arms behind her head and pressed into her. They both groaned, and he began to pump deeper into her. He moaned and shifted to pinch her breasts. His pace was steady, but Cori demanded more, so he quickened the pleasurable punishment until she screamed out.

Ethan woke from his nightmare to the sound of his own screams. He panted and wiped away the sweat on his brow. He ripped off the blanket to his cot and sat up. He had moved into a cell on the part-time level. The privacy was still minimal, but he at least had three and a half walls.

Unfortunately, the dream feeders were having a heyday with his insecurities. He had been having more sex dreams than when he was going through puberty. Unfortunately, Efrat always had the starring role.

He supposed he should be thankful that was the worst of it. Belus was being subjected to so many nightmares that he was only getting a few hours of sleep at night. It wasn't surprising, given the type of skeletons he kept in his closet.

Danato was still underplaying his risk of long-term exposure to the persistent psychic invasions. The only thing working in Belus's favor was that his immunity to Mezula also made him resistant to the dream feeders. However, the longer he was subjected to them, the easier it was for them to bypass his natural defenses.

"Hey boss." Duke popped his head into the doorway, startling him. He looked sallow, tired, unshaven, and a little too thin. He knew he probably looked the same. They had all been doing overtime on bloodletting, and there wasn't enough food to keep anyone plump. Luckily, the medical staff had enough saline and nutrient IVs to keep them nourished despite the sparse calories. They were doing everything they could to keep people from stealing more than their share of food, but they were living with the threat of starvation.

"Nightmares," Ethan explained his obvious state of unrest. He grabbed a black t-shirt and slipped it on.

"I'm sure she's fine. Cori's mighty clever under pressure," Duke said, and Ethan nodded. He honestly wasn't worried about her safety. Cori always found trouble, but she always found a way out of it, too.

His son squawked from the bassinet by his cot. He moved to check on him, but Duke waved him off. "Uncle Duke's got this one." He picked up the baby and bounced him a little. "This little man's getting big."

"Yeah, he is." Ethan frowned. "I was kind of hoping the bubble would slow his growth a little bit, so Cori wouldn't see how much she's missed."

"Hey, cheer up, boss." Duke sat down beside him. "I know this isn't the ideal situation, but we're over halfway through. Once the bubble's down, we can start putting this place back together."

"She'll never forgive me for not telling her the truth."

"Yes, she will. She'll see what you went through, and she'll understand why you wanted her to stay away. Besides, who else was going to save our asses?"

"Yeah, I know. It's just going to be hard to convince her of that when she sees that her son is a year older than when she left."

69

E FRAT PULLED CORI CLOSER as he continued to deepen his kiss. He wasn't forcing himself on her, as she anticipated, but with their joined hands behind her back, and his other hand cradling her neck, he was definitely making retreat a little more awkward. She was trying to just let him make his point and move on, but somehow the kiss had turned into a moment rather than a statement.

She relaxed against him, surrendering to his desire. Not because it was the right thing for her, but at the moment, it was the right thing for him. He needed to know what it would mean to finally have her the way he wanted.

He shifted, pressing his tongue past her lips for a taste of promised passion. It was a haunting repetition of the first time he kissed her. Only now the only intrigues between them were potentially broken hearts.

It was all very simple for Efrat: seek out the one human being he could touch. It wasn't love or passion; it was basic instinct, and even logic. He wasn't thinking about anything beyond this kiss, though.

For Cori, it wasn't as simple. She had a husband and a baby to worry about. Not to mention that Danato would never look at her the same if she became an adulteress. Where would she go without Ethan? Live in the barracks on a cold metal bed with Efrat? Would he try to be a father to a child he could never touch?

Efrat's life was beyond pity. He was in a living hell. She didn't doubt that the only relief he felt was when he could touch her, but why did she have to break Ethan's heart and her own, just to heal his? It was too much to ask.

Since she wasn't fighting him, he moved his hand to cradle her face. That's when he noticed the part he was missing. The part of her that wasn't keeling to his desire. His lips stopped, and he reluctantly pulled away from her.

For a moment, he just looked over her face. The red eyes and tear-streaked cheeks. He took in a deep breath and wiped away one of her tears. He frowned at the torment on her face. "I love my husband, Efrat."

He closed his eyes for a moment, as if hearing that hurt him to the core. "I never doubted that."

"I can't cheat on my husband just to give you a reason to live." He nodded, showing more maturity than she expected. Or perhaps he already knew the answer. "That's too much to ask of me, Efrat."

"I know it is, kitten, but it's also too much to ask me not to try." He moved his hand to caress her hair. Despite her rejection, he hadn't moved away from her. "I suppose it's not even about you, really. Shit, some days I think I hate you."

"Thanks."

He chuckled. "You know what I mean. I know I don't make it easy on you, but it's either yell at you or kiss you, and until now I wasn't sure I would survive the latter. It's just... life has dealt a lot of bad cards, and I keep thinking that maybe someday I'll get a good hand." He pulled his hand away from her face to look at it. "A better hand, at least."

"I want that for you too, Efrat. I really do."

"I know you do."

She huffed and raised her hand to touch his cheek, where she had only recently slapped him. "Then trust me. Let yourself be a part of this place. I know you don't want to be here, but I know how amazing you could be if you just let go of that imagined life in your head. We will figure out a way to make things better. I know we will. If I can get Rodan a cage outside and Cleos a glass cell, then I *will* find a way to shut those hands off. I promise you I won't stop trying."

He smiled at her determination. "I'm starting to see the difference between stubborn and tenacious."

She shrugged. "It's my thing."

"I think I'm also starting to see the advantage of having you... as a friend." He smirked at her. "Thank you." He leaned in to kiss her again, but this time she dipped back slightly, moving her hand to his arm. "Last one. I promise." He pulled her back slightly, and she didn't fight him.

Once again, he placed a soft, unassuming kiss on her lips. She assumed he would keep it fairly chaste, but his fervor increased, teasing her lips with his tongue.

She tried desperately not to enjoy it too much, but he was a really good kisser. She pressed her free hand to his shoulder, warning him that he was trespassing on her good graces. He obediently drew away from her and grinned down at her. "There, that should be just the right amount to keep my lips memorable."

She was about to make a playful comment about still remembering their first kiss, but she was interrupted.

"Ethan and Cori, I assume?" a woman asked from behind her. Cori whipped around and stared at the complete stranger standing at the entrance of her house.

70

"WHO THE HELL ARE you?" Cori asked. She and Efrat immediately repositioned to face her together.

Cori was certain the green pant suit the woman was wearing was probably expensive and intended to look classically retro, but it just looked old to her. The short, ash-blond hair was overworked to the point of looking like a fro. Her gaunt frame and sharp facial features might have made her a good model thirty years ago, but now her fifty-something was easily misinterpreted as sixty-something.

"My name is Renee Braxton." The woman brandished a smugness that demanded sycophancy. If Cori hadn't hated her instantly, it was only because the house didn't throw her out upon passing the threshold without permission. "Was I correct? Corinthia and Ethan Pierce?"

"I'm Cori. This is..." Cori flushed, realizing why she had probably assumed Efrat was her husband.

"Efrat Alston," he answered for her.

"Interesting," Renee said, looking over their still conjoined hands.

"Ma'am, I'm sure you are someone of great importance," Efrat continued, "but you really need to start talking before we're forced to remove you from this facility."

"I'm not going anywhere." Renee picked up an oversized piece of luggage and tossed it into their path. "Be a dear, Efrat, and put that in one of Danato's spare bedrooms. When you two lovebirds are finished, you might want to step outside."

Before either of them could respond, she shut the door behind her.

"What the hell was that?" Cori squawked. "Where did she even come from?"

Before they could get to the door to check out what was going on, it slammed open and Trevor came running in. The excitable young man tripped over Renee's luggage and landed face first before them. Efrat leaned down to help him, but he was up again like a jackrabbit. He must have been a former junkie or a getaway driver, because he never seemed to stop moving.

"Ah, yeah, there's something going on out there." He pointed his thumb toward the proverbial *out there*.

"No shit," Efrat snapped. "What?"

"Trucks are coming in and they got loads of supplies."

"Great, maybe we can eat," Cori said, relieved.

"Yeah, but it ain't food, yo."

"What is it?" Efrat asked before she could.

"The drivers said it's construction supplies. Drywall, brick, and tools n' shit."

"What did you tell them on the taps?" She turned a frown at Efrat.

"Oh right, I do remember asking for a McDonalds Play Place. What do you think? I asked for food, water, and medical supplies."

"Why would they send construction supplies?" She looked at Trevor, but he was just as baffled.

"That ain't all, ma'am." He paused and listened intently to something. He pointed to the ceiling. "Trucks ain't the only thing comin' in."

"Get the men together, get armed, and meet us out front," Efrat barked before Cori could even comprehend what she was supposed to be hearing.

Trevor ran off, ready for any order that required forward movement. "Wait, what?" Cori said just as she heard the distant thrum.

"Helicopters," Efrat explained.

"Okay, so they brought the supplies—"

"Food doesn't come on helicopters. *Men* come on helicopters."

"Why would they bring men in? We don't need more men. Where's our food?"

"Exactly; that's what we are going to go ask. At gunpoint."

71

E FRAT BARELY FLINCHED AT the shivering breeze the three helicopters produced when they arrived inside the courtyard not far from Danato's home. His reserved stare and statuesque puffed chest pose reminded her that the military was still in his blood.

Cori was not as graceful or imposing, since her hair was whipping her in the face. Her men had arrived; twenty-three black-on-black, armed, and dangerous men. They lined up at her back, prepared to shoot at her command. There was something exhilarating about it, but also something terrifying. She had never been in a war or even a standoff.

She looked over at Efrat. Despite the drama she had just been through with him, she was grateful to have him standing next to her. He didn't look back at her, but he squeezed her hand—a tiny reassurance that he knew she was still there, and probably wouldn't get her killed.

That put her mind at ease, but it waned as the black hawks spilled out nearly thirty men before they even reached the ground. The fully-equipped infantry squads cleared the blades and lined up before them like a British brigade. They raised their weapons without cause and started barking orders for them to surrender their weapons. Naturally, the men behind her raised their weapons in defense.

She and Efrat stood in the middle of it all, useless barriers against their bullets. Efrat didn't even flinch, though.

"Identify yourselves!" Efrat demanded, barely audible over the looming massacre. "Where's your commanding officer?"

"Right here! Lieutenant Colonel Alexander Maddox." A broad-shouldered brunet, matching Efrat's height, stepped from the crowd of men. The long scar across his left eye seemed archetypal for his position, but the missing left hand was not. "Who the hell are you?"

"What branch?"

"None that you would have heard of. Who the hell are you?" he repeated.

"Lieutenant Sergeant Efrat Alston, Special Forces."

"Congratulations, I still outrank you! Not that it matters here."

"And *I* outrank *you*!" Cori yelled before she became completely invisible in the conversation. Maddox looked at her without the annoyance she expected, but the confusion he held for her told her he wasn't used to eye candy having an opinion.

"And who might you be?" he asked, giving her a slight smirk.

"I'm the acting warden of this facility. You, my friend, are trespassing in restricted airspace and unless you want this altercation to escalate, I suggest you tell your men to stand down and give me a full debriefing of your purpose here." Cori knew she was taking liberties with her title, but it wasn't necessarily wrong. She was the next in line for warden—outside of the bubble.

"You're outnumbered, little girl! Give the order or I will, your choice!"

Cori raised her hands in surrender—the appearance of which was diminished by the intense blue crackling from her hands. She could hear Efrat chuckle as the energies combined and bloomed into a flattened sphere. She had thought their attachment would hinder her ability to wield the electricity, but even with Efrat's power suppressed, their connection seemed to feed her vigor.

The men before her backed away, unsure of how to attack this threat. "Somebody shoot this bitch!" Maddox yelled, and she increased the energy, allowing her anger and fear to feed its magnetism.

Two shots fired before the guns aimed at her were ripped away from the hands holding them. The metal clanked, and a few more errant bullets fired as the guns clustered in her magnetic field. She let them drop to the ground in front of her.

She couldn't afford a glance at Efrat, but the strictness in his body suggested he was vicariously peacocking. The men blanched at her demonstration, but more than a few of them pulled handguns from behind their backs. She wasn't sure she could repeat the performance, since someone was liable to shoot her before she got the energy produced again.

For a moment, everyone just held steady, waiting for the arguing leaders to come to a compromise or order the bloodbath.

"Impressive." Maddox tipped his head and pulled a cigar out of his front pocket with his recently emptied hand. Cori had thought he couldn't get any more stereotypical.

"Need a light?" Cori raised her fire-filled left hand. She was more than pleased to see him shaken enough to forget how to light his cigar.

"Now, now," Renee's flinty voice peeled a path through the men before Cori could see her. "No need to continue your performance, Mrs. Pierce." The near six-foot woman stepped out of the crowd, freshly vomited from her seventies soap opera set. "Maddox, take your men and do a preliminary sweep of the area. Then map the entry points."

Maddox gave a wave, and the men marched toward the bubble to do her bidding. Cori glanced back at her men, and they lowered their weapons. "Are you going to tell me what's going on, or just continue to be inscrutable?"

"I'm here to relieve you of your duties," Renee said it as if she should be thanked.

Cori shook her head. "You don't have any authority here. I think I've proven that."

"I agree that in Danato's absence... *and Ethan's... and Belus's*...that you would be the next in command, but I assure you, I am fully authorized as a representative of the board of directors to take over this... mess."

"You're a board member?" Cori's heart sank. "Why did they send a board member? I asked for supplies. We need food and water. The men trapped inside don't need more people to give them orders. They need to eat."

"The food is on its way. We will air drop crates into multiple locations in the bubble. Hopefully, they can get to some of it before the wizards discover it. We'll need to put together a plan to reduce the bubble."

"We already have a plan. The electrical supply is still beneath the bubble's reach. We've been reducing it incrementally, to wean the entity. With the power decrease, she'll back off."

"Do you have a time estimate?"

"Within the next twenty-two hours." Renee paused as if she were calculating something. "I appreciate the food drops, but we have the rest of this under control. I don't understand why the board sent you."

Renee checked her gold watch. "I admit that my timing isn't the best. It's always been an involuntary flaw in my character, but I am here to stay."

"What for?" Cori asked, exasperated.

"The audit."

72

"This is ridiculous!" Cori dragged Efrat into the house after Renee. She had not only invited herself inside, but was taking liberties with the fridge as well. Cori hadn't considered her refrigerator to be part of her jurisdiction, but it was just one more liberty the woman was taking without consent. "Why the hell would you start the audit while the prison is in the middle of a crisis?"

Cori kicked the fridge door shut, nearly taking the woman's hand off as she retrieved a bottle of water.

"The prison is always in crisis," she snapped and set the water on the counter before pulling out a small pillbox from her pocket. Cori felt a glimmer of regret for begrudging the woman water to take her medications, but then her catty side decided that it was probably just the woman's appetite suppressants and the guilt disintegrated back into hostility.

"I don't have time to answer your ridiculous questions while my family is trapped inside that damn thing."

"I would say you have plenty of time, then." Renee downed her pills with an excess of water.

"Okay, bad choice of words. I don't have the *tolerance* for your questions."

"Listen, Cori, I don't know if Danato has explained this, but you are not the only one under investigation here. The prison is in unprecedented territory. With two outsiders about to take control of the prison, we need to know that you are loyal to this arrangement."

"Are we back on this? Recruited, kidnapped, who gives a damn! This is my home now."

Renee slapped the counter. "And what about your children, and your children's children? Are you prepared to surrender their futures to this prison? Have you thought about how your son will continue his lineage? Mail order bride? Or will you track down the *wandering village* like Danato?"

Cori quieted as the questions seeped in. She had considered how raising her son might be difficult, but she hadn't considered the quality of his life beyond her rearing.

"That!" Renee's finger popped up into her face. "That right there is why I am here." She glanced at Efrat. "Your soft heart and pervasive morality have already gotten you in trouble."

"And what if you find that my soft heart can't be hardened? Demote me to hunter and send me to Mexico?"

Renee took in a long breath and gave her the best motherly scolding she had witnessed in a while. "You need to start taking me very seriously," she said in a low tone. "This is not the type of organization that lets loose ends waggle in the wind. Wiping is quickly becoming a non-option for you."

Cori could feel Efrat tense beside her. He was getting ready for a fight, even though the threat was far from physical.

Cori swallowed back the last of her animosity and spoke carefully. "Are you threatening my life?" she asked as coyly as she could without allowing her fear to show through.

Renee snapped her gilded pill box shut and slid it into her pocket. "As I said, Mrs. Pierce, you need to start taking me very seriously."

73

"D O YOU THINK SHE'S serious?" Efrat asked, pacing her small living room. Their connection had worn off shortly after she had absconded to her apartment to mope.

"I know she is." Cori touched her right hand. It felt strange being free—not that she preferred being tethered, just strange. She imagined that would be what it would feel like if she went back to the real world: strange, but good.

She wiped away another tear. They weren't coming fast, but she couldn't shake them. She hadn't once considered leaving the prison since she had returned to it the first time, but the walls had never felt quite as confining the second time around.

"What do we do?"

"Nothing." She looked up at Efrat.

"She's threatening to kill you. That isn't an audit. That's murder." Efrat's hands percolated with blue energy. The cockle in his brow hadn't released since the moment he heard Renee's threatening innuendo.

"Yes, it is." Cori stood and placed her hands over his, letting the excess power absorb so he didn't start her apartment on fire. "It's her job to make sure this prison stays safe. But she's not going to kill me."

"You don't know that." He glanced down at her hands.

"I do, because Danato would never let that happen."

"Putting your money back on the big man."

"I never should have taken it off him. That's what got me into this whole mess to begin with."

"*I* got you into this mess."

"You planted a seed of doubt, and I let it control me. You were justified, but I shouldn't have let your opinion of Danato influence me. They might be able to challenge my loyalty to this prison, but my devotion to its warden is constant."

He nodded. "Okay, so what? We just play nice until Danato can save the day?"

"First, we have to save him." She glanced at her watch. "In about sixteen hours."

74

"DO YOU FEEL THAT?" Cori asked, Efrat between the bursts of illumination.

"Yeah," he murmured beside her. "A tingling."

Cori looked over her hand, but the tingle was not visible like it was in the giant sphere before them. The pulsing ripples that shimmered through the half orb sent nerve-awakening needles through her right hand where she had been connected to Efrat.

"Residual?" she asked, even though she knew he didn't know any better than he did.

He glanced at her. "Sure," he said with pessimistic hope. "Maybe we should split up a little," he said, taking an exaggerated step away from her.

The bubble had been becoming increasingly more active over the last few hours. With the sun long gone, the light show was broadcasting across the compound, drawing everyone in to observe and volley questions no one could answer.

She could only assume that the bubble was about to shrink, but the mammoth pulses of energy seemed to be increasing in strength rather than decreasing. Maddox's men were taking readings off the dome, which they were frantically discussing with him, but so far, no one was reporting anything to her.

"Fall back!" Maddox ordered his men after looking at one particular device

"I don't like this," Cori said, feeling the angst that was quickly spreading through the crowd. She moved through the clusters of mobilizing men. No one tried to stop her until she was inches from Maddox. "What's going on?"

Two men thrust out their forearms, blocking her at her collarbone and waist before she could grab the man and shake the truth out of him. "Whoa, toots!" the one blocking her neck said.

"I wouldn't advise pissing her off," Efrat said close behind her. She hadn't realized that he had followed her, but she was once again glad for his company. "She's already castrated one man this week. Or should I say dismembered?" The man chuckled at his presumed exaggeration. "Not even remotely kidding," Efrat said earnestly. The man's smirk slowly died away as he took in her peeved expression.

"Easy, gentlemen, the lady just asked a question," Maddox interjected and waved his men away.

They released her to pass, but her desire to manhandle him had passed. "What's happening? Why are we drawing back?"

Maddox looked her over carefully before looking back at the bubble. "He hasn't told you about the borehole, has he?"

"What are you talking about?"

"We're going to lose her."

"Lose who?"

"The entity."

"What does that mean?" she asked, but Maddox had no chance to answer her. The pulse from the bubble trilled into a high-pitched sound that made everyone cover their ears protectively. The next pulse brought a deep bass that buried her eardrums into her brain.

"It's gonna blow!" Maddox yelled between thrums and waved his men to fall back farther. The men who hadn't already moved ran away from the undulating orb. Hers followed suit as well, not requiring an order to protect themselves.

"What are you talking about?" She grabbed Maddox's shoulder before he could walk away.

He turned back, brushing her hand off him as he did. "It's a no-go! She's pulling out."

"What does that *mean*?" Another throb that shook the ground at her feet covered the question up. She looked down and found a tiny crack in the earth beneath her. She looked at Efrat. He was just as alarmed by this as her.

"Move back or you're going to end up at the bottom of a crater!" Maddox grabbed her arm and pulled her along with him as he put more distance between them and the sphere.

"What the hell is it doing? Is it about to shrink?" she yelled near Maddox's ear.

"No, the weaning isn't working. She's leaving."

"Is that good?" she asked, hoping that a lack of time bubble would be better than an oversized one. When Maddox didn't answer, she ripped her arm away from his grip. "What happens to the prison?" she yelled.

Maddox glanced over to Renee, who was standing well away from them, observing the entire scene with knitted, white-knuckled fingers. The woman wasn't a pinnacle of sympathy for Cori's potential death, but she *was* worried about *someone's* death.

Maddox waited for the ripple to pass before he answered. "The entity is going to draw back. She's going to pull out of this dimension completely. When she does, everything within the time schism will perish."

Cori shook her head. "You can't know for sure."

"Yes, I can. It's happened before."

Cori stared at him, unable to fasten herself to even one of her mounting questions. Regardless of the queries, she understood what was about to happen. She was going to lose *everyone* she loved. "We have to do something!" Cori screamed. "Don't just retreat! Do something!"

"We can't!" Maddox took her elbow, drawing her forward again. "She's pissed off, Cori. We've been feeding the bitch for nearly a century and we just cut her off. How do you suppose she feels?" Cori ripped her arm away again. "You can't save them!" he warned her.

"Then I can at least die with them!" Cori turned back, fully prepared to run into the time bubble, back to her family. If they were about to die, then she was going to be right by their side. Efrat's arm latched around her waist, once again preventing her from running directly into the path of a *bullet*.

This time, however, she didn't want to be saved. She elbowed him in the face and he released his grip. She ran full speed toward the turbulent collapsing bubble. She was seconds from being inside when a different orb enveloped her.

The static blue energy blocked her with the sheer strength of a pain-inducing force field. She turned back to Efrat and screamed out her wrathful words. "Let me go!"

"Not a chance, kitten!" he yelled back. "He knew this was a possibility, and he made me swear to protect you. I know you'll hate me for this more than anything else I've ever done, but you will *live* to hate me."

Cori turned back and saw the prison showing through the bubble—as if it was in real time and space. It was there and gone with each resonation. So close, yet so far away. The pulses were so quick; it was practically just one long vibration. The ground shook beneath her like a tiny earthquake. She couldn't tell if it was the bubble that was causing it, or if it was the earth rejecting the entity.

The field around her moved, forcing her away from the sphere. Away from her family. Away from certain death.

"Efrat, let me out!" her voice was raw with desperation.

"I'm sorry, Cori. I have to." He shook his head somberly. She might have respected his devotion to his duty if it wasn't days and months too late to be appreciated. Not to mention he was standing between her and her child.

She glared her contempt at him through the hazing blue. She gritted her teeth and pressed her hands into the force field he had created around her.

"Cori, no! It's too much!"

The agonizing power crackled around her hands, scorching her fingers, igniting her rings, and singeing the hair on her arms. She could see the concern in Efrat's eyes as his cage wavered around her.

"Cori, don't do this! Let me save you!" Efrat yelled and increased his output, but her rings were already compensating.

The walls of the field faltered and fell, bleeding into her rings. Efrat's energy, intentionally or not, continued to feed into the connection, tugging on the last vestiges of the time bubble that had glued them together.

Efrat's energy was being sapped, not unlike when he was trapped inside the den. He looked over the thick blue rope, connecting them with confusion and concern. He looked at Cori's outstretched hand, absorbing more than she was capable of producing on her own. Even the rings on her free hand were glaringly bright, trying to balance the threat against her.

But it wasn't a threat for her. It was just a hell of a lot of *Twinkies*.

Cori's fingers were burning like hot lava, but she refused to release the energy building in them. She may have been about to cook her hands like a Thanksgiving turkey, but Belus was right—every headstrong, idiotic, fortuitous mistake she had ever made was because she cared too much. Stubborn, tenacious, or otherwise, she had to try.

The energy building up in her rings circulated and balled around her fists, begging to be released. The whipping tentacles snapped in her face until she focused on them, tethering the energy into tightly bound spheres.

The deep rumble behind her turned to a wailing screech. The time schism was fracturing, and it was about to kill everyone inside, maybe even outside.

She could hear Efrat and the others demanding her to fall back, or give up, or something like that. But she was long past the option of self-preservation.

The bubble's shrieking pitched so sharply that it left the range of human perception. The soundless sound waves muffled all the other sounds. The eerie silence stilled everyone.

Cori looked down at the energy she had palmed. She had wielded a power stronger than any storm cloud could produce. Every last fear and hope for her future had boiled to the surface in the form of dancing blue energy.

Somewhere between the teeth-clenching pain of holding the power and the rigor-mortis-inducing voltage she could no longer deflect away from herself, she screamed.

She released the bolt. Singular and pure. Powerful and magical. A *Twinkie* to a starving man.

A debt.

A pact.

And a plea.

FELICIA JEDLICKA

FORK IN THE ROAD

Book 10

THE WARDEN

FORK IN THE ROAD

Sneak Peek

GYPSY WATCHED THE FUSION of the shimmering orb and blue lightning explode into blinding light. The pilot cussed and slammed down on his rudder pedals, turning the helicopter away from the detonation. The blast wave was as much sound as impact. If she hadn't been wearing a headset, her eardrums might have shattered right along with the windows of the helicopter.

The pilot cursed again and adjusted for their aircraft suddenly becoming an open top convertible. "I need to land!" he yelled through the headset.

"Keep going," Gypsy drawled before spitting glass shrapnel from her mouth. She could taste blood, but she wasn't sure what part of her mouth was cut.

"That was an explosion! I can't land over there!"

"Then *you* can carry the comatose bitch six more miles to deliver her." She turned slowly, eyeing his reaction carefully. He might have been afraid of her by pure reputation, but he was more afraid of the woman she had brought on board. If she'd been smart and joined the Air Force instead of the Marine Corps, she wouldn't have needed to put up with pilots that were easily distressed. What was the military coming to if their men were startled by flying dragons and supernatural sonic blasts?

"I'll do a flyover, but if I can't find a place to land—"

"Just land on the roof." She pointed out the building standing in the center of the walled off installation.

"How the hell is that still standing?" he mumbled and shifted the chopper back to his previous course.

The pilot circled once to survey the grounds. Gypsy could see three black hawks and at least six semi-trucks crowding into the open acreage surrounding the main prison building. The vehicles and outbuildings weren't in much better shape than their helicopter, with broken windows and mangled roofs. Only one outbuilding seemed to be immune to the damage.

"Looks like I'm late to the party," Gypsy said, as she made a mental inventory of her ammunition.

The pilot offered her a furtive glance and lowered them to the roof. Once they touched down, he adjusted his switches for a shutdown. "Don't shut it down. You aren't staying."

"I can't go back with shattered windows," he objected.

"I don't think they have a helicopter repair shop. You need to go back immediately and report."

"What do I tell him?" he muttered.

"Nothing, just shake his hand. I'm delivering the girl to Danato. The others are coming in with the witch. By the looks of the parking lot downstairs, your project has arrived."

"What do you mean, my project?" The pilot frowned at her as she reported to him as if he were an answering machine.

"Shut up and listen. There are three black hawks too. I'm not familiar with the insignia. I'm sure it's a private party, and I'm about to crash it. Not sure what's going on with the light show, but by the looks of this chaos, I don't think you're going to be welcomed back. I would advise postponing your arrival, but I know you won't listen. I'll know more in a few hours." She started to grab her gear and get out, but stopped and turned back. "Oh, and download this guy's flying lessons. I'm sick of dealing with panicky pilots."

"Nut job," he grouched as she got out. If she cared about his opinion in the least, she might have punched him for the remark, but it wasn't the first time her sanity had been put into question and it wouldn't be the last.

She slipped out of the cockpit and looped her duffel bag over her shoulder before maneuvering the petite cocooned woman from the back. She was light, and Gypsy was strong, but she was not looking forward to flights of stairs with her and her pack in tow. She could have lightened the load, but what would the warden say if she just left a near-god-level sorceress just lying around? Someone was bound to trip over her.

Gypsy offered a salute to the pilot and slipped into the stairwell. If there were supposed to be guards available to greet her, detain her, or otherwise annoy her, they were too busy with whatever the hell had just happened in the courtyard.

Thank you so much for reading. I hope you enjoyed the ride and if you aren't getting off here, I encourage you to sign up for my newsletter so I can return your generosity with new release updates and special offers.

Sign-Up

You can also find me on Facebook or visit my website. Keep reading!

Website

Facebook

AUTHOR

As a Nebraska native, and a small-town girl at that, I have very little to occupy my time beyond imagining a world outside of my own reality. By the grace of God and the seat of my pants, I have kept my waning attention span on the task of becoming an author.

So here I am, an indie author, peddling my words in cyberspace and enduring my comeuppances with an unwavering determination. I may not be a professional, and I certainly am not perfect, but if you've made it this far, you have to admit, this smartass yokel does spin quite a yarn.

From the self-inflicted sweatshop conditions of my unairconditioned childhood home, to the arthritis reaping positions of a sedentary lifestyle, I bring to you: my sarcasm, my oddity, and my heart. Take it with a grain of salt or a teaspoon of sugar, but take it for what it is: a story born of the mind, translated to paper, and gifted to you.

I thank you for your readership and even more for your support. Please recommend this book to your friends and family via any social media that you use. Word of mouth is still the best advertising and is greatly appreciated.

Most importantly, keep reading. I'll keep writing.